Als

Writing as Hanna Earnest

Night and Day:
Book 1: *All the Best Nights*
Book 2: *End of the Day*

QUEEN OF DUST

H.E. DARE

carina
press

Recycling programs
for this product may
not exist in your area.

ISBN-13: 978-1-335-62192-4

Queen of Dust

For questions and comments about the quality of this book, please contact us at CustomerService@Harlequin.com.

Carina Press
22 Adelaide St. West, 41st Floor
Toronto, Ontario M5H 4E3, Canada
www.CarinaPress.com

Printed in U.S.A.

To small pleasures
(may there be many)

QUEEN OF DUST

Chapter One

Mara would not clench her fist.

Let the damsel glitter. Even in the low light of the ship's humming overheads, the woman's silvered skin sparkled like morning sun on frosted glass. She was painted from head to toe, including the bottoms of her feet—which Mara could see as the damsel knelt in front of Liam, her head bobbing up and down while he watched. His eyes weren't the only ones on the damsel; the observation deck was filling with passengers the way it always did before dinner.

And that was what threatened to close Mara's hand, to set her mouth in a hard, tight line.

That he'd done it with an audience.

A dalliance was fine, expected, healthy. But Liam had chosen to broadcast this one to an entire ship full of people who looked up to him, and not just because they had to. Liam Pent, CEO of the Pent Corporation, was as ubiquitous and powerful in the universe as the Dern Empire. But here, on his ship, he was admired. A manifest full of high-class passengers who could afford a Fold, and had chosen this one, to spend the time with the man who'd grown a business to span the universe. And what was he telling them now? That he'd had to outsource his Balti Temptress. That Mara wasn't what she claimed to be.

Mara flexed her fingers and forced her features to relax. She kept her face pliable, refusing to flatten her pouty lips. Instead she parted them, sipping something bitter and tart out of the heavy-bottomed coup glass she'd carried from her room, aware that eyes had pulled from the spectacle and found her. Aware that people were waiting on her reaction.

The ship's front viewing deck was part lounge, part boardroom, complete with a throne-like chrome-and-leather chair reserved just for Liam. Typically, Mara's place was right beside him. And she knew why. Despite the skeptical whispers about their relationship, Mara knew the strength of the threads that tied them together. They both had legacies that set them apart. Legacies that were impossible to escape, that were better to embrace—showing people what they expected to see had its advantages. And then there was their shared, open disdain for the Dern. If there was one part of her Balti heritage she didn't have to learn, have to work at, it was despising the empire that had cost her a home. That came as naturally as breathing.

Liam's past was different from hers, but he hated the Dern as she did. A ship like this had been his childhood home. He had no land, and his loyalty to the Dern crown was entirely financial. They'd tried to convert him, of course, but subjugation wasn't one of Liam's interests. When the pushiest of his Dern partners was last aboard to discuss the renewal bid for military supplies, Liam had proven his disinterest in Virtue by taking Mara on the glossy boardroom table. Midmeeting. Mara remembered it in a rush, how Liam had bent her forward, water sloshing in the pitcher at the center of the table with each of his thrusts.

Liam Pent was no Dern. Liam Pent did as he pleased, when he pleased. And Mara Leanor was happy to help, happy to show the Dern her equal disregard for their oppressive Virtues. How good it had been: the Dern watching them, shifting uncomfortably in their loose, simple tunics, needing the deal to go through, forced to allow Liam his theatrics. His display of power. Mara remembered best smiling and coming hard.

Now he was putting on a show with someone else.

Sauntering through the room, her feet crossed with each step, the way she'd been taught by Jimma. The only other Balti she'd ever known. Mara hoped no one registered that one faltered step when she'd spotted Liam with the damsel. He must have picked her up on Satsume. But why not leave her there when he'd finished? Mara assumed they'd been docked long enough. It was hard to tell. Time in the Black was weightless, as unbearably useless as up or down. This "morning" seemed ages ago and she had slept the whole "day," only to awaken to another stomach-churning lurch from the ship's nuclear reactor. Another nauseating jolt of power thrusting her forward, correcting and maintaining their course in spurts and spasms.

With her face composed, and her grip on the glass as light as she could get away with, Mara kept her struggles to herself. Why had Liam brought the damsel here? Mara looked again at her painted skin—paint that had yet to smudge—meaning Liam had saved her for this display, the same way he waited until they were almost out the door to don a fresh white shirt. He was not generally a patient man, but he cared how things looked. And this was something he wanted Mara to see.

"Fine evening," she said, the common greeting practiced on her tongue. Though it wasn't. Not fine nor evening, just more cold, dark Black.

Liam looked up from the damsel and smiled, a guiltless offering that dared Mara to question what he could and could not do, on his ship or anywhere.

"What's this then?" she continued.

Jazzy notes of a song she'd heard at least a hundred times bounced around them. Even the musicians on board were recycling stale product.

"Just a little entertainment," Liam said, trailing off with a satisfied grunt. His pale fingers threaded into the damsel's braided hair, linking them further.

Entertainment. Oh. So Mara had brought this on herself.

"I hate space," she'd told Liam that morning. "I can't breathe in this lifeless air anymore—and can't they do something about the cold? I'd think I were dead if I weren't so bored."

"Bored, cold, in need of livening? I can think of a remedy or two," he'd said and reached into the slit of her silk robe.

Mara had forgotten herself and jerked back from his icy hand.

The recycled air that tasted of laboratory O2 had felt thin before, but Liam's hard stare seemed to collapse her lungs. Mara reached out a remedial palm for him at the same moment his attention shifted to the communication stone glowing on the table. Normally she resented its constant presence, but the interruption had been a relief.

"We're landing on Satsume, for supplies," he'd said, standing up. Mara had stood too, pressing the pad on the wall to open the closet. She had held his shirt for him as he stuffed his arms into the sleeves. "Are you coming?" he'd asked, looking her over as he secured the buttons. She should have loosened the knot of her robe, let the shoulder slip to reveal the tight bud of her nipple, let him think the shivers that started from her bare feet on the cool floor were for him. But she tightened her arms across her front. Maybe if Satsume weren't full of covered cities, maybe if it were open to the elements, the air and the sky, but she'd only have been locked in another layer of tin.

"I'm tired, I—"

"Suit yourself," he had said and was already at the door, the metal panels opening like a concertina at his touch. They'd flattened shut and Mara had been alone.

If only there were a button she could push to flatten the layers of anxiety that spiked her moods. Mara had been trying to contain her agitation for weeks and it had only been getting harder. She longed to do what she'd been taught: balance feelings like these with pleasure, let raw need wash out the tension that plagued her. But it was as if she couldn't focus on desire, she was too overwhelmed by her nerves to feel anything else.

When she complained to Liam, it was easier to claim the Black as the cause—and she did hate it. Hated the windows that showed her nothing, the view always the same. Hated how stifled and restless eight months on the ship made her. Hated the repeated jolts that accompanied every nuclear reaction propelling them forward. It would have been harder to admit that the pressure making her so reactive was an unexpected dread that built as they neared their destination. As she neared her home.

Balti waited for her, growing closer every day.

The planet that had all but dissolved in her memory would be tangible soon. She'd feel the sea wind on her face, taste the salt of the air, hear the rush of vital water from every direction. For eighteen years she'd been drifting so far from it; now she was caught on a tide that had finally turned, bringing her back.

She should have been excited. Wired and ready. Instead her energy flagged as trepidation rose to the surface of her mind. Today she had given in to it, sleeping the entire time they were docked on Satsume. But when she woke, still on the ship, alone in the dark, she knew she had to do something, and soon, before the feeling drowned her completely. She'd showered and poured herself a drink strong enough to burn her throat, tried to heat herself up for Liam's return, thinking she could make them both forget. Forget the moment that she'd refused the distracting pleasure he offered her. But Liam never forgot a thing.

So Mara watched, along with the rest of the people on deck—employees, partners, and travelers who were posh enough to afford a ticket on one of Pent's Folding ships, the people who made up Liam's corporate court. Watched as this done-up damsel slopped her tongue all over Liam's hard cock.

Mara wasn't sure if it was comforting or insulting that the damsel's technique was so very bad. It amused her slightly to see Liam reach for his stone, his attention pulled from the performance in his lap as it never would have had Mara been starring in the role. Of course he often multitasked—but his attention never wavered when she coaxed his cock from his pants. Pleasure was her heritage. She should have drawn on it this morning, to avoid the embarrassment now.

But embarrassment was internal—and she wouldn't show it. Would never admit this was anything that bothered her. Let Liam make a wet mess of his damsel. Let him stamp his hands on her painted skin. Mara had been taught to accept bad with good—both were fleeting. And it was in her power to create more pleasure than pain. That was the Balti way, and Mara had committed herself to it.

Smiling at a board member she knew, at a stranger, too, Mara let everyone see how unbothered she was. How relaxed, how uninvested. With a magnetic click, she set her glass down on a long side table and made a show of choosing an edible from the bowl next to it. The zyng-root flavor filled her nose even before she'd bit through the gummy square, felt its spicy heat on the back of her tongue. Having another drink would make it look like she needed immediate relief—the edible would prove to them that she had time, that she could take it.

Mara caught a raised eyebrow from across the room—Harper, one of the security personnel Liam insisted on. He prized loyalty and Harper was incorruptible. Her face was round but her eyes were sharp. She was a presence just like the Black, always waiting, always there. Her skin as rich in hue, her reach as penetrating. Liam's shadow, she saw and heard everything. And if she didn't buy what Mara was selling, Mara had to elevate her pitch.

The Balti let a better smile pull her mouth open, one cheek at a time. She squinted at Liam like they were conspirators. "Am I next?"

Liam didn't grin like she'd expected him to. He didn't react at all for a minute, his mouth moving with the quiet murmurs that told her he was in the middle of composing a message. Some urgent missive about inter-planetary ore deliveries or updated trade treaties that opened new markets. Nothing that mattered to Mara very much. There was only one planet in the system she cared about. And she was almost there.

When Liam did focus on her, he closed his fist around the stone and rested it under his chin. His other hand stroked the damsel's hair, following the ribbon that wove through her braid to the knotted end. Mara mashed her tongue to the roof of her mouth—the only way to express the tension she was feeling without it showing. She'd never risk a furrowed brow, or any line that would illustrate what she was really thinking.

As Liam considered her, his eyes a foamy green, deceptively soft, Mara felt the cold of the ship again, the thinness of the air. She'd told him she was bored. But she hadn't meant of him. Liam had been her rock since Rozz had died. And there was more than that fueling their attraction, sustaining their connection. What the Dern had done on Balti had impacted both their lives.

But since Liam had taken over his father's company at sixteen, he hadn't spent a day without everything around him exactly to his liking. Mara usually reveled in that power: his ability to create the world he wanted for himself. What she would give to do the same. He watched her now and she knew he was trying to figure out what that was.

What would Liam like next?

"She's all yours," he said finally.

"I can hardly wait." Mara didn't miss a beat, allowing a hint of relief to shine through her eyes. She didn't mind letting the damsel have a go at her cunt next. A bit of pleasure to balance the negative trend of her day. And it would work for Liam, too, smooth his ruffled feathers. It wouldn't bother her to let him and any other interested parties watch. She was not bound by abstract Virtue. Liam was ready to get over their tiff. Mara would be getting off easy—

The metal doors surged open and Liam glanced at the new arrival. A grin split his face as he returned his attention to Mara. She stood straighter in response, a wire charged by unexpected current.

"Why should you have to wait?" He beckoned to someone behind her and Mara craned her neck to see who it was. "I've got an assignment for you, Captain— Ms. Leanor requires a little warming."

Nerves fizzled in Mara's chest. "Liam—"

He interrupted her. "Isn't that your complaint about space travel, my dove—too dreary, too cold? Too boring? This will be interesting."

Mara didn't trust herself to protest again, not until she had control over the rapid-fire pulse of her heart. She'd caught sight of the man Liam had addressed, a grunt, a Dern soldier, this one with a shell of dark hair smoothed over his head. And she knew when he turned her way she'd see black eyes and thick lashes and the resigned face of a man she'd been determined to dismiss.

Chapter Two

The Balti had been eerily pale in the first moment he'd seen her. So pale she glowed, ethereal and unreal. He'd blinked, rubbed his eyes, and blinked again, not trusting his own sight. That had been in the unpredictable light of the tram tunnel, and he had no reason to think her a vision now that he'd caught up to her on the deck. She was real—real and fired up—an invigorating color enlivening her face. Her hair was as striking as before, red-gold and set off against all that phosphorescence. He supposed the contrast was exaggerated by deep space, where there was no sun to bake her skin, only an internal heat that flushed her cheeks in Liam Pent's presence. Liam Pent, who was unaware of the conversation that had just transpired between them. Liam Pent, whose Balti Temptress had already piqued Calvy's interest.

The ship's internal tram had brought her right to him. It should have been empty, what with his stop being on the lowest of decks. The end of the line where he'd found himself, with only one direction open to him. Instead, through the car windows, the Balti had stood. Glittering. Glorious. Shocking him. And that was all before he'd noticed her hand spreading open the folds

of her dress, caressing herself just below the trim patch
of red curls that glinted at the apex of her thighs.

Virtue be damned.

It wasn't the first time Calvy had had that thought in
recent months. Recent years. The further he got from
home, the more he saw of the galaxy, the harder it was
to be that boy who'd tried so diligently to find solace
in the rules of his people. It had worked for him—for a
time—when his family and their advisors had told him
to wait. Wait until they'd figured out what they should
do with him. It had worked because, at his core, he believed in patience and compliance and dedication—he
believed he had a purpose. He could feel it, looming, a
little further off. Someone he was meant to be. A promise between him and the unknown. It was only later he
realized those qualities could—and did—exist throughout the galaxy, without any connection to Dern Virtue.
Without the inflexibility of Dern demands.

The Balti was a perfect example of life outside those
rigidities. Her ensemble had made that clear enough.
She was traversing the ship in a dress not much different from a robe—the slit skirt and plunging neck gathered together in a narrow swath from above her navel
to barely below her pussy. When the tram droned into
view, the material, a metallic auburn, flickered in the
passing tunnel lights like flame.

The car slowed, the doors hissed open for Calvy to
enter, and then shut, without the Balti paying them—
or him—any mind. Lost in her own world, she parted
her painted pink mouth and scraped her teeth across a
full bottom lip.

Calvy coughed. "Fine evening."

The Balti ignored that too.

He pressed on, undeterred. "I hate to interrupt."

"Then don't." Her voice was lower than he expected, slower too. The words drawn out, lazy and detached, like driftwood.

"Where are you...getting off?"

The Balti opened her eyes, grey and rimmed with kohl. Her hazy gaze slid to the silver panel of buttons. Calvy pressed the furthest one to the right, for the observation deck, and she frowned.

"And for you—"

"That's fine." She took a sip from a glass in her free hand.

The Balti swayed as the tram kicked back into motion, and Calvy slotted the pieces into place. She must have forgotten to push the button wherever she had gotten in and the tram had taken her the opposite way, to the back of the ship, where he had joined her.

Slanting against the car wall, her eyes drifted closed again. Calvy stood straight and tall, his shoulders as square as the jaw he'd inherited from his father, forcing his eyes to fix on an innocuous spot above him and not the continuous motion of her hand under her dress. He was tested when the dress shifted open, displaying a lovely, plump breast, exposed to the air, to him. The sound of the tram whirring through the tunnel filled his ears like static as he held, and then those grey eyes opened, narrowing in accusation and then widening with surprise. "You're not staring."

"No—" He shook his head against the lie. "Yes, I was. At your hair."

The thick bob sprang away from her face, settling

above her shoulders like pulled sugar, popping against the background of dull metal.

Calvy swallowed. "It's very vivid."

"Is it," she replied without inflection.

"You're a Balti."

An explosion from the ship's propulsion engine caused the tram to lurch from side to side, sloshing the drink over her hand.

"I know what I am." She sent the drips to the tram floor with two sharp shakes of her wrist and looked him over again, taking in the details of his appearance. He saw the moment she formed her conclusion with a long blink and a sideways glance. Dismissing him as a witless enlisted Dern. Someone who didn't know how to conduct himself. Calvy could represent the Third better than that.

"Pardon me. I meant—you, yourself, are striking. I studied Balti. And I've traveled quite extensively and never met—"

"Yes, well, that's what a P bomb does."

Calvy's throat tightened. The feeling he knew best in the world washed over him. The intimate shame of his presence unrequested, unwanted. "My apologies again," he choked out before clamping his jaw shut.

But he had the Balti's attention now, whether he wanted it or not.

"Again? And what are these pardons for? Your rudeness or your part in the destruction of my people?"

"My part?" Calvy balked.

"You're dressed as a Dern soldier."

He looked down to check his structured green uniform. A foolish gesture. An unnecessary one, as if he could forget he was wearing it. So stiff and fitted compared to the loose jumpsuit he'd been allowed on Theos.

"Unless it's a costume," the Balti continued.

"Is yours?"

It was her turn to glance down and review her outfit. The liquor in her glass tipped, gathering close to the edge as possible without spilling over, as she used two fingers to adjust the thin fabric and recover her breast. "This? A costume? And what part would I be playing?"

"The Balti Temptress. My grandfather's first wife was a Balti. Not a Temptress, mind."

"It's not for everyone."

"Some are called?"

"Chosen." She swallowed something back. "To inspire. To set an example of how to live pleasure to pleasure."

"I've heard the stories. In private of course. The kinds of things that would burn a priest's ears right off."

"Your priests, perhaps—religion in Dern is awfully restrictive."

"Everything in Dern is restrictive." His eyes flickered to the one hand she'd casually retucked under her dress. "You'd be arrested for such a wild display."

"Must the Dern categorize any simple pleasure as wildness?"

"What would you call it?"

"This?" She set her hand moving again, circular strokes that Calvy imagined held just the right touch of pressure. "This is serenity, this is only taboo if you're told reward finds you once you commit to being wound with burden. A Balti creates her own reward."

The thrill of debate quickened Calvy's response.

"Virtue isn't about pain at all. It's meant to bring you peace. To help you surrender your agony. To let it go."

"To let go of control?"

"Yes."

"So some D'Aldiern king can take it? No. I decline. I more than decline, I'd counter that instead of taking, you all might give us a break. Keep your Virtue to yourself."

Calvy breathed into his nose and steadied his stance. "It bothers you—that the Dern are devout?"

"Hardly. It is your corrupt politicians forcing that devotion on the rest of us that bothers me."

A long whistle escaped his lips and he turned to face the doors. If this was a Temptress's mind slowed by drink, he didn't want to know what she was capable of sharpened and more alert. "My grandfather used to say there's nothing like the tongue of a Balti woman."

This one was voicing, proudly, things he'd only heard whispered, far from Dern, in private spaces. In the back of his own mind.

Her cheek twitched. "No doubt what inspired your scholarly interest."

"It wasn't that."

"Oh?"

"I didn't believe him."

"Why not?"

He caught her eyes in the glass, trying to ignore the unwelcome sight of his own untanned skin. "I was skeptical—that anything could be so powerful."

She held his gaze through the reflection, the two of them a pair of would-be ghosts. Her airy tone was as dismissive as the once-over she'd given him earlier. "You don't believe in the power of controlling a person's satisfaction—the power of having them beg you for release?"

"Not if you're the one on your knees."

A sound caught in her throat. When she spoke, her disinterest sounded forced and Calvy felt a prick of satisfaction. "I shouldn't expect a Dern to understand. Haven't you done away with the carnal in favor of automated reproduction?"

"That seems to be what's trending in high society, certainly."

Her gaze settled on the left breast of his jacket. An empty space where the fabric was dotted with tiny holes, a constellation that mapped the shapes of two chevrons. The evidence of embroidered patches recently ripped from their place. He watched more conclusions form in her mind. Watched her see what he was: a demoted officer. Someone who had started at this low rank and recently returned to it. Someone who'd earned position but didn't have connections strong enough to keep it.

She confirmed her assumption when she jabbed again. "Not yet trending in *your* circle?"

Calvy held his hands behind his back and widened his stance, at ease. He'd missed this—the back and forth of conversation, the spirit of interaction. A basic amenity his situation on Theos had lacked. He'd been right to get out of there, whatever the cost. It was worth it simply to find himself here. Trading words with this woman, he was starting to feel free again. Free like he hadn't felt since he'd first enlisted. When his father couldn't do anything to stop him. He wanted to hold on to that feeling, the memory of possibility waiting just ahead of him. "I'd offer to prove it to you, but you seem to have everything well in hand."

The Balti laughed, her head falling back to reveal a slender neck he suddenly imagined catching in his palm.

Not that free.

"I've never found a Dern amusing before. Never known them to be as clever with their tongues as I am with mine."

Calvy's heart thumped, forcing blood that had gone thick and syrupy through his tightening veins.

She watched him through heavy lids. "It's not my experience that a Dern knows what he's doing. A pity for your lovers, but at least they don't have to suffer long."

"Maybe you can share some knowledge, help the poor people of Dern." He smiled back at her and she frowned in response, like it displeased her that he was enjoying the exchange.

"Some things can't be taught. And I'm not available for practice."

"No, you look like a professional."

Her hand fisted and her mouth opened, but she snapped it forcefully shut, letting his attempted quip spiral lower in the air between them, an obvious, embarrassing end to their sparring.

"I—" Calvy had begun, but the tram doors had hissed open again and the Balti had breezed down the hall and away from the stop.

The two men at a security desk had let her pass unbothered, but one had stepped in front of Calvy. Frustration had simmered under his skin as they scrutinized his credentials and insisted he check his sidearm. He had wanted to catch her. Wanted to apologize.

It was clear that what he wanted didn't matter to a Balti. He was only a Dern grunt, after all. She hadn't even looked back. He was sure she'd spend the rest of the journey avoiding him completely, looking through him like so much space dust. But the security team had let him through, the deck doors had zipped open, and Liam Pent had grinned, forcing her to meet Calvy's searching gaze again.

Chapter Three

A black-eyed gaze set in a face that missed the sun watched Mara for an answer to Liam's challenge. Let the grunt warm her? Not if she could help it. She would give the Dern no more amusement. He'd proven in the tram that one couldn't expect anything from a Dern but insults—their prejudices were as deep as their pockets and the only thing they liked more than repressing themselves was forcing worse suffering on everybody else. She'd told him as much.

"Liam, please, you're making the poor boy blush." Mara looked the soldier over again. He was most definitely not a boy—he had a manly build, tall and athletic, albeit slim. His coiffed coal hair added to his impressive height. But he was Dern and that was enough to classify him as inexperienced, craven.

Liam lifted his chin and spun the stone in his hand, ignoring her. "Go on, Captain, that's an order."

The music had stopped, the duo hired to play caught up in the new entertainment. Mara took a step forward to approach Liam, but the soldier, already in her path, moved slowly towards her. She froze. The Dern, who had all but called her a damsel minutes ago, dared to act as though this was going to happen.

She looked at Liam, trying to conceal the anger that salted her blood. Though his face was formed in amusement, she could see this was more than diversion to him. It was as serious as a contract negotiation—every line was under scrutiny. He'd walk away with everything as he wanted it or smash the unsigned tablet to pieces.

Mara hadn't simply bruised his ego this morning, she'd ignited a question in his mind. He was testing her now, seeing how she responded to the challenge— how far she'd go to please him. She'd never needed to say no to him before—she'd never wanted to. She connected with Liam, admired his strength. When she'd faced the rocky unknowable ridge of the future, he'd paved her a path. But the trip was almost over, and he'd noticed her drawing herself in. She understood completely that underneath his bravado was fear: fear that he'd been played for a fool, that she'd only been using him for a free Fold. She had to prove to him that wasn't the case. If only coupling her with the grunt wasn't what he wanted.

But she was no Dern, forced by Virtue to conform with regulations stipulated by uptight men in buildings that speared the sky billions of light-years away. So when the soldier reached her, the square unadorned pads of his uniform shoulders blocking Liam temporarily from view, Mara tilted her head up to meet his eyes.

"If you don't want me to—"

"On your knees, Soldier," she said loud enough for Liam to hear, adding more quietly, "Was this not what you had in mind in the tram?"

"I didn't require an audience," the soldier said in a low voice that matched her own.

"Well, you've got one." A flood of unfamiliar sympathy washed through her at his lined forehead. "Look, just tell him you won't do it. You're Dern—this goes against everything you believe in, it offends your Virtue, what have you. He'll understand." Maybe if she could convince the soldier to back out Liam would relent—

The soldier shook his head. "Purity through patience, clarity through compliance, deliverance through dedication." He recited the Three Virtues of Dern. The rules they'd made up to extend their control where it did not belong. Virtues that emphasized idleness and obedience in return for the promise of betterment. Virtues that stopped anyone from making waves.

"But if you don't want me to. Say. Say and I won't." He lowered to his knees in front of her, exposing her to Liam's scrutiny again.

Mara pushed her tongue over her dry lips, drawing the chemical perfume of her lipstick into her mouth. Her breasts, rounded from the cold, rose heavily in her lower periphery as she looked down at the soldier. Despite herself she felt anticipatory heat spread from her stomach. A low throb threatened to push thought out of her mind as her body began to take notice, take over. She'd been taught that shame and dishonesty had no place in pleasure, and she knew not to discount the telling slickness that coated her cunt. That was real. That was her body informing her: she did want the Dern soldier. She liked the way he looked down there, awaiting her command. Not that his inexperienced touch would be all that enjoyable, but she could let him give it his best attempt for a few minutes, to appease Liam. To ease the desire that was rushing in her veins.

She needed the release, the catharsis of pleasure.

Craved it like she craved fresh oxygen. Maybe she could wring something from this nobody.

"Thank you for thinking of me," she said, flicking her gaze back to Liam momentarily. And then, addressing the soldier but loud enough for Liam and the others to hear, "Is this a lesson in patience? You should know I don't care for practicing Virtue myself. I'm not accustomed to waiting."

A determined look hardened the soldier's eyes. Her cunt contracted, and she felt its emptiness gnawing at her. It had to be the power, not the Dern himself, that roused her interest. Or perhaps it was all the buildup, the length of delay that had her in a state of anticipation. Mara placed a hand on the starched stiff jacket as he pushed her dress off her thighs with both hands. It was almost a shame, that the Dern soldier wouldn't be able to—

Oh. Mara's head fell back at the first brush of his curious tongue. She spent a long, open-mouthed moment with her neck bent, dark space filling her vision as she looked up to the deck's triple-paned dome above her. Then she brought her chin down to see him, meeting his black eyes, reading the question dented in between his eyebrows: *Okay?* Mara nodded, her face flushing, words too complicated to form, and the soldier's eyes sparkled. He took her cue to increase the pressure of his mouth, then his tongue teased into her and Mara gasped, her head dropping back again, the force causing her to lose balance. She gripped his head for stability, pushing her fingers into his hair, through the waxy crunch of the top layer, into the soft thick bristles at his scalp. The soldier's hands moved to cup her from behind, holding her to him. As if there were anywhere else she wanted to be than here, right here under his hot mouth, wet to wet with her aching cunt.

Some internal fire burned the bottom of her feet. Her eyes locked on to him. She couldn't look away. That strong, dark brow had unfurrowed, like he didn't need to concentrate, like this came naturally to him. Knowing what to do for her.

That annoyed her. She lost the rhythm of pleasure for a moment. How irritating, that he didn't have to work at it. That he looked so comfortable, so good obscured by her cunt. She pulled on his hair and his chin pushed harder against her in retaliation.

A low note throbbed through her, out of her. There, she had the beat back. The soldier's tongue dipped into her again, drawing up over her center with a twist. Her body contracted, and she clutched him closer, urging him to do it again. He obliged, and suddenly he was taking her through the flood of release. The soldier kept his mouth hard against the bone of her pelvis as the waves of pleasure washed over her, as she rose, higher and higher. Momentum before a fall.

The force and timing of her orgasm surprised Mara and she tumbled inwards. It hadn't taken long at all for her to come—when she'd implied the Dern were quick, she'd meant with their own pleasure. Standing on unexpectedly weak legs, she found herself wishing she'd let it go on a little longer. Drawn out the experience. No Dern had made her come like that before.

No one had made her come like that before.

It had to be the exhibition of it, or the work she'd done to prime herself on the tram, any little touch would have made her crack. There had to be something, some other reason—something besides the someone—to explain her reaction to that magic mouth.

It took longer for her to remember herself. To remember Liam. Her audience. His cock was still in the damsel's mouth, his stone balled tight in his fist, but his full attention was on Mara, and it took her muddled brain time—too much time—to decipher the hard look in his eye.

She blinked, trying to focus. She'd done something wrong, she realized, her heart hammering. While the soldier was on his knees in front of her, she'd kept the pleasure to herself. Liam had been expecting them to share. He'd paired her with the grunt so he could watch. Her breath caught, out of rhythm. Liam had watched as she'd parted her lips for the soldier. Liam had seen that she'd forgotten he was there.

The Dern braced his hands on her hips as he stood, and Mara fixed her breathing in his shadow where Liam couldn't see it. Then she plastered a smile to her face and leaned around her human shield.

"There, now, we can—"

"No." Liam's knuckles stretched around the stone, tight and pale. "His turn."

Not even the flush of ecstasy could stop Mara's cheeks from losing their color at Liam's words.

His eyes softened. "Not that, my dove. But it wouldn't be fair, would it, for the captain to remain so uncomfortable through dinner."

Mara took note of the large lump raising the front of the soldier's pants. She swallowed, relieved that Liam wasn't suggesting she get on her knees for the stranger, perform a Balti Kiss for him. She wouldn't. A Balti

Temptress was known for her tongue—but she didn't lavish it on just anyone.

The soldier began to loosen his hands on her waist but Mara planted hers on top of them. They were in this together for the moment, and he wasn't going anywhere. She took a step back, pulling him with her into the wall. She'd seen the nonnegotiable look on Liam's face—this wouldn't be over until he was satisfied. Liam's satisfaction: that was her objective. It should have been her objective all along.

"I'm not going to—" the soldier started.

"Don't be stupid, of course you are."

"Am I?"

His resistance made her pause. There were rules to pleasure—all parties had to be willing, invested. "Do you want to?" she asked genuinely, for the first time addressing the soldier without bite, without sting.

The soldier took his time answering, considering how his options affected his Virtue, no doubt.

"Yes," he said. And that settled it.

Mara perched herself on the long side table, the surface cold under the thin fabric of her dress. She refused to shiver. Instead she'd pull the warmth from the soldier's skin and take it for her own. She parted her legs, waiting for him to fill the gap. He stayed at a distance and she fell back on her training, letting her cheeks pull apart one at a time, that smile that told a lover she was scheming, colluding just with them. Creating an intimacy, a secret intrigue. Making him forget the rest of the world—or at least the rest of the observation deck. She looked at his hair, the strands all out of order, forced out of place by her hands. The wax meant to keep it flat now charged it upright. Distracted, she swallowed a laugh at the disorder of it.

He stepped closer and her smile grew—another thing she and Liam had in common. They both liked to have their way.

The soldier unbuttoned his jacket and Mara met his hands at his pants. She tugged his blouse up as he undid the fastening and groped her hands over his hip bones until he guided her to the spot she was looking for. He pressed her thumb against the circular indent under his skin—his health regulator, ensuring her that there'd be no result from their encounter, that he was healthy and he'd handled protection.

"You're sure about this?" he whispered and she hesitated. Not because she didn't know her own mind, but because she didn't understand his. She'd expected to hear apprehension in his voice. The Dern were known to be uncomfortable even during private acts, and this was anything but. Instead he seemed unfazed, as if his concern were for her. Which was impossible. He was a Dern—this situation had him so far out of his comfort zone—see there, his hand was trembling against her thigh.

She pulled him closer, positioning herself over his shoulder, so she could lock eyes with Liam, see his reaction to her getting fucked by this poor grunt who'd stumbled through the door at the exact wrong moment.

The soldier didn't move. He stalled, waiting for her answer. "Are you?"

"What? Oh. Yes." She ran her palms up his shoulders. "Liam's right, it's your turn."

Still the soldier held his ground.

What did a man need to hear? Same as a woman.

Up close his hair smelled sweet, like the white curled flakes of dried coco Jimma liked to toast and scatter over thick breakfast cream. Mara sighed into his ear, knowing truth was the secret to seduction. "You made me feel so good."

Had she been looking, she might have known to brace for the impact of his smooth cock pushing into her. He'd done his job well earlier and her cunt was wet and ready for him, but the shock of its size, the tap of his tip against her back wall stole her breath, a gasp cut in half by surprise. Mara forced her eyes to stay open and narrowed her gaze on Liam, who at last offered her a small smile. He sat forward in his chair, pushing the damsel's head flush against his pelvis, her jaw opening wide for him. Mara smiled back and matched her hips to his from across the room—finally understanding what he'd wanted: proof that connecting with him was her priority.

Which—of course it was. It had been from the start, since before he'd set up this stunt. Liam didn't like to talk about it, but Mara had to remember that he'd been affected the same as her—both of them orphaned by the events on Balti. Sometimes he was that boy again, afraid he was alone in the universe. Who knew better than her how that felt? Mara licked her lips for him— they were in this together. Liam grinned and his grip tightened on the damsel's hair. He was getting close and Mara could feel the proximity of his finish as if it were her own. Because she was enjoying it—the charge of his gaze, putting on the show for him.

But then the soldier slowed, his last thrust falling short, failing to nudge that spot that sent jolts up into her lungs.

"Don't stop," she hissed.

His whisper was strained but clear. "I could easily give my dick a tug in my bunk."

"What are you talking about?"

"I can do this alone myself."

"You're not alone." Mara rocked against him to urge him back into motion. Liam was so close.

"You're not—I lost you somewhere. And I'm not going to—"

Mara let her head rest on the wall as she rolled her eyes to meet his. It was exasperating dealing with men—they made everything so complicated. "I'm right here. I'm with you. Okay?" She nodded at him, drawing one hand up to his cheek and sifting the other into the hair at the base of his neck.

A moment stretched between them as his eyes fixed on hers.

Desire swelled in her as she waited. He was filling her, expanding her, and yet it was his focus that made her breathless, made her want. Finally he began to move again. Mara didn't dare look away as tension knotted in her cunt. Now *she* was close—so close to bursting. He tilted his head and for a wild moment she imagined kissing him, sliding her lips against his, still glistening with the taste of her.

They'd been hurtling through space for months, fast enough to rip her body apart were it not for the thick panels of the ship. But the journey thus far had seemed static. Like being trapped in a giant icebox. Now, suddenly, it was as though she could feel the ship's speed, vibrating the screws in their sockets, the sheer uncontrollable force of it making her dizzy, making her weak. And for once the voyage felt like flying, like she was soaring through endless velvet space, locked into a collision course with the twin orbs of light reflected in the Dern soldier's black eyes.

The first time he'd made her come had been a surprise. This second time, even as she felt it rising inside of her, the indulgence still registered as unexpected, a force as powerful and hot as the nuclear explosions that rattled the ship, throwing her off balance and forcing her to right herself. This was the pleasure she needed, to push the hard thoughts out of her head, to focus her in the moment. As the soldier thrust into her, Mara clamped down on him, moaning wordless curses. And only when he squeezed his eyes shut and unloaded into her tight cunt did she turn her head to find Liam, to let him see the pleasure shudder through her. She watched him push further into the damsel's mouth with a groan.

Mara smiled at Liam with the soldier's damp forehead resting against her neck. She scratched at his scalp absentmindedly and he shivered against her. Liam sat back, gliding his cock from the damsel's mouth. Then he smiled, he nodded.

Good, Mara thought fuzzily as she untangled her hand from the soldier's soft hair, it was done.

Chapter Four

"That's better," Liam announced from the head of the table. "Just what we all needed. A little activity to stimulate the appetite." He lifted Mara's hand to his mouth and kissed the back of it. "Warmer now, my dove? You're pink as a shell."

He meant it as a compliment. But Mara wished the color from her cheeks.

A Balti Temptress does not blush, Jimma had told her. *Blushing is a surprise, a Balti Temptress maintains control of her pleasures.*

Mara had made the mistake of looking over at the soldier across the table from her, and the involuntary flush of her cheeks had been the result.

Because she'd been stuck on the moment when his forehead had landed hot and sticky on her shoulder. A moment when his cock had continued to throb, warm and solid, tucked inside her, tight and safe. When she'd been relaxed and relieved and forgotten that he was a Dern, an enemy inside her walls. Until he coasted his palms up her sides and she experienced simultaneous urges to pull him closer and shove him away.

"That was—" he'd started.

"That wasn't for you."

"Right." He'd lifted his head. "Is he going to want anything else?"

In answer she had pushed at the soldier's hips and he'd backed up, freeing himself from her.

His shoulders stiffened into that militant stance of his as he watched her fix her dress. "That seems to be a trend for you."

"You'll find I'm not insulted by reminders that I do as I please," she'd tossed at him as she pushed past to Liam, who'd stood, kissed her cheek, and nodded at the bathroom where she'd cleaned herself up and returned in time for dinner.

"Captain—" Liam began, slicing into a vegetable that had been boiled lifeless, drained of all its color, and inexplicably still served to them under the guise of a "salad" course.

Mara licked dressing from her thumb. At least vinegar kept its flavor. "He's not a captain."

The soldier nodded. "She's right. I thought they'd told you. Of my situation."

"They might have—small things fall through the cracks." Liam took a sip of his wine, his cheeks twitching in response to the sour tannins. He was lying. He knew everything that happened on his ships and off. With that ever-present stone, he was completely plugged in, in constant communication with one team or another. If he was "mistakenly" calling the soldier captain, it was to needle him. Demean him. Mara understood the urge. "Private, then—or do you prefer Prince?"

"Prince?" Mara rolled her eyes. How many games would Liam insist on playing tonight?

"Oh, dove, don't you know whose cock just pegged you to the wall? The private is a prince of Dern."

Mara fisted her fork so it wouldn't clang loudly against her plate. "He isn't."

"Not technically, no," the soldier said. "Calvy D'Aldiern, cap—private in the Third." He pronounced the contraction with an upper-class inflection, smooth as a mouth-warmed spoon through iced cream.

Mara shook her head. "The D'Aldiern name doesn't make you a prince. The heirs of Dern are numbered— the process regulated. Each has a role before they're born and each is accounted for."

Liam egged her on, though he must have known the catch. "One through ten, isn't that the custom?"

"So which number are you?" Mara asked, knowing he had none.

"I was not expected. And not subject to the same treatment."

Someone must have mentioned it to her once because the story buoyed up from the depths of her memory— the story of the surprise prince. The king and queen weren't scheduled to mate and their health regulators had been offline for reprogramming. The child was born of passion and coincidence—an affront to the very core of Dern policy. How Jimma had laughed. Mara missed the sound, but she shook that part of the memory away.

This man couldn't be that babe. "Royalty can't participate in the military—they have ministries assigned to them before birth."

Calvy had another answer ready. "Under the law I'm a commoner. Dern have a calling to serve. This was my path. They could not stop me. Because I am no prince." His cheeks flashed a smile like a wink. "And you know how it is—the best way to fix a mistake."

Don't make one, Mara thought.

"Destroy the evidence," said Liam.

Calvy nodded. "I think they hoped the problem would clear itself up. But it hasn't. And they didn't have the pull to make me quit. Until now."

Mara leaned back as a waiter collected her plate. "You're an eleven. I've never met an eleven." She hoped he found the statement as vexing as she had when he'd told her he'd never met a Balti.

"And you still haven't. I'm not an eleven. I'm unnumbered."

"That's ridiculous." She felt the need to argue with the very core of him. "You're still an eleven and a prince. Born to a king and queen. After the tenth. It's what you are."

"I agree with Ms. Leanor, sire," Liam said. "You are what you are—no matter what they call you." *Sire*, another dig. Liam was almost giddy as he said it.

"Well, then. To anomalies." The soldier—Calvy—lifted his glass at Mara in salute.

Mara lifted hers in return, if for no other reason than to quench her thirst.

"But what is he doing here?" she asked Liam, noting the way Calvy's eyes lowered at her as she spoke of him in the third person.

"I bought his contract—I hope you don't mind, you were supposed to be released entirely, I gathered."

Calvy gulped his wine. "Don't mind at all. It worked in my favor."

"Mine as well."

No need to wonder why Liam had done this. Because he could. Because he'd seen an opportunity to own a piece of the royal family. To make the Dern comply and serve Pent. It was a flex at his Dern partners and he'd relished taking it, as he'd taken her on this very table in front of them. Mara eyed him with understanding, sharing in the thrill of his purchase. She swept her fingertips over the glossy table and he raised his eyebrows. That hungry grin of his was her reward.

"Tell me, Private, how did you find her?"

Calvy wiped his mouth with a napkin. "Pardon?"

Mara beckoned the waiter for a refill. She should have known Liam would want a debrief from the soldier— she was surprised he didn't request a written report for his files.

"My Balti Temptress—your first, I presume, as she's the last one in the galaxy. An experience I'd wager you won't soon forget."

"Yes, a very fine pussy," Calvy admitted flatly after a moment of consideration.

Liam leaned forward and Mara back as they laughed, hers the sharp burst of someone delighted by another's misfortune.

"I haven't heard that term in ages. How quaint," Liam said.

Mara squeezed his hand before bringing her elbows to the table. "You pet a pussy, your grace, you fuck a cunt."

Liam hummed appreciatively. "I do love that mouth."

Calvy stared at her across the table. "Your cunt. Noted, Ms. Leanor."

Wine stung the inside of her mouth. His affect lifting the ends of his words, it had almost sounded like a contraction. *You're a.* Surely she'd misheard him. Surely he hadn't the acuity for a grammatical slight. A bowl of pale, watery soup was placed in front of her, and she ignored it. Calvy tore off a piece of bread and ate with

the gusto of a starving man. If this was Liam's entertainment, seeing how far he could push the Dern, she
could play too.

"I was surprised to find you game," she said to Calvy.

"It was an order."

"Still. Most Dern can barely look me in the eye."
They glanced at her to judge. Not to know her. They
wanted to keep her in the periphery, forget about her,
and what they'd done to her, so she took any chance she
could to force her way into the spotlight. "You must
have been uncomfortable."

Calvy chewed politely before answering. "I've
strayed from my Virtues before. I dare say I will again."

Not with me, thought Mara.

He looked away and then let his focus drift to the
dome above them. "I think about the first ambassadors
from Dern. Invited to a moonlit orgy by the Balti queen?
I can't imagine the culture shock."

Mara would not allow the change in tone. "The Dern
are only shocked because they are so rigid. You refuse
to recognize that there are other ways. Other Virtues
besides compliance. Other expressions of patience."

"Like what?"

"I thought you said you've studied Balti?"

"When did he say that?" Liam asked.

Calvy leaned in. "Refresh my memory."

Mara was happy to oblige. "Balti religion teaches
rhythm—the push and pull of nature, that life is tidal,
temperamental. We can wait, not to prove our purity,
but as part of knowing we must accept what comes. All
anyone can do is respect the mercurial quality of life
and seek pleasure wherever they can. There is balance
if you know when to let go—"

"Oh, dove, spare us the theology. At least until this starts working." Liam plucked an edible from the dish on the table and Mara clamped her mouth shut, her unspoken rant colliding against the back of her teeth before she swallowed it back down. It wasn't worth it anyway. No matter what he said, Calvy was a D'Aldiern, a prince of the Dern Empire, as embedded in their society as it was no doubt embedded in him. One of the stubborn many who refused to understand a Balti Temptress was not a child raised to bring pleasure, she was a child taught to seek it out. There was a misconception that the training was sexual, inappropriate. But Mara had simply been taught to embrace what made her feel good—as a child that had been swimming and sweets and daydreaming about open night skies. She learned the power of her own physical pleasure as she grew up. The Dern scorned both their fallacy and her reality.

And on top of that: Calvy was the son—the blood, the extension—of the man who'd exiled her from her home, who'd ripped her from family. And she'd shared pleasure with him. She shook off the regret before it could cling to the memory—satisfaction wasn't something to taint. It was to be exalted. He'd been on his knees for her first. Often the salt made the sweet tastier.

Mara pushed her untouched soup away and sipped her carbonated water, exaggerating a grimace when Liam caught her eye. "Citrin—again. Is it the only flavor they stocked?"

"The pilot reports that we'll be to Balti by week end. One last stop first, on Lita, for the passengers who prefer the predictability of warmth and sunshine."

For the passengers who paid for a ride on a Fold and

traveled for months just to vacation somewhere exotic at the edge of the universe.

"I shall have to try to stay alive until then," she replied dryly.

"I quite like citrin. Peachy blush on the outside, bright pink underneath. Reminds me of something." Mara lifted one shoulder to her chin: *Wonder what?* Liam warmed her with a tender look before he turned and added to Calvy, "Mara doesn't like space."

She wished he would stop including the Dern, inviting him to interrupt. It wasn't that the game grew tiresome for her, more that she was overly stirred up by the playing of it—forgetting it was diversion, forgetting to be amused. Mara needed to let him fade away, before the torrent of emotion he triggered broke free.

"It's your first journey?" the soldier asked her.

"My second. You have to leave first. To return. I'd never know I didn't like space travel if I hadn't had to flee my home."

"Of course, my apologies."

"You say that a lot, your grace, as though the words are easy for you."

"They are."

His sincerity chipped at the dam that held her back. "Because they are meaningless. To you and me. Your latent amends have no impact on my experience. I do not need them."

"You don't need apologies?"

"I don't forgive. It doesn't change anything. It makes nothing better."

"One might argue it allows you to let go." He twisted her words in his mouth.

"I make ample opportunity for release."

"Let go of your anger, I meant."

"Anger is a passion like any other. Why let it go when you can burn it for warmth."

"That seems a very loose interpretation of Balti ethics."

"I said we embrace the good and the bad."

He leaned closer, his eyes eager with interest. "Yet how can you. *How* can you still believe that? Commit yourself to it, when what happened to your people was so bad—so unthinkably bad?"

And that was it—that he dared bring up her tragedy so carelessly—that released the overflow of emotion Mara had felt building since she'd first seen him.

"How can I? *How can I?*"

"Mara." Liam tried to stop her again. He may have liked the scene he'd created earlier but he could tell this one would be hers and hers alone. And he was right; heads were turning her way from the other end of the table. She dropped her voice to a harsh whisper, but she couldn't keep her feelings from spilling out.

"No, he asked, and I am answering. What else do I have? You've taken the rest. My planet was destroyed. My people wiped out. By you and yours."

Silence followed the accusation. Mara could hear it ringing in her ears.

Calvy retreated in his chair and she let out her breath. There. She'd told him and finally shut him up.

But then he spoke, his words hoarse with what had to be defensive pride. "You're right. Even though I was not there. It was terrible what happened—"

"You don't believe that. You think us all damsels and pagans. Not a one of us worth saving."

"And yet here you are. Who saved you?"

Mara frowned, not caring about the tension that lined her face. She did not owe the Dern her story.

But Liam answered for her. "She was found. By a Dern. Put on her ship."

Rozz. She was a historian, studying the Spread— humanity's path outward from galaxy to galaxy. She'd been interested in Balti and the other outer planets because of their proximity to the Rim, their relative youth. Though they all began in the same place, it had taken longer for settlers to reach the Rim, giving Dern, one of the Center planets, a head start. On technology, on "progress." While the future Balti traveled, Dern had grown from seed to tree. By the time Balti had been established the Dern were already spreading their branches to other planets near the Center, like Støsh, where Rozz had brought Mara after the bomb. Balti had been safely out of Dern reach until the Fold was invented. Then the Dern's unwanted interest covered Balti like a shadow.

"A Dern," Calvy repeated, "pulled a damsel from the—"

"I am no *damsel*!"

Liam slammed his fist on the table, and the woman next to Mara jumped. His voice was dangerously controlled as he spoke. "Private, remind yourself that you are no guest here."

"Forgi—" Calvy looked at Mara, who smirked at the overused phrase. "I meant no insult. It was an attempt to use Ms. Leanor's own words to prove a point. The Dern aren't everything she thinks of us."

"Well, if that's the case—" Liam took another edible from the bowl—as if that would make the first one work sooner "—quit now, D'Aldiern, you won't change her mind."

Chapter Five

"Quite an evening, don't you think, Mara?"

Evening. She'd come to hate the word. As if there were a difference between dusk and dawn in the endless Black. But she knew why they had to be out here. The ship had to be in the deepest nothingness to Fold space, to jump clear through the universe without damaging anything. And it was worth it. They'd arrive at their destination months after departure, instead of hundreds of years. Even if lately it felt like she'd experienced the Fold with no ship to protect her, like a million little fissures under her skin had cracked open, because she'd been unable to endure the pressure.

Liam set his stone on the rimmed table next to the bed.

"In the drawer," Mara said. Sometimes it bothered her that committing herself to the Temptress doctrine meant forgoing devices like health regulators, but seeing how attached others were to stones, how reliant and distracted, helped her understand the choice.

Liam left his stone where it was, still in sight. Instead he reached up and pressed his thumb behind his ear, turning off the chip that connected him to the device. "Better?"

She nodded. They were alone, truly alone now. Now she could get down to smoothing the bump she'd created before Satsume. She'd fight the darkness around them the way she'd been raised to: with connection, with pleasure.

She'd fight it like a Balti.

"You're not angry with me? For the damsel?"

"You know I'm not."

"Because it was just an expression of pleasure, to balance a long day?"

"Exactly."

"You've been distracted."

"So have you."

Liam watched Mara unwind the thin metal chain she had threaded through the seven pierced holes along her earlobe. She had to do it by feel as there wasn't enough light in their cabin to see—the ship's sensors were set to conserve energy during "the night"—which was otherwise indistinguishable from "the day."

Except now, for the first time in weeks, Mara was aware that time had passed, something had changed distinctly from then, to now. Something had happened. She felt different about the endless trudge that had bogged her down this morning. She felt awake. They were nearing Balti. They were almost there.

Liam noticed too. "I haven't seen you riled up like that in months."

"I thought that's what you had in mind, when you told me to take him?"

"I meant at dinner."

The silver chain caught and Liam stepped forward to help her untangle it. He smoothed the hair back from her neck, his hands cool against her skin.

"I'm not sure what to do about it."

"About what? We'll get to Balti, you'll put him to work—it's done." It was more than done. She'd had enough Calvy D'Aldiern.

Mara started to unlatch her dress but Liam took over. She let him, he liked to help, it was one of the quiet ways he showed his affection. And it was his hands traveling slowly across her navel—not the talk of what happened with the soldier prince of Dern—that caused her breasts to pucker against the silk of her gown.

"I'm not staying on Balti."

Mara shook the growing fog of lust from her head. "What? What do you mean? I've waited eighteen years to get back there, Liam—I don't want to visit for a day and then—"

"*I* am not staying on Balti. I have a business opportunity in another outer planet. It's not safe that close to the Rim, so you'll stay behind until I get back." He pushed her dress off her shoulder to take her breast in his mouth.

"Liam, we need to talk about this—"

"You liked it." Liam blew across her nipple, wet from his mouth, and she shuddered as it tightened another degree. "What he did to you."

"I liked it because you wanted me to like it."

Her hands slipped through his short hair as he bit down on the tip of her hardened bud, pain doubling as pleasure.

"And you do what I like?" he asked, his green eyes meeting her grey ones, sea at the edge of a storm.

"You know that I do."

"Then you'll stay on Balti. With the private as your bodyguard."

Mara tried to focus on the argument while Liam walked her back to the bed, his lips on her neck. She was horizontal, his body leaning over hers, by the time she was able to form a response.

"I don't need a bodyguard."

He lifted his head to meet her stare. "Oh, you don't? It's not the home you left, Mara. What were you—seven? When Rozz found you at the station?"

"Six."

It had been eleven minutes before detonation. She could have left Mara there, huddled on the ground between shuttle bays, but Rozz had carried her onto her ship, brought her back to the Center planets, near the heart of the Dern Empire. Mara's only memory of Balti was watching from above as the atmosphere clouded over. She'd imagined it as ash at the time, dust from the razed buildings, but the P bomb was poison, no explosions, just gas that filled the air like toxic smoke breathed into a lung. It had taken time to clear, the planet only becoming habitable again ten years later. And she'd had to wait eight more before she'd come up with the means to go home.

"Even if you had memories of Balti, it's changed—there are tensions on the surface with the new Dern governance. They've established a military base. They manage the immigration, production contracts, energy. They are doing everything they can to maintain control."

"They don't belong there—on our planet. How can they just take it?" Mara fisted the back of his shirt.

"They don't want your planet. They want your oil. If Balticourt had only negotiated—"

"You only negotiate when the other party has something you want." Her people didn't care about Dern wealth or Dern ways. The Balti had had everything they needed. They had enough energy from ocean turbines, and no desire to dig for oil they could ship off to some other planet.

"Well, she lost her people and her planet. She might have wanted those."

A strangled noise escaped Mara's mouth. "It's our planet. The Dern have no right to it. We can manage it ourselves."

"Who, Mara? There can't be more than a hundred Balti in the entire system now. You couldn't populate the Pearl, let alone the planet."

"The moonclan—"

"Mara, enough."

She understood the bite in his tone. The moonclan had relocated to the planet after the poison had cleared. They didn't need to farm the domes any longer. Because half a million people were dead. And the dead do not eat.

He paused, holding her in the soft focus of his gaze, as if he could protect her from the sharp truths of his next words. "The Dern have taken the planet. The moonclan has no power, no leadership." He nuzzled at her neck. "I admire your devotion to your culture, but the planet *has* changed. The Balti you want died with the Balticourt line."

"Maybe," Mara said and regretted it as Liam rolled his eyes.

"This is more from that tutor of yours, isn't it? It's a good thing the skills she taught you are worth the other nonsense," he teased. "Tell me again how the Balticourt family was chosen to lead by a flock of gulls."

"Raptors," she corrected. It was her favorite story. Though Jimma and Rozz always disagreed on the telling. Rozz said that Pry Balticourt had been a settler and scientist. One day when exploring the new continent she'd gone south and stumbled into one of the planet's existing electromagnetic fields, which the birds naturally circled at different times throughout the year. "No, no, no," Jimma would start. "Pry Balticourt was carrying the first child that would be born on the planet. That's why the birds *found her*." Mara was fascinated by the two versions of the story, the way time and belief blurred the truth in each.

Liam busied himself testing the skin under her jaw with his teeth. Mara closed her eyes, letting the sensation wash over her, breathing in the cool spice of his body.

Jimma had told her other stories, one of which she made sure to share only when Rozz wasn't around to dispute it. Because it wasn't a story really, but a rumor based in stardust and hope. That Queen Balticourt had lived, survived that terrible day, and escaped. That she would return. And that was how Mara knew it was just talk—it was too good to be true. Jimma was also the one who'd told her, "Life is a bitter fruit—learn to pucker or apply as much honey as you can find."

Liam was honey—sweet and golden and ready to pour into her mouth. They'd had a tumultuous day and she'd wanted to throttle him for the nonsense he'd started by hiring that damsel—but when it was just them, just Liam and Mara, just like this, everything worked. She could forget Calvy D'Aldiern, she could focus on Liam and the gift he'd given her, ushering her home to the planet she'd lost. Staying by her side, so she wouldn't have to do it alone, so she'd waste no more time. She tugged his face to hers and pulled his lip into her mouth, biting into it as he pulled away.

"There's another thing. He won't just be your security."

"Who?"

"D'Aldiern."

"Liam." She sighed, dropping her head onto the mattress. "Can't you see I'm not in the mood for talking?"

"That's exactly the issue—your moods. While I'm gone—"

"How long are you planning to be gone?"

"Six weeks, at least."

"Six weeks!" Mara's tongue skimmed the roof of her mouth. "I can wait six weeks."

"Does Mara Leanor wait? That's news. You didn't always on Støsh."

"Neither did you."

"I know how you feel—about seeking out pleasure."

"There are other ways to do that, Liam. I'm sure the food alone will be enough to keep my legs shut for six weeks."

"But why would you want to when there's such a lovely, sticky cunt in between them?"

She pushed his hand off her hip. Then she cupped his cheek. "I'll wait. To be with you."

"But I won't, my dove. And so I wouldn't expect you to—oh, come on, Mara, I don't want there to be lies between us." He put her hand back against his cheek. "Should you want to bed someone while I'm gone—"

He couldn't be serious. "I'm quite capable of finding someone on my own—"

"No. Not there. It's not safe. It's not like Støsh. The

planet is a step away from frontier. Anything could happen to you." His fingers tightened around her wrist. He captured the other and brought them both above her head, securing them in one hand. "You came for him. Twice."

"I'll—" She tried to articulate another argument, but it kept coming back to one thing: "He's a Dern."

"He is. And a prince at that."

"Not even being born to royalty could make him a prince."

Liam murmured approval into her hair.

Mara glared up at the ceiling. "And I hate them. All of them."

"I know. You don't have to sleep with him. But if you get that feeling—and we both know you will—when you need to fill that tight, dark space that keeps you up at night, use him. Only him."

"Why, Liam?"

"I want to know you're safe. And satisfied." He had that look in his eye, the one he had negotiating contracts. He would not back down, not without getting everything he wanted. And she knew there would be more—details and clauses meant to protect his interests. The rest came out as a whisper, intense and intimate, catching Mara's breath in her throat. "I want them to know what they are to us—where their compliance puts them. Make no mistake: this arrangement is not for his benefit—it's for yours. He won't touch you unless you want it—and you won't touch him unless it's for you. I'm not paying him to get his cock sucked. I want his father to know we owned a piece of him. And we did with it what we pleased."

Mara felt the pulse of lust beat within her. *We did*

with it what we pleased. Liam's words had her wet and wanting. His free hand worked his cock from the confines of his pants and he tucked her knees up and to the side. Her cunt was still swollen from Calvy and Liam groaned when he pressed into her tightened folds. In and out he moved, harder than she expected, his loose hand alternating between groping her breasts and gripping her top thigh. The angle wasn't such that she could feel him against her clit, and she longed for his hand to circle the hot spot and bring her with him. But Liam pushed into her again, just as another nuclear explosion rocked the ship, and she felt the liquid heat of him streaming inside of her. Only then did he slip his hand between her thighs, finding her slick with his own come.

"You'll think of me—when it's him inside you?"

"I don't want him," she insisted.

His hand stopped and she twisted to grab it, moving it against her clit herself. He found the back of her neck, tugging her hair so that it tingled at the roots. His fingers slid into her again on their own accord and she let him slip out of her grasp. "Let me take care of you, Mara."

She moaned his name and he brought her to release. He kissed her ear and let go of her hair to trail his hand down her spine as she clenched around the other.

"I'll think of you," he said, as if that were necessary. But Mara wasn't jealous, she understood the need for pleasure. That he'd think of her while with another woman was flattering, sweet.

"I know you will." With a soft, satisfied sigh she added, "I'll think of you too."

And Liam smiled—he believed her. He hadn't had

Jimma to teach him not to trust words coaxed from ecstasy. Because Mara had already decided: she'd rather
forgo pleasure than let the Dern under her skin again.

Chapter Six

"Did he tell you?"

"I received my orders this morning."

Calvy watched Mara closely, trying to gauge her response. At dinner last night he'd noticed the way she spoke to Pent, never concealing her enjoyment, not even of her own quick wit. Now she revealed nothing, tucking her hands into a quilted muff, covering the safety belt he'd seen buckled at her waist. Mara secured. That was his job now—her welfare. He was glad for it. For something constructive he could focus on, if she'd give him nothing else.

Since leaving Theos, everything seemed surreal, especially his first night on the ship—a wild dream that he relived whenever he closed his eyes. It had been a command, to service this Balti Temptress, and he knew where shirking orders got him—off his path, back to another. And he hadn't wanted to disobey. Even with all those people watching, with Liam Pent watching, Calvy had wanted her. As far as orders went, it was arguably the best he'd ever gotten. A close second had come this morning, when he'd stood before Pent and heard his assignment—at attention, eyes straight ahead, not a glance at the sideboard where he and Mara had—

"You were an officer." It wasn't a question, jarring Calvy back to the present. He liked that—when she didn't pretend to know less than she did.

"A captain, yes."

"So what happened? You don't seem to have a problem with compliance."

"I do. When following an order will cost someone's life." He'd always questioned those. He'd followed most of them, sure. He'd been trained to. But he'd questioned them all the same. Questioned them more on Theos, when he'd had nothing but time to reconsider his choices.

Mara appeared unmoved by his honesty. "Not likely to happen during this assignment."

"Unlikely, yes, you don't need to worry about that." Calvy tapped his knee. His mind had always been full of questions—not a great quality for a soldier—and more plagued him now. What did she think of the arrangement? Did she think that's why he was here, to have a go at Pent's Balti Temptress? She might not have been impressed by his honesty but he wanted her to know where he stood. "I didn't know. What the job would be. Maybe a night watchman. In one of his factories. Not this—"

"You wouldn't have agreed?"

Everything she said hung between them like bait. Every question a sharp-toothed trap set to ensnare him, leave him dangling by the ankle, upside-down and exposed. His pulse quickened and his palms grew hot.

"That's exactly what I'm supposed to be learning— you don't have to agree to follow orders." Another question emerged in his mind. Had she requested Pent allow it? That would make things easier. He smiled slowly. "I can't say I understand Mr. Pent's directives, but I—I'm happy to be of use. The assignment is not without its perks."

"It is. Without perks." She lengthened her throat, tilting her head from side to side as though her collar were too tight.

His own neck burned. Of course the arrangement wasn't her choice. She was the epitome of desire and as a Dern, he was assumed to be a living representation of the opposite. The two of them together was the setup of a joke he'd heard countless versions of in the barracks. In this one, the punchline was him, foolishly hoping that Mara had come up with this idea.

"I see. Well. I'll be up for—that is, I'll do what I'm told," Calvy told her, suppressing a shiver as he remembered the way she had scraped her nails against his scalp after he'd released himself into her. He could still feel the soft bristle of her red curls on his cheeks, the silky tenderness his tongue found inside her. Even in his embarrassment, he knew, if the opportunity presented itself again, he'd do what she asked, not because of some soldierly compulsion to comply, but because he'd gotten a taste of her and wanted another. "If you change your mind—"

"I won't. I don't know exactly what Liam told you—"

Pent had told him plenty. All about Mara, that she was obstinate and could be…unappeasable. He needn't have bothered with the warning: Mara made all that perfectly clear herself.

"He told me I was responsible for your security. And your…satisfaction. And in that regard, he told me I was to do what you asked. And to take no liberties."

"Well. There's nothing I can do about you being appointed bodyguard, but your other services won't be necessary."

Calvy exhaled. Done. That was Mara's call. He'd put it out of his mind.

There was a part of him that was relieved. Her desire for distance made things less complicated. It was an easier job to get right if her security was his only mission. When Pent was explaining the rest of it, panic had gripped his chest. Because it couldn't be real. And if it wasn't real, maybe he was dreaming. Maybe he'd wake up and still be on the hard floor of that prison cell, the cold that sank into his bones emanating from the stone floor, not the empty space that surrounded the ship.

But he wasn't there. This was real. He was on his way to Balti. One lucky son of a bitch.

Calvy nodded. "Whatever you say, right?"

"Right."

So he'd only have to work with her. That would be easier still if she didn't hate him so much. He tapped his knee again. He could do this. He'd done scarier things than try to make amends with a woman. "Mara, I—"

"Mara?"

"That's your name."

"It's awfully familiar."

"I thought we were."

"Not like that. You will call me Ms. Leanor."

The pilot's voice crackled over the speakers then, announcing their departure in a few minutes. Calvy couldn't see her hands inside the muff, but he imagined them folded together, the knuckles white. Mara kept her face relaxed but her furtive glances at the window betrayed her. At first he'd thought she was impatient, tired of waiting. They'd been in the shuttle for ten minutes, ready to head for the surface, waiting for clearance. But her chest rose and fell too quickly as she stared out the window. She was nervous. To go home.

"I have twin sisters," he said, hoping to distract her. "They share a name. Differentiated by their numbers. Luca Five and Luca Six. We call them Lufee and Lucee."

Mara turned from the window to look at him. "How unfortunate for them."

"I could give you a nickname. You could be—" he paused and then sounded it out "—Misslee? Milean—Millie."

"No, I couldn't."

"You're not a Millie? You're sure?" She rolled her eyes back to the window, and he must have imagined the smile that pulled at her mouth because it never surfaced. Tension tightened his forehead and he looked down at his hands before meeting her gaze again. "Mara, then? When we're alone?"

"If you must," she relented. "But we won't be alone."

"Oh, Millie, we're alone already."

Calvy knew immediately he'd said the wrong thing again. Her face went perfectly blank, hiding whatever thought had come to her. Was it fear? Of being left with him? She had to know he wouldn't hurt her. Pent would—oh. They were alone because Pent wasn't here. She missed him. The man she wanted at her side.

Calvy should have known better by now than to think conversation with her could be easy. That anything with her would be easy. Mara, for all her light-hearted redirections, was an emphatic opponent. And it had been too long since he'd seen combat. He was woefully unfit against her.

Calvy would stop trying to engage with her. He

needed to keep his head down, anyway, focus on the real mission: getting back where he belonged. He hadn't been entirely truthful discussing his reasons for joining the army at dinner with Pent. The decision had been less about following a calling and more about finding one. He couldn't live the life of an unwanted son anymore. It didn't matter that he was smart, dedicated, driven to serve—that he would have been a perfect prince— he was a blemish. A problem to everyone around him. People who thought he was born without a purpose. People who were wrong.

He hadn't found it exactly in the army. But he'd gotten closer. There he'd been something else, useful and mostly anonymous—except to a few higher-ups who'd made it their personal sport to test his "royal" resolve, who'd intended to reduce him still. For all his trials and reservations, Calvy *was* a good soldier, gaining rank, responsibility. He'd earned a position on his merit—making him more of a target to the members of command that despised him on principle. He'd even let himself imagine rising higher, above them, all the way to the top, until he held a position that even his father had to respect, to rely on. But that hadn't happened. He hadn't been able to follow blindly, suppress every question, not when it meant abandoning his unit, the people who already relied on him. The people who accepted him for who he showed them he was. People who'd let him earn his own place, earn their respect.

Mara turned back to the window, but he was sure she'd memorized the pattern of the surface by now. As he had. As a boy he'd fall asleep to a screen of Balti rotating, a night-light that did little justice to the scene below him. The projection had been flat, unable to capture the wild, tossing ocean, the height of the cliffs that cut out of it, the texture of the trees, how they danced in the wind. The city grid was more intriguing in his memory, clearer. Looking down now, thick clouds blocked the map he knew by heart from view.

"You can barely see anything," Mara complained.

"Smoke—from the factories—"

"Yes, I had deduced the cause. It reminds me of—" She cut herself off. But he could guess what she had seen. A memory layered over the present.

"What happened to you? After the bomb?"

Her response was practiced, devoid of emotion. These were the facts. "I was taken to Støsh by Rozz, the woman who found me."

"You were lucky."

"Lucky," she repeated, without looking at him.

"Støsh is an affluent planet. You must have been comfortable."

"Comfortable."

She was impossible to speak to. Yet he kept trying.

"You must have been happy there."

"Happy."

She picked him apart, one word at a time, sharpening her echoes with spite. The repetition, the way she mocked him, ground his teeth together.

How he'd fooled himself again, into thinking they were alike. Both remainders. Her without a family, him systematically ignored by his. Both lucky. He'd readily admit it. In his darkest moment, he'd given up on the dream of purpose. He'd relented, and offered himself back to his father's control, not knowing Pent would step in and he'd have another chance.

But she was closer to the spoiled courtiers that had

surrounded him for the first seventeen years of his life. The way she cut through him—he recognized the blade. The weapon of those who considered themselves so much better than him, so superior. Those who had always thought him less than.

Frustration clenched his jaw; if only it held his tongue in check. "Yes, I think it's apparent that a certain amount of comfort has always been afforded to you."

Her head snapped towards him. "I was an orphaned refugee at six years old."

"And still you think it's preferable to starve than eat stale bread."

How could it be that she seemed to tense, though her face remained relaxed. It was something in the air around her, the way she charged it with her anger. This wasn't going at all well. He exhaled and tried again. "What I mean is: I have been hungry. I have seen men starve—"

"And I have seen a world and its entire population dissolve into mist."

He didn't want to argue with her. Not about that. She was entitled to her pain. So he nodded. "I remember the uproar—when we heard of the accident—"

"The accident? You don't believe that."

He leaned forward, his own belt tightening about his hips. "Of course I do. You can't really think we did it on purpose—our society was outraged—"

"Outraged—how outraged? So angry that you did what in retaliation?" Another calculated head tilt, as though he were so biased he'd gone off center. "Passed stricter regulations?"

"What else would you have us do? We tried to make

sure that it couldn't happen again. Balti was already lost."

She waved her hand at the oil rigs that studded the coast. "So you might as well capitalize on the error."

Who was impartial now? "We aren't the only ones. It may have been a Dern bomb, but the poison was manufactured by Pent. It's his father who shares in the blame."

"At least his father had the deference to die with us. Yours has continued to take."

Falling back on rationales he'd heard and repeated before, Calvy argued, "People need the fuel. To keep warm. To—"

"It does not belong to you!"

Calvy's jaw pushed forward. *Belonging.* Of course she was concerned about ownership, she shared a bed with Pent, after all. "Now, there's a typical Balti response. Your queen was the same way—only caring about her own."

"You think the Dern are different? Concern is the pretense you use to bring others under your control. We bothered no one here. You would have left us alone if you hadn't seen our planet as a ripe citrin ready to squeeze."

Calvy sat back, feeling himself losing ground, scrambling for footing in the argument. "Is that why you dislike citrin so much?"

"Who cares if I dislike citrin?"

"I thought you'd express more humility."

She leaned forward, pressing her advantage in the face of his disorder. "I'm at the edge of my seat to hear why."

"You said it—you were orphaned at six years old."

"And that gives me no right to opinion? To preference? I was so *lucky*—nothing should ever bother me again. Here's some advice: don't think about me." She was beyond facts now, fueled by as much passion as he'd ever seen, without Pent to remind her to hold any of it back. "Tell me, is it only Dern royalty who are justified in their judgments?"

"I'm not—you're the judgmental one. You've looked down on me from the moment we met."

"I looked down on you when you got on your knees. How did that feel, your majesty, divesting yourself of your Dern-sanctioned privilege? I must admit I enjoyed that aspect at least."

Calvy had had enough. He'd do the job. He'd make it back to his unit. He'd get past Liam Pent and his Balti Tempest. But there was no need to make nice with her—it was impossible. "You can mock all you like. I don't care what you call me. I know what I am. I know my purpose. I found my place. There are lots of things I am, Ms. Leanor, but I assure you, entitled is not one of them."

"Is that anger I detect, your grace? Have you tried just letting go?"

The shuttle lurched, finally taking off, and Mara shut her eyes, ridges forming across her forehead.

"Liam told you to do what I say?"

"He did."

"Then shut your mouth—don't talk about what you'll never understand."

Chapter Seven

Balti was a small planet, attended by two even smaller moons. Mara could see them from her window, curved nails dug into the sky over the city. She could have seen them clearer on their descent from the ship, but she hadn't been looking, her gaze fixed on the surface instead, all that ocean and the one long landmass rising out of it. The city took up the south of the continent, while the north was devoted to natural space—a sanctuary of sorts, for the birds that prowled the planet, raptors, all of them, known for their ability to snatch fish from the water with their sharp talons. She'd seen a pair of them on the way down—the grey-blue wings blending into the sky like brushstrokes on canvas.

The hotel was near the city center, just west of the boulevard that ran from the shuttle port to the Pearl at the land's southernmost tip. Mara had watched the sun set, expecting the buildings to light up, like on Støsh, but most of them remained dark, the lit windows scattered like stars.

She turned around to survey the room—the third she'd seen that afternoon. Private D'Aldiern had vetoed the first—he disapproved of the balcony, calling it "an obvious risk." Mara had protested, liking the idea of standing out in the open, looking over her home, but on security matters she had no say. She, in turn, vetoed the next room just to watch his jaw set with annoyance.

"There's no view," she had sighed, waving a hand at the west-facing window. In truth, Mara felt a thrill looking down at the buildings. From this distance she couldn't see the disrepair of the crumbling sand plaster, and the overgrown vertical gardens, spilling down the open back porches, looked lush instead of neglected. The continent was edged with cliffs, except for the western side of the city, where the ground sloped and curved around a cove. And there, jutting out into the water, were the docks. Jimma had told her about the fish, as large as a man, that they brought in some mornings. Light had danced on the waves and even though it appeared flat from her vantage point she imagined the feel of the current pulling her in and pushing her back.

"You've been staring at nothing but space for months, certainly this is good enough."

"Private, you'll find that I prefer better to good. And I think we can do better."

"Of course, Ms. Leanor," he had said, his voice carefully even, and went to find the concierge.

The suite she'd ended up in, from where she now regarded the bright crescent moons, faced south, offering a view of the Pearl on the hill and the grounds surrounding it. A view arguably better than the others. So she'd made a point to complain about the old-fashioned doorknobs for Calvy's benefit.

"You'd prefer to be locked in? If the power surges or fails?"

"Ocean turbines make constant—"

"Ocean turbines require maintenance. They've shut

down. The army has set up a fire plant to power the city."

"That's ridiculous."

"There's plenty of oil."

"It's unnecessary." The Dern, for all their professed interest in progress, in efficiency, were cheap. Careless.

"Ms. Leanor disapproves—would you like me to alert the authorities?"

She had shut her old-fashioned door in his face.

The room itself was spacious—in that it reminded her a little bit of space. The air conditioning was on full blast, and the building displayed typical Dern style— all glass and steel. It was sterile, the ceilings too high, making her feel small. She wished they could stay somewhere more authentic instead of the hotel, which was newly constructed to accommodate the influx of corporate interest in Balti, but Liam had made the arrangements.

And this wasn't space. She wasn't stuck in this room. She lifted the cloak she'd slung over the couch that faced the wide windows and made for the door. A hand caught her elbow as she stepped into the hall and she jumped.

"Where are you going?" Calvy D'Aldiern asked.

"Why are you standing outside my room?" She wrenched her elbow away from him but he had already let go. He had changed into a navy blouson jacket. The ribbed bottom fitted to his waist just above a pair of dark slacks, but it bulged on the right around his firearm. His hair was slicked back as usual, not a strand out of place. He still looked like a soldier, even out of uniform.

"You seemed like the type of charge who'd try to leave without telling anyone."

"Did I misunderstand your purpose—are you a body-guard or a prison guard?" Mara walked to the elevator, jabbing at the button long after it had lit.

"I'm here to keep you safe. Which is why you won't be leaving the hotel without one of us."

"Us?"

"Your security team—you must have noticed the people carrying all those bags from room to room this afternoon."

"They don't work for the hotel?" She feigned ignorance.

"They work for the Pent Corporation. But you knew that. Our room is down the hall. They're getting settled. I took the first shift."

He followed her onto the elevator and she narrowed her eyes.

"If you don't want me, I could go get—"

"No," she interrupted, nodding for him to press the button for street level, bypassing the lobby on the second floor. "Dannos has friends everywhere, I doubt he's still in the hotel, and we should let Harper sleep. She'd never admit it, but she's had terrible ship fatigue since before Satsume. She needs the rest."

It was a hard choice, but as unpalatable as she found Calvy, he was preferable to Harper's brand of rigorous scrutiny.

He looked like he was trying to figure her out. Her motives at least. "I saw. Real gravity, unprocessed air. Should help."

"Well, at least she'll have the gravity."

The elevator doors opened and the sulfuric smell of metal production filled Mara's nose. Jimma had described Balti as a natural place—fresh and green and bright, filled with life. Mara had returned to a hazy, smog-filled wasteland. What had become of this place?

She felt the same panic she'd had in the shuttle on the way to the surface, engulfed in the haze of cloud cover. Panic, that even though she'd made it back, there was nothing left of her here. Nothing left to find.

She thought she'd feel something as soon as they landed at the station—the one place she knew she'd been before. Where Rozz had found her, saved her. But it had felt like any other shuttle port on any other planet. From above, when they'd finally broken through the fog, she'd seen a canal cut across the continent, separating the station from the city. What else had been carved away?

The elevator doors started to close and Calvy stuck out his arm to hold them open.

Mara pulled up her hood against the cool night air and stepped onto the street. She looked right and left, her tongue moving against the roof of her mouth.

She could do this. She started south.

Calvy asked over her shoulder, "Where are we headed?"

"The Pearl. I want to see the Pearl."

"Not tonight, Ms. Leanor—you have to arrange for a tour. Clearance comes from Dern."

She stopped and faced him. "Does it?"

"Dern runs the planet, in the absence of native governance."

"Because you killed our native governance."

He didn't respond. The last time they'd discussed this she'd told him to shut his mouth. He'd been gloating about his perfect place in the world when she was so unsure of hers and she had snapped. To someone else she might have considered offering amends, but she owed the Dern nothing.

Mara headed west instead, towards the water she'd seen that afternoon. She held it in her mind, the sparkling surface that almost blinded her.

The street began to slant down and she knew they were getting close. Yet she didn't see it. The buildings faced out on the side of a hill, the levels stepped, connected by the sloped road that snaked back and forth towards the shore. Everything was dark. Too dark to see the colors of the houses. Too dark to even see the water. More black emptiness. Mara closed her eyes. The Black. It haunted her. But as she took a few deep breaths she focused on the sound of the waves, the brine of the air. This was not the Black. This was home.

She had time. Tomorrow, when the sun rose, she'd see it all then. She'd fill her eyes with it. Her mouth and her ears. She'd touch and taste and steep herself in everything Balti had to offer.

Calvy was waiting patiently behind her when she turned. He had a familiar look on his face, one she was getting used to seeing—he held the question between his brows, just for her: *Are you okay?*

She refused to think about the first time she'd seen that look on his face. The heat he'd lapped over her aching cunt—the climax he'd persuaded from her.

Now, again, she'd had a tense day. What she'd like, what she needed was a dose of something pure and rapturous. Her eyes followed the curve of his lips, another crescent moon the Balti in her was drawn to worship.

"Can I help you with something?" he asked when she didn't move.

Six weeks. Liam would only be gone six weeks. All

she had to do was remember what else that mouth was good at: insulting her.

"I'm hungry," Mara said. Though it wasn't exactly what she meant.

He nodded right and she set off, threading up a set of stairs between a quiet pub and a shop that had seen better days. Most of the storefronts had. There was no one left to run the businesses—no one left to patronize them. It was like seeing a sketch of the city, shallow and toneless.

They walked a few blocks in silence before coming to the main boulevard. There they took up the middle of the empty street because they could. Jimma insisted that Mara always walk with her head up, her chin high, but Mara couldn't help looking down. The street was an intricate mosaic, bright orange lines separating eight lanes of mixed blues, wide enough for a person or—

"Hoverbikes," Calvy said. "Balti transportation was singular."

Singular, he said. But she knew what he meant: self-serving. The Dern hated the Balti autonomy. In all of its forms.

"Where are they now?"

"Military had them all locked up."

On the next corner Mara stopped. The street was torn up, the displaced mosaic mixed with gravel in a pile next to a sleeping digger. Lying beside a raw hole in the ground was a Dern street sign, declaring the road High Street.

"It's the Queen's Road," Mara said. It didn't need a sign. None of the streets had needed them before—Balti had been insulated, everyone knew where to go. Everyone had had a place.

"There'll be a lot of this. Dern changes to the infra-structure."

"I saw the canal," Mara replied.

"Standard procedure. Section off the assets, set a perimeter. That one will bite them though."

"How's that?" She hated how much more he knew about it than her, but not enough to quell her curiosity.

"In a storm surge. The continent is high, cliffs all around."

"Not the cove on the west side."

"No, but the buildings are made to withstand a storm. Set into the hill. Sloped roads. Stone breakers. The doors and windows seal—built-in bulkheads. They just have to wait for the water to recede. The canal gives the water a way into the middle of the continent. It'll flood. If a storm is big enough."

She didn't know enough about it to argue more. Just that the storm season was months away.

So she did what she always did, and kept moving.

The boulevard curved in a circle around the city center, the Ring, they called it—and the Dern would have no luck changing that. And here: here were people. Excitement quickened Mara's steps. She found an opening that led into the circular block between the buildings, following the smell of hot oil to a stand off the center of the Ring's open square. Mara had been too nervous to eat lunch and it had been hours since the paste of ground meal the ship's cook had served for breakfast. Her mouth watered as she drew closer.

"Fine evening," Calvy said to the vendor, a man with white hair and a weathered face. He grunted a reply. He was probably used to these Dern invaders. Mara felt the sudden urge to distance herself from Calvy's ignorance.

"The moons rise well," she said, repeating the phrase Jimma had used, even on Støsh, where there were no moons. No natural tug outward, upward.

The vendor lifted his head and stared at her. His gaze caught like a hook in the tangle of her red-gold mane. He smiled at her and nodded. "Very well," he agreed.

"This one." She pointed to one of the rice cakes on the cart's small counter. "Is it pinasche?"

The man nodded again. "My grandfather's recipe."

Mara held her finger up for one and the man slipped an uncooked cake into the oil, frying it fresh for her. Calvy opted for a sweet variety, covered in powdered sugar, which the man chose from the display pile while Mara's cake sizzled, the rice taking on color.

She couldn't stop herself from staring as Calvy bit through the crust, revealing a seedy fruit filling. But her own hot, golden cake was worth the wait. It was savory, tasting of green: the deep earthiness of pinasche and the brighter notes of herbs that teased her taste buds, tantalizingly familiar. Mara could feel recognition tickling the tip of her tongue and she closed her eyes to let it wash over her. But it stayed there, just out of reach. She exhaled the threat of frustration. It was only her first night. Something here would stir up her past, she was sure of it. She had tomorrows on Balti, as many as she needed.

"It's good," Calvy said. "Really good. What is it?"

Mara was pleased to know something he didn't. Something from Jimma. "Fica pear. It's a traditional dessert. I'm finding myself more and more doubtful of your assertion that you studied Balti culture."

"I studied the planet."

"I don't see the difference."

"I know the weight of the moons. Mika, the smallest, is also the heaviest. I know the deepest point in the ocean, the length of the great cephalopod rumored to live down there. Over fifty meters, but that was on its last sighting. I'm sure it's grown. I know the birds we saw today—they were blue ospreys. Out hunting. Probably jackfish, based on the direction, the time of year, the migration patterns. I know the planet. I didn't read the menu."

Mara chewed quietly and swallowed, refusing to be impressed that he'd memorized facts and ignored the customs of the people that made Balti what it was. "It's pronounced My-ka."

They stood in the square side by side, watching people pass. A group of men and women covered in factory soot left a busier pub across the square, keeping their heads down as they passed two Dern soldiers on patrol. Mara's heart throbbed as she recognized them as members of the moonclan. She'd never felt this sort of immediate kinship before. Never seen this many people *like her*, people who shared her history, her culture, who looked—well, no. Nobody looked like her. They had similar features, but their skin was pale from generations of living under the rock, no atmosphere to protect them from harmful gamma rays. And none of them had her signature red-gold hair. Only honey-colored curls.

In her mind she'd imagined Balti as a paradise—where people like her, people who had gotten away, had returned to start over together. But how many people was that? Barely a fraction of the population had been off planet when the P bomb detonated. A remainder that bordered on negligible.

The pasty had been light and warm as she ate it, but now it grew heavy in her stomach.

Mara took a different route out of the square, Calvy jogging to keep up. She kept walking, narrowly missing a stray supply truck as she walked blindly across the curved street surrounding the Ring. Calvy swore behind her but she didn't turn. The hotel was in this direction, wasn't it? But the street she was on was different, littered with garbage and stinking of urine. She passed another pub, the entrance dark and seedy, and ignored the whistles from the men smoking on the stoop.

"Take a right," Calvy said, when they reached the corner. He was closer now, not letting her have as much space. It helped orient her: they'd gone too far east.

She stepped over more trash. "Maybe the Dern should try keeping the soldiers to their barracks."

"That wasn't us. It's the toughs who run Pent's plant."

"Of course, the Dern are governed by Virtue."

He didn't speak again until they were in the elevator, rising up like the smoke from the stacks of the factories she'd seen on the city's rim.

"Is it not how you remember it?" he asked quietly. She didn't have to look at his face to know the question stitched between his brows.

"I don't remember it."

"Nothing?"

"You don't believe me?"

"You were six."

"Your point?"

"That seems old enough to—"

How dare he try to tell her about *that*. She replied defensively, her shoulders hitching up. "I hit my head. I fell. I was—I think I was rushing. Rozz says I had my shoes on the wrong feet. That they were too big. I must have tripped. My first memories are space." Cold, empty, dark—months of feeling trapped, being trapped. On an unfamiliar ship. Missing something. Missing everything. It had to be the shock of what she'd found on Balti that had her explaining to him, "Everything I know about Balti I learned from Jimma. I have more of her memories than my own."

"Jimma?"

They'd made it to her door. Mara answered as she pushed it inwards.

"My tutor. She was the real last Balti Temptress. Rozz found her. Or she found Rozz. I don't know how. Jimma found me." Sometimes Mara wondered if she'd been chosen as a Temptress, if she'd have made the cut if she weren't the only little Balti girl left. "Jimma found me and she tried to keep me connected to this place. She wanted us to return together—to be here, for the—" Mara cut herself off. In Jimma's last year she'd had trouble remembering that the story of Queen Balticourt's return was a myth; she'd talked about it like it was real. Mara had almost said it like it was real too: *the Resurrection.*

Because here, seeing her home laid bare, overtaken, she knew—she felt—why that rumor mattered so much. How much better this place could be. If only the Dern were gone.

Mara turned to look at him, gripping the edge of the door as he brushed crumbs of sugar from his jacket. She had stood apart from him in the elevator and on the street and now their faces were close—closer than they had been since he'd pulled out of her on the observation deck, and she'd returned to Liam's side, her inner thighs sticky with his come and her ears ringing with the harsh words they'd exchanged. She thought about running her finger down the length of his nose, hooking it behind his bottom teeth and pulling him into her room. She almost surged forward, ready to let him wash the day away.

But where did he get that nose? Whose black eyes had he inherited?

His father had given an order once. To kill the Balti-courts. And what was Calvy? The kind of soldier who'd follow it.

"Mara, can—"

Mara let go of the door and it fell shut.

She sat on the couch, still in her cloak, and looked out the windows. Her first night in Balti left her feeling lonelier than she'd felt since she was a little girl. The city was changed. The people were gone.

What had she thought she would find here?

Chapter Eight

Mara did her best not to see Calvy after that. When he split the extra-long day into shifts and assigned himself the stretch of night when she was asleep, she figured the separation was mutually agreed upon. Harper (the better alternative, she realized now) or Dannos was waiting outside her door during the long bloom of daylight hours. They accompanied her whenever she left the hotel, which was just about whenever she wasn't sleeping. After two weeks of walking the city's streets she'd become familiar with the geography, if not the people. If not herself.

Her favorite part of the city was west of the Ring, where the moonclan had settled in the tight buildings that covered the hill leading down to the docks. They must have been like her. Obsessed with the water, wanting to be near it. The way it changed from day to day, a kaleidoscope of colors and moods. She could stare out at it for hours. She did.

The sky was equally captivating. And equally changing. Some days it was open and bright, warm enough that she could stand and bake her arms in the sun, while others she had to wrap her cloak securely around her shoulders against the grey cold. She loved to see the shoregulls swooping through the limitless vault above the black sand beach. And it delighted her to catch sight of the ospreys further out, diving into the water after their prey. One day she and Harper were enthralled watching the blue-grey birds take down a drone that had whizzed by on its way out to a drilling rig.

"Not one of ours," Harper said.

"How do you know?"

"Ours don't go down. The birds are drawn to electromagnetism." That Mara knew, thanks to Rozz and her version of the Pry Balticourt story. "Mr. Pent had ours outfitted with blockers, they emit a repeller signal."

"Liam won't tell the army about the tech?"

"Not until they're willing to pay for it."

A rare smile covered Harper's face and Mara shared it internally. They both liked to see the Pent Corporation triumph over the Dern.

Another day the tide was out, the black sand stretched before Mara, studded with green and grey. She watched a woman walk out on the glossy beach, her reflection pausing over the deep puddles that pocked the surface. Mara had been hesitant to get too close to the water— it seemed too willful, the depths too unknowable. But today the edge of it was so far and she was curious enough to follow.

The woman noticed her and beckoned her over. That was the way it was with the people on Balti. They saw her hair and either pulled her in or pushed her away. It was the older people who opened up to her more often. They would look at her and it was like they saw so much more. They saw what she wanted to see: Balti as it had been. She'd get that look from the younger set too, but it was often tinged with skepticism. Like they didn't believe what they were seeing was real. Like they didn't believe she belonged here anymore.

The woman pulled a rock from the pool. Not a rock, Mara realized, as the woman used a stubby knife to pry the thing open. A shell.

"Oesters," the woman said, offering the bottom half to Mara like a bowl. "The thing I missed most up there." She nodded to the moons above them, the ones they couldn't see, but knew were circling. "Did you miss them too?"

"I never had one," Mara admitted. "You drink it?"

The woman smiled and nodded. The shell was rough against Mara's lip and tasted of the ocean. The oester itself was cold and slippery, sending a shiver of bliss down her spine.

"Small pleasures," the woman said as she continued to the next pool, to fill the net that hung on her arm.

"May there be many," Mara replied, the automatic response coming from deep inside her.

There were a few encounters like that. People would notice her. But limit their interactions. She remained separate from them as she gathered information, searching for her place among them.

She longed for a deeper connection. But she had no one but Dannos to lament to, staring at a row of vacant buildings, paint peeling off the wall in great colorful flakes, revealing the rough sand plaster beneath. "Those damn Dern spend all their time on street posts. But what about these walls?"

Dannos shrugged. "What's the use? Unless the buildings require weatherproofing—what does it matter how they look?"

"You're as bad as—" Mara stopped herself before she said his name.

Another afternoon she'd stumbled into the preparations for a gathering. A table set in the street ran the length of the block. Was it the full moons already? It had to be. Full moons were celebrated on Balti. The moonclan would dine under them tonight, after they were done in the factory. She imagined them here, sharing stories, passing plates. The laughter, the flicker of candles. She almost went back that night—to see it in action. To see it for real. But she didn't go.

It wasn't her place.

Instead she stood by her window, staring at the twin orbs. They were impossibly round, impossibly bright. She'd never known the moons would glow like that. She thought for a moment that she must be dreaming, that she was back on the ship, and hadn't yet made it to Balti. Who had she been the last time she'd stared up at these moons?

Every passing day, it became harder for Mara to ignore the knot that pulled tighter inside of her. She needed to loosen it. And the small pleasures weren't enough. The relief of stable ground was short-lived. The thrill of fresh food did not last. At first she slept too hard to be bothered, her body unused to the exertion, the way sunlight and wind drained and energized her at the same time. But as the weeks wore on, as her days of exploration, of searching, came up empty again and again, her mind grew restless. And so did her body.

That afternoon, in an attempt to settle herself through exhaustion, she'd walked from the stacked shipping container barracks the Dern built across the canal at the city's northern edge, through the Ring, down to the empty mansions at the foot of the Pearl's grounds. Those wide streets were almost entirely deserted, except for the Dern crews working diligently to post signs on the larger corners. She was forced to stop before she reached the southernmost point of the continent. A series of fence posts connected by crackling red lasers had been built around the grounds. The Pearl remained distant, untouchable behind them.

Now, weary but wired, Mara stood at her window, looking south to the Pearl on the hill. Built in the shape of a sphere, it was round and pale and grand. A natural jewel where the royal family had lived, where the people of Balti had been invited to gather. So far, she'd had no response to her request for a tour from Dern officials. When Liam got here—in just a couple more weeks— she was sure he'd get them in right away.

She could wait. He was almost there. She could wait. She hated waiting.

Mara sighed, turning away from the window and searching for a tin of water. Kneeling in front of the refrigeration unit under the table behind the couch, she was low enough to catch the conversation that stole under her door from the hall.

"I'm thinking of asking Cap for the night shift. Not sure how much more wandering I can take," Dannos was saying.

"Just do your job," Harper shot back. It was that easy for her.

"You're right, he's suffered enough."

"That's not what I said. Stay sharp, I'm going out."

"Where?"

"Some of us serve Mr. Pent's more lucrative interests."

Wandering. That's what it seemed like to them. Mara

wasn't wandering. She was hunting. She wanted to find a clue, something, anything she remembered. A door or a park or a smell that would jar something loose in her mind. Make this place feel like home.

She'd walk every inch of the city until she found it.

The knot inside her looped and tightened.

What if she didn't? What if no matter how long or where she looked, she never found out where she came from? In a way it had been easy to claim her Balti heritage on Støsh—she looked the part, she'd learned from Jimma. But here, she felt like an imposter, because she couldn't say for certain where she'd begun. Her chosen abstinence made the disconnect worse—it wasn't the Balti way to resist temptation, but to indulge.

Life was giving her another dose of citrin, and it was honey she needed to distract her, to provide a reprieve from the bitter rind she'd been chewing since she arrived on Balti.

And she planned to get it tonight. Just as soon as Liam screened in. He'd made it to Theos, and finally had a stable enough connection for a video call, not the short texts she'd been receiving. With any luck he'd find everything to his liking, sign his name with an impatient flourish, and be back on his way to her in a few days. But until then: Mara had plans for the call. Her hands slipped down her sides, the navy satin that barely reached the tops of her thighs rippling like the ocean under moonlight.

The mirrored surface of the coffee table began to glow and the speakers chirped to announce an incoming call. Mara nearly tripped over the armchair between her and the table as she jumped to tap the display on.

And then he was there, projected in front of her. He

was as real as a mirage in the desert and Mara could feel thirst spread through her at the sight of him.

"Ms. Leanor."

"Mr. Pent." She breathed his name, her heart beating double time.

"Fine evening."

"The moons rise well," she agreed.

His mouth opened in a hungry smile and he leaned forward, as if the urge to touch her made him forget the screen. "I think it's the sun that has done you a service."

Mara skimmed a hand up her tanned arm. "Dannos says I'm so bronzed I could be painted."

"He's wrong—it's unmistakably natural on you. You're stunning."

They stared at each other for a long moment and Mara felt her cheeks heat with longing.

"Oh, my dove—you need something."

"I do. You."

"You've not made use of the private, then? Your on-Balti Tempter."

"That's not a thing. A Tempter. Men are too selfish in their pleasures, too quick to release. There's not enough to admire."

"That's quite a stance—even in your black-and-white world. But you are a Temptress."

"Meaning?"

"You're a zealot, Mara. An extremist. You and the Dern you oppose, both abiding your binary doctrines. There's a topic you and D'Aldiern might discuss." He straightened a thoughtful finger against his lips, then directed the point at her. "You're more alike than you'd ever admit."

She sat back. She did well enough avoiding Calvy,

she didn't want Liam bringing him up. "We don't talk. I hardly see him. I wish you were here. I thought we might pretend you were."

"It's too bad you don't have one of these," he said, tilting the stone between his fingers. "A damsel in town showed me a way to link them while we fucked—it was like being one mind."

It had been a few weeks. She knew how Liam was— of course he'd already needed someone—for him that was a woman. For her, it was someone who wasn't Calvy D'Aldiern—and that's what she'd get from this call: someone who'd proven he could ease the ache that twisted inside her.

So she shrugged. "We've never needed gimmicks."

"No, we haven't." She let her knees drift apart and he rolled the stone in his hand. "But it would help us close the distance."

Mara huffed out a sigh. "I can't. You know that. Jimma said the Balti kept their bodies free of all tech. No chips, no regulators—"

"Nothing that can interfere with the natural rhythms of the body. I remember. My dedicated Temptress."

"You don't seem to mind my dedication to certain other practices."

"I mind nothing that benefits me. And I am the only one who benefits from that skill of yours?"

Irritation crept into her voice. "I already told you—I haven't even seen him. I'm waiting for you."

Liam didn't respond. He'd become distracted by the glowing device.

"Can you put that away?"

"No. I'm waiting for a message from Mi-isk."

"I thought your contract was with Theos?"

"It's not a contract until I sign, my dove, it's an offer. And if a better offer comes my way before the thumb-print is on the screen, what sort of businessman would I be to ignore it?"

"But you said Theos-made weapons sell at a higher markup."

"They also cost more to make—this planet is too proud, too slow. Production here takes too much time." He tapped the stone to his mouth and looked at her. "How's Balti—everything you hoped?"

"It's… I don't know—I'm—" Mara drifted from answer to answer, her hands twisting in her lap. She wanted to tell him, wanted to open up about her doubts, but she couldn't get the words out.

Liam wasn't listening anyway. In a burst of energy he fisted his stone, holding it up in triumph as it glowed red for an incoming message.

"I almost don't want to ask what that was."

"I got a better offer."

"What does that mean, Liam?"

"We're off to Mi-isk, to make sure this goes through."

"That's another three weeks, just to get there!"

"And then however long it takes to ensure our in-terests."

"And then five weeks to get back? That's months, Liam."

He blinked. "What would you have me do, Mara? Business is—this is necessary."

"I know, but I'm—"

But his eyes weren't focused on her, his mouth was moving, already replying to the message, making plans.

"Mara—I've got to cut this short. Need to get out of Theos before they hear I'm in bed with Mi-isk. Don't pout—you know I'd rather be in bed with you. You look like you're going to burst—take my advice, don't wait. More soon."

And then the projection cut out. The coffee table's mirrored surface went still. The silence rang in her ears.

More soon. He'd be gone for months. She needed *more now.*

If only he cared about her needs as much as he cared about his—

But Mara couldn't finish that thought. Because Liam did care about her needs. He'd seen this coming, planned for it, as he did for all things. Liam was a smart man. A thoughtful man. He knew her—knew what she needed and he'd tried to provide.

He'd arranged for a substitute.

If only it weren't Calvy D'Aldiern.

Mara put her feet up on the table and sank low in her chair.

Why did it have to be *him*?

What options did she have? Even if she managed to sneak out of the hotel, it would be a betrayal to Liam—it would be reckless for her—to try to find someone else on this planet where she knew no one.

Mara's foot tapped as she thought it through. Liam had given her parameters: that anything that happened was to be for her benefit, not Calvy's. That box was easy to check—she knew she'd benefit from a release. And she knew—it would be so much easier if she didn't know—that Calvy could provide it.

But the other rule was harder: that she had to initiate it. They weren't exactly on the best terms. Still, it was his job. If she told Liam he refused, Liam would deal with him. But she knew Calvy wouldn't refuse. He'd said as much on the shuttle down to Balti. He endeavored to please.

She didn't have to do anything for him. She could take what she needed and run.

Mara shifted her hips in the chair. Restless.

She needed to feel like herself. She needed to feel like a Balti.

Use him. That's what Liam said. *Think about me.*

That's what she'd do.

That's what she had to do.

Chapter Nine

"Where's Calv—where's Private D'Aldiern?" Mara asked Dannos when she opened the door to the hall.

One of his eyes narrowed as the other went wide, expressing his confusion. "The captain?"

"He's been demoted, has he not?"

"I heard the story from some gents stationed with a gal from his squadron. He's the captain—no matter what the bastards above have to say about it."

"What sto—no, never mind. Do you know where he is?"

"Sleeping, miss. If you'd like to—"

"Down the hall?"

"Miss? He'll be on in an hour—it can't wait? I'm to see to you until then."

No. She couldn't wait.

"I'll need the key." She held out her hand. "The captain will understand."

The room shared by her security team was smaller than the living area of Mara's suite—three long beds lined against a wall. Two of them empty. One pillow on each. Even the blankets seemed thinner than hers. It was just down the hall from her but she felt as though she'd left the hotel and had arrived at a military barrack.

Calvy lay in the bed furthest from the window, closest to the door. He slept on his stomach, his arms bent above his head, which was buried under just enough pillow to cover his eyes, block the sunlight while he slept. Mara felt like an intruder, catching him disarmed, unaware.

The thinning dusk cast the room in a half-light as she made her way to the bed. Since the moment she'd decided to do this her body had come alive. The memory of their first encounter primed her desire, excitement coiling in her muscles. She longed for pleasure and she was here to claim it.

Calvy woke disoriented when she lowered herself onto the bed's edge. He propped himself up on his elbows and Mara could feel the hectic rush under his skin when she put a hand on his back, her palm flat between his shoulder blades. Her pulse raced to match it.

"It's Mara," she said.

He rolled onto his back and pressed the heels of his palms into unfocused eyes. She hadn't had a chance to admire his body the last time she'd found pleasure in his embrace, but now, with him lying there, his breathing hitched and uneven, she could see the chiseled form that had been hidden beneath his uniform.

His straight hair was loose, slanting across his forehead, and for a moment he looked so boyish and kind that Mara felt she didn't know him at all. She combed his hair back, the strands soft and smooth between her fingers, until his face appeared again: the face of a Dern prince who thought her a Balti brat.

Which was absurd. She didn't need him to look more like Calvy, not when he was meant to be Liam.

Mara skimmed his abdomen with her knuckles,

the rippled plane grooved like sand ridges beneath the ocean. She followed the thickening line of dark hair below his navel and pushed the thin sheet out of her way. His cock was already drowsily rising to half-mast and all it took was a quick cupping of his soft scrotum to bring it to full attention. Mara ran her finger from the thick base to the rounded tip, following the seam of his cock's underside. She watched appreciatively as it swelled just a little larger for her, a drip squeezing out of the tight tip. He was responsive, she'd give him that.

He didn't ask what she was doing. And she was glad not to have to explain.

Mara climbed over him slowly, straddling his hips, opening herself up to him.

Their eyes connected, her eyebrows raised, and Calvy nodded. His black eyes were alert now, trained on her face, filling with longing. She knew what it was to be wanted, and Calvy was as eager as she was. Still, his hands hovered at her sides, as though he wasn't sure he could touch her. As though she were a phantom in his dream.

His skin was warm, like laundry fresh from the dryer and smelling as good. She wanted to bend forward and press her nose to his collarbone. But she kept herself upright—maneuvered him into position and felt him slide into place, his cock pushing deep inside of her at last.

Calvy gripped her hips, crushing the navy slip, and Mara's teeth sank into her bottom lip.

Fuck.

She closed her eyes and pictured Liam beneath her. But she couldn't fool herself. Her fingers slipped across Calvy's skin in search of any looser spot to twist into her fist. Liam was muscular and strong, but she could always find a soft place to pull. Calvy was too lean. Too hard all over. She finally found leverage, fitting her palms against the curve of his pecs, her fingertips covering the even numbers of the military identification inked over his heart. Even as she rose to her knees to roll her hips over his, she felt the difference in his narrow waist, felt the increase in her own power because of his shape.

A thin navy strap slipped down her arm, exposing one of her peaked nipples. Calvy leaned up to capture it in his mouth, circling his tongue around the tip and then sucking it flat. Mara's hands found their way into his hair as she moaned and held him close. He breathed into her. "I've wanted to do that since the tram on the ship."

She pushed him away, down, ignoring the flex of his jaw. She moved her grip to his shoulders, smaller than Liam's, but dense and stiff with compact muscles. Every detail added to the chant that pounded through her mind: *This is not Liam.* And the dark shadow of realization that followed it: *But I like it.*

Mara shifted back, gasping as his cock found the end of her, prodding against the sensitive spot deep inside her. She rubbed forward, the swollen bead of her clit against his hard, flat abdomen. Prod and rub. Prod and rub. Again and again, her eyes shut, her mouth open.

She had no excuses this time: no alcohol, or spicy edibles, or rushing space to explain the dizzy blur of her mind at his touch. She was weightless with lust, spinning above him like a kite, tied down only by their connection.

His hands feathered over her breasts, thumbs swiping under their curves. But he stayed lying flat, beneath

Chapter Ten

Mara spent the next day convincing herself it had been enough. It didn't need to happen again. She was better now. She could wait some more. Then as night approached, she watched the sun lower and her resolve faded with the light.

She let herself into his room and fit herself over him again, coming just as easily, just as forcefully, expecting it this time. Craving it.

Then she did it again. And again. A few times a week she'd slip into the Dern's bed at dusk, waking him before his shift. She was there just long enough for him to set her off, never staying through the full impact. She stayed upright as she rode him and he seemed to get the idea that his participation was limited to the thrust of his cock inside her, though his hands fluttered over her body in the unavoidable way that wind ruffles the feathers of a soaring bird.

She'd walk back to her room on shaking legs, her thighs tingling, no longer bothering to swear off the next night. This was what she had to do, to combat the sadness that threatened to drown her every day she walked Balti's empty streets.

In the morning, Harper was always waiting outside

her. Mara shivered, her focus on the tightness building from below. Hot palms returned to her sides, fingers splaying around to her butt under the slip. The skin between them was slick with sweat and wetness from her excited cunt. She rocked forward again, and then, as though he'd been waiting for the moment, Calvy lifted his hips, prodding deeper into her, rubbing harder against her. Mara bent forward, spine curved. Her nails dug into his skin, her face flamed, and she released the most pathetic whimper of relief.

She came hard—infuriatingly, marvelously hard—untangling the knot of tension and anxiety that had worked itself around her. As always happened with him, she surprised herself with the force of it, the pleasure somehow out of her control.

Mara sprang off Calvy, and he uttered a groan of protest, but she was already stumbling into the hall. She leaned against the wall, her cunt still contracting, until she was steady enough to make it the rest of the way to her room.

Dannos opened the door to her suite without meeting her eyes.

That was fine. He didn't have to understand.

What she did was for herself.

And she had needed it.

Mara's door, switching off with Dannos after lunch. She only saw Calvy in the half-light, through half-drawn lashes. The day was divided, the experiences separate.

"No word about the Pearl yet."

Mara looked up at Harper. She'd been staring at the landmark again, this time from the hotel's rooftop restaurant where they were taking their lunch. She'd finished every bite of a kelp salad with raw orange fish and sat idly scraping her spoon against an empty dish of fica pear sorbet.

"Why do I feel like that isn't going to change?"

"Just wait until Mr. Pent arrives, Ms. Leanor—he'll get you in."

"I wish it could be sooner." She pulled the spoon from her mouth one last time. She'd enjoyed that sorbet to its last drop, the definition of small pleasure. The little seeds popped between her teeth, adding a satisfying crunch. Unbidden, the thought came: Calvy would have liked it. She coughed, a seed sticking in her throat. Mara tried not to think about him during the sunlit hours. As far as she was concerned, he only existed in that darkening room, in the hazy moments between day and night. But now that he'd entered her mind, she couldn't help considering him in the context of the conversation. He was a Dern—she could not forget it. "You don't think the captain could help move things along?"

"I wouldn't think so." Harper yawned. She'd been tired all morning and Mara wondered if she'd been out with Dannos the night before. More likely she'd been collecting information somewhere for Liam. Always of use, always watching. That was more like Harper.

"But he's a prince. He must have some sway."

"He's an eleven."

"Dannos says he's well respected."

"With his unit, maybe. Not with Dern officials."

Harper's mutual disgust of Calvy was normally something Mara took part in, so she wasn't sure what made her argue now. Maybe it was her desire to see the Pearl up close, so strong she'd even stoop to wishing Calvy had the power to make it happen.

"But he grew up at court."

"That means nothing to them. Dern only respect the position you're born into."

It was little comfort that his own people didn't like Calvy any more than she did. Except his soldiers, who were still devoted to him. Mara swished water in her mouth, trying to loosen any stray seeds that might have caught in her teeth.

"Did Dannos tell you what happened to Cal— D'Aldiern?"

Harper threaded her fingers together in a move that reminded her too closely of Liam. "I think you can call him by his given name."

Of course Harper knew what Mara did when it wasn't her shift—Dannos loved to talk. And Mara loved to fuck. She wouldn't be made to feel ashamed of it. "I think you're close to overstepping."

"You're right—a woman does best in this world if she knows when to keep her mouth shut." Harper stood, looking down her nose at Mara with a pointed glare before waving Dannos over to their table. "Ask him yourself."

"Ask who what?" Dannos said, settling into the chair next to Mara.

"Nothing." Mara stewed. Dannos would have told her. She should have waited. Then she wouldn't have

sniped at Harper, giving her more cause to strengthen
her case against Mara's presence in Liam's life. And
what did it matter what Calvy had done anyway? She
didn't need to know.

Dannos opened the warming basket next to her plate
and was rewarded with the last flatbread.

"Why was Calvy demoted?"

"Miss?"

"You said you had friends who told you the story.
Tell me."

"Oh, I don't know if—"

"Please."

That was all the prompting Dannos needed. He tore
the flatbread, folding a piece in half and biting into the
crust, answering around it. "A bunch of his soldiers got
caught by Theos with counterfeit weapons. Nasty business. They don't take well to being crossed. If they think
you deserve it, they will take what they are owed. Supe-
riors told Cap to stay out of it—this General Hardcase
has been trying to catch him out for years."

"And he fell for it. He intervened."

"Intervened himself right into a Theos prison. That's
right, miss. I bet those were a few long months."

Mara worried the frayed edge of her napkin. "How'd
he get out?"

"He agreed to put his contract up for sale. So his father could buy him out."

I found my place, he'd boasted to her. And what?
He'd given it up so his papa could rescue him? She could
never imagine doing that. If she knew where she belonged, she'd never give it up. The story proved Calvy
was every bit the weak-willed Dern she assumed. Nothing like her, nothing like Liam.

"And Liam got there first." She didn't conceal her pride as she said it.

"Good thing for Cap—now he's got a second chance at the army. His father must be furious. His soldiers will be glad to see him back. Because of him they only spent a day away from the unit. Instead of rotting in some Theos zoo."

Calvy had chosen to rot in that Theos zoo to save them. The bowl was empty, her craving satisfied, but Mara spun the spoon in her hand, catching light across its curved surface. That was the part of the story that didn't make sense. "He didn't have to do it."

"No. He didn't," Dannos agreed, wiping his hands on the tablecloth. "Where to this afternoon? Or is it a sit-and-stare-at-the-Pearl kind of day?"

"The Ring, there's a soap shop." She sat straight, back to business. She was running out of places to look. Things to taste. It was time to try smells—some of her strongest memories were linked to them. The steamy waft of menth tea Rozz and Jimma liked in the afternoons sent warmth buzzing through her. Less appealing, but just as evident, since the sweet scent of the wax Calvy used in his hair had stayed on her skin for hours after their first night together, the slightest hint of the scent now could trigger a flood of lust in her veins.

Calvy. The story stuck in her mind as she tongued one last seed wedged between her teeth. She shouldn't have asked about him. It didn't matter what he'd done. It wouldn't change what he was to her.

Mara excused herself and made for the washroom, using the mirror to dislodge that last speck of dessert. Standing with her hands on the edge of the sink, she looked down at her feet. The floor was as flat as it had ever been, so why did it feel as if the world had tilted on its axis? What entitled prince would sacrifice himself for a few army grunts? His orders had been to leave it alone. And he'd traded himself for his unit anyway.

That was the man whose room she visited each night—he wasn't such a Dern about that. And it didn't feel much like he was acting on orders either. When he was looking up at her, there was something in his eyes she didn't want to name. How could she abide that look, knowing what she did now? Knowing him to be the kind of captain who'd surrender his position for the sake of those without, who'd accept a punishment that wasn't his. How could she pretend not to recognize it for what it was? Genuine virtue, that made him inconveniently less deserving of her scorn.

The faucet next to her automated and Mara glanced up. The hotel clientele was almost entirely Dern prospectors and subsidiaries looking to claim a piece of the growing industry. So the woman in the bathroom stood out—her red hair against the black tile a bonfire in the night. That hair. Mara had been looking for weeks and the only other time she'd seen a color like it was looking in the mirror.

The woman finished coating her lips in a bronze shimmer and raised her eyebrows at Mara's reflection. She blinked.

Mara started. "Oh—I'm staring. It's—your hair. I've looked for it. All over the city."

The woman took her measure in the mirror. "You're searching for red-haired Balti?"

Mara nodded, not trusting herself to speak without rambling.

The woman turned to face Mara directly. "Are you a patriot?"

"A patriot?"

The woman lowered her voice. "Are you loyal to the queen?"

"Queen Balticourt?" The surprise Mara displayed caused the woman to withdraw.

"I shouldn't have said—it was your hair. I thought you supported the cause. The dye is the best I've seen yet."

"It isn't dyed."

"Like I said: my mistake." The woman dropped her lip color in her hurry to pack it in her bag and Mara bent with her to the ground, catching her hand by the wrist.

"What cause?"

Mara bit into her cheek to conceal her urgency and waited. Hoping. Hoping the woman would say what she longed to hear. And the woman delivered, her eyes brimming with purpose.

"The return of the queen."

Chapter Eleven

"Oh!"

Mara's exclamation caught Calvy off guard. As had her door opening to the orange glow of the hall in the middle of the night. He eased his hand off his sidearm and stared at her, as surprised as she appeared to be, face-to-face somewhere other than his bed. Her pillowy lips came together with a swallow and parted again, her breath stuttering with the too-quick swelling and dipping of her chest. It was clear she'd forgotten he'd be there, standing guard. Or perhaps she was used to looking down at him. Wasn't used to seeing him upright, clothed. Stiff and composed.

Stiff she should be used to.

Calvy sniffed sharply, fighting the instinct to come fully to attention, hands immobile at his sides. Mara had enough power, there was no telling what she'd be capable of with more. Even if her eyes lacked their normal focus, the iridescent grey dulled by an uncharacteristic fog. She half turned, returning to her room, and he noticed the damp hair at the back of her neck. The way she remained a little breathless.

Oh. Now he understood—too well—recognizing the specter of fear that agitated her movements. He was acquainted with the feeling of jolting awake in the night, lungs aching like he'd been screaming. Of surfacing out of the kind of nightmare where the details fade immediately but the emotion remains, vivid as a flare in the night sky. What would it be for her? Loss and pain and terror as bright as fire, however distant.

"Mara?"

She pivoted back to the hall, her gaze concentrating on him. "I'm out of water."

"I'll get Harper—"

"Let her sleep. I'll go myself. Better yet, you can go. The vend is on the second floor."

He hesitated.

She sighed. "You think I'm going to run off?"

Thinking it over, Calvy tapped his thumb on his leg. "Unlikely. Where would you go?"

Mara blinked. He hadn't meant it as an insult but there was no mistaking that she'd taken it as one when she snapped, "Then go."

His arms locked involuntarily to his torso.

With some of the frustration filtered out of her voice, she added, "Please?"

Please. A word so simple it would be foolish to give it more meaning than it deserved. He considered her for a long moment and then headed for the elevator. She wanted water—he had no reason to deny her that.

"Cal," she called after him, so unexpectedly he froze in place. She faltered for a moment, as though the nickname on her lips was as jarring for her as it had been for him. He turned, waiting for the rest, pretending he hadn't noticed her slip of the tongue. "Not citrin—get gilderberry."

"Gil—what?"

"The one with the blue top."

At the vend, he had the urge to select citrin despite her request. There'd be some satisfaction in showing her she didn't always get her way. But his satisfaction wasn't the job. And deep down he liked pleasing her.

Mara was waiting in the door when he returned, blue-lidded tin in hand.

"Still here," she announced.

"I wouldn't have gone if I'd doubted it."

"Ah, and you know me now? Because I've found a use for your cock."

He should have brought her the damned citrin.

Calvy folded his arms, tucking the tin away from her under his elbow so she couldn't take it and go, the way she normally dealt with him. Not tonight. Not when he had a chance at equal footing. "You're having a hard time pretending everything is fine tonight."

"Everything is fine."

He wouldn't let her get away with that either. "Dannos reports that you spend your days alternating between staring out at the horizon and wandering the streets. Says it would be easier if you dropped something. At least then you'd know what you were looking for. What will you do when Pent gets back, and you haven't found it yet?"

"Why do you care?"

She'd probably respect him more if he shrugged, feigned disinterest, but Calvy couldn't help admitting his curiosity. He wanted to know more of the story she held so close to herself, afraid to lose what was left of it. "I want to understand. I know why he wants you.

Beyond the obvious. You're a status symbol to him—a commodity—the last real Balti Temptress in the galaxy."

Calvy's jaw clenched when Mara stifled a yawn. "Are you saying I'm priceless?"

"I'm saying you're owned. Why do you let him keep you? When you don't need anyone?"

"I am not kept. My company is a gift." She crossed her arms, mirroring his stance and preparing to square off against him. "And Jimma said a Balti Temptress cannot be bought. She is earned."

Calvy leaned his shoulder into the wall. "And what did he do to earn you? Passage on a Fold?"

"Liam gave me what I wanted without me having to ask." She put her hand out for the water he'd gone to get for her.

He kept his grasp tight around the tin. "And your Jimma knew everything?"

She exhaled, releasing some of her hostility at the same time. "My Jimma. You say that so respectfully."

"Should I not?"

"You most definitely should." Mara cocked her head and ended the digression. "Yes. She knew it all. But she wasn't without her faults. She loved a Dern."

"Good of you not to hold that against her. Of course, he was probably the reason she survived?" He checked his assumption with a question. "Why she wasn't on Balti?"

"I see the point you're trying to make, but in another, more accurate sense: forcing her to leave with him shortened the time she had here. When the P bomb detonated, she'd already lost her planet, her heritage, her home."

"How do you know he forced her?"

"It's what the Dern do. They get off on control."

Calvy warmed under the burn of her gaze. Slowly, he peeled back the blue lid and placed the tin in her hand. He let the tide of emotion he felt ebb away before he spoke, changing the subject. "Citrin is typical of long voyages. For nutritive reasons. It wasn't an oversight, of whoever did the stocking on Pent's ship."

"Fascinating," Mara replied, taking a long sip. She had no reason to stay now, not after her needs had been met. But she hesitated in the doorframe. "I know how I sounded—how it seemed. About the water, the flavor. It...it reminds me of the worst time of my life." She looked down, fingering the edge of the tin—were the nightmares he'd guessed at still fresh in her mind? "When I was alone and the darkness was all there was."

The change in her voice twisted his stomach. Yes. Those feelings that had chased her from her bed were still with her. His fingers drummed against his forearm, this time an expression of his barely contained uselessness. "I should have realized. I'd heave faced with stewed yarrow."

"Aren't you going to pry into my personal life some more? I'm sure you've another scathing commentary about my lifestyle you're dying to share." She poked, but only half-heartedly. He knew she was capable of more force. That she didn't use it could only mean she wasn't in the mood for a fight.

Cal wasn't supposed to take any liberties. But her defenses were down, and the opening she'd given him was too tempting. "You think Pent earned you. You think he'll make you his wife?"

Mara surprised him with a laugh. A thrill of desire

rose into his throat at the unselfconscious way she displayed enthusiasm. The freedom she felt to show her pleasure, whenever she felt it. "His wife? That would not benefit me in the least."

"You don't require a promise from him?"

"What's this? The scholar knows something about Balti unrelated to migration patterns?"

"My grandfather's first wife," he reminded her.

"She took a promise from a Dern king?"

"He gave it. To protect her home from invaders. And he kept it. Well after she died and he'd taken another wife. Kept it even as tensions rose in the Empire. Kept it even as oil stores dwindled and density reports came back that Balti was thick to the core with it."

"And then?"

And then the inevitable. Calvy had lost the one person who'd ignored the controversy of his birth, who'd treated him like he mattered, just by being him. The person who'd first put the thought into his head: *What were the Three Virtues of Dern compared to the promise of Balti?*

"He died. And my father made no such promise." Calvy caught his breath, preparing for the fallout that normally followed a mention of the Dern king Mara despised.

Mara activated the door's anchor and stepped into the hall. She moved sideways, keeping her back protected. He widened his stance and his eyes, watching her slide down the wall, stretch her legs out in front of her, and cross them at the ankles.

That was not the reaction he'd been expecting.

"Sit down," she said. "You'll strain my neck if we keep talking like this."

"Keep talking? You're talking to me now?"

"Are you busy?"

Calvy looked up and down the hallway but it was late and they were alone.

"I won't tell," she added.

No, he'd be the one to put this in his report.

He knelt down, squatting, ready to spring into action if the need arose.

Mara shoved him and he fell to the side. "I said sit." She approved when he straightened his legs out and leaned against the wall next to her. "That's better."

Calvy wiped his palms on his pants. "You don't make it easy," he said after a moment, "to see that there's a considerate person under all that shiny fabric, all that forced frivolity."

"It's not very much fabric," she deflected.

The end of her robe's belt rested on the floor between them and Calvy picked it up, rubbing it between his fingers, waiting for her to snatch it away. "You know my father offered for Queen Balticourt. She refused."

"You misremember your history again. It was he who refused her terms."

He disagreed, hoping they'd be able to argue objectively without exchanging personal blows. "Her terms? Were made in jest. She could have simply said no."

"It was no jest. It was the promise she required. In exchange for her soul and her body, she respected herself enough to demand it."

Calvy tugged gently at her belt. "Demand that he give up his throne?"

"Give up anything in exchange for her."

"Her expectations were unrealistic."

"So were his."

He shook his head, releasing the length of fabric. "He wanted an alliance—"

"Political allies are not only won through marriage contracts. He wanted her. And her submission."

The yellow lights buzzed as he considered her point. It would have been no hardship for Calvy, to renounce something that was never his. His captaincy though— the position he'd fought to earn—he'd been forced to give it up twice now, and he wasn't sure he had it in him to let it go again, "He was a king. He had his kingdom—"

"And she hers. He could have relinquished his position for a place at her side."

"He had a service," Calvy tried to explain. "He is a Dern—"

She cut him off, impatient as always to have her say. "And taught that that makes the difference. He would not serve her. So he did not deserve her."

Calvy lengthened his neck. "And, if he were worthy, she would have served him?" Did she think Pent worthy? Is that why she did what he asked?

"If a Balti Temptress binds herself to a partner, she devotes herself to them. But you know that. Isn't it what started your fascination with us? The way your grandfather talked about his first wife's devotion?"

"No. It was the way he talked about his."

She slipped forward, losing balance, her shoulder bumping into his. Then abruptly pulled herself straight, sipping at her water. He knocked his toes together, feeling self-conscious, his all-terrain boots—army-issued and Pent-made—thudding dully.

She surprised him again, passing him the tin. He watched her note his hesitation, the gleam of awareness in her eyes growing brighter. It seemed to amuse her still, how carefully he took it from her hand. But she was offering him something more than a water tin— with this conversation, to him, they were building something delicate, easy to break. A truce.

"Much better than stewed yarrow," he said after cooling his throat. "To be fair, the nutritive powder they added made it chalkier than it would have been."

"Is that what they served you? In prison?"

"Who told you—"

"Harper and Dannos don't only report on me to you. Information flows in all directions."

"Harper barely reports to me. I don't believe you got anything from her."

Mara brought one shoulder up to her chin and a small smile flashed across her face, giving everything away without saying it. "How long were you there?"

"Three hundred bowls of yarrow."

"Three months?"

"Ten."

He watched the calculations behind her eyes. Her throat worked through another thick swallow as she reevaluated the assumption that he'd had three meals a day.

I've been hungry, he'd told her. That had been an understatement.

"That's why you agreed to sell your contract?"

"Quit soldiering or stay in prison. It wasn't that hard of a choice."

"I thought it was your calling. Your place."

So she thought it cowardly that he'd offered himself back to his father. The decision hadn't been easy, but it was the only one with possibility attached to it. And it had gotten him here. "It was my way out. I guess I'd rather starve my soul than my body."

She spoke with the automatic ease of someone repeating a lesson learned long ago. "The body and soul are united, what pleases one pleases the other."

"Then they are both pleased. That I get a second chance. If Pent returns my contract with positive marks the Third will have to reinstate me."

"And if he doesn't?"

Carbon fizzed in his mouth. "They'll have cause to terminate. And the king will be pleased instead." He'd have Calvy back on a shelf.

"Then we'll have to make sure Liam is happy with your work. I'd hate to contribute to your father's happiness."

If she'd have looked at him, they might have shared a smile. But she didn't. Maybe it wasn't something she was willing to risk. Maybe the reminder of his father's presence hovering over them prevented her from feeling true amusement. He didn't tell her she was one step ahead of the king—she'd already found a use for his superfluous eleventh.

Mara didn't hold a monopoly on grievances with his father—Calvy harbored a few of his own. The man may have given him life, but he'd also tried to take it back. Before Calvy'd been sentenced to a Theos prison, he'd lived in a Dern one. That king, his court, his generals all believed, all declared Calvy born without a purpose. They'd been wrong. And he still had a chance to prove it.

In the elapsing silence, the other implications of Mara's words hung in the air. To keep Liam happy, to keep herself happy, she'd visit Calvy's bed, take her pleasure from him. And Calvy would keep a secret: there was relief under his resentment. Acquiescence coupled with the consolation of being good for something. More than that, because Mara didn't hold herself back, because the purity of her desire for Pent was so strong, so boundless, Calvy could almost feel it transferred to him. She wouldn't want to know she was giving Calvy something he'd ached for at every stage of his life. She wouldn't want to know that there were moments she made Calvy feel irrevocably wanted.

The water tin had grown light in Calvy's hand. He handed it back, expecting Mara to take the rest and leave him where he was. But something kept her in the hallway. He wasn't fool enough to think it was his company. More likely she was avoiding what had driven her out of the curtained dark of her room. It was only in comparison to that that she'd choose him.

She rolled the tin between her palms, the metal crinkling softly. "Your father—the man *you* serve indirectly as a soldier. The one you claim isn't responsible for the wreckage of this planet. He installed the military here. To make decisions?"

Calvy nodded. He shifted to look sideways at her, trying to guess at what was on her mind. "They needed someone to handle the details of restructuring, oversee the drilling rigs."

"There shouldn't *be* any restricting. There shouldn't *be* any oil rigs. And making decisions doesn't require some prowess, some ability only the Dern possess. Conviction isn't another market you've cornered."

Calvy didn't respond. He couldn't. Not when the conviction in this Balti's voice forced the air from his lungs. His chest constricted while she pressed on.

"What would it take—for them to let us govern ourselves? Have our planet back?"

"For my father to turn over control? A leader he couldn't deny. The Balticourts were the only ones to ever rule here. And the Balticourts are dead."

The thin metal buckled under Mara's grip. "I know that."

He faced her fully, surer now of the self-indulgent thought she was embarrassed to speak aloud. "It's just a rumor, Mara. The queen was at the Pearl—they all were. My father had them count the bodies, down to the last toe. She didn't escape. None of them did. She's dead. Queen of dust, that's what my father called her."

At the mention of his father in that context—so closely linked to the tragic past that informed her very being—the delicate truce slipped out of their grasp.

Mara shot to her feet and Calvy scrambled up after her. The anchor latch stuck when she tried to shut the door. Once. Twice. Her elbows winged wide with frustration and he eased her out of the way to fix it.

Her breath was harsh again, like it had never settled, like he'd done nothing for her since she'd appeared in the hall. But with her eyes fixed on the door, she gathered herself.

"Thank you," she said, the final surprise of the night. "For the water."

A courtesy. Maybe their truce had only cracked, not broken. Risking another allusion to his father, another fissure, Calvy admitted the truth he believed, a truth that no royal Dern was permitted to speak. "Accident or not, it shouldn't have happened. And if there were a way to make it right. To make it better. I'd do it."

He waited for her to turn, to see the unmasked sincerity he was offering her. He waited for her to give some sign that she believed him.

Mara stepped inside and closed the door without looking back.

Chapter Twelve

Small waves knocked the boats together with a gentle splash. There was a thud of wood and a clink of metal and then another crest pulled them apart again. Mara was obsessed with the water's power, especially on days the waves shattered into mist against the rocky walls of the cove.

"Can you swim?" Harper had asked her yesterday, when the waves were choppy and rough.

"Of course." Støsh had pools.

Harper had shrugged. "It was worth asking. D'Aldiern can't. If you want to go in, don't come with him. I won't let you drown. I'd lose my job."

Of course Liam's factotum would drag her back to shore. Anything for Mr. Pent.

"That's reassuring."

"You've been staring at it for months."

"Your point?"

"What are you waiting for?"

Mara hadn't answered. She didn't want to admit that she was afraid. Not just of the water's power, but its depth. That she looked out to the darkest blue and imagined the ocean monsters Jimma had spun stories about. More of the planet was underwater than above it. Mysteries had to be hidden beneath.

If she was going to go in, this would be a good time—with the waves lapping gently at the shore. When the tug of the undertow at her heels wasn't strong enough to pull her down to the waiting clutches of some giant squid. Thanks to Calvy for giving dimensions to her fear.

She thought suddenly of the academic inflection he'd used when rattling off facts about the planet's eco-system. A theory had formed in her mind, without her permission, that it wasn't hostility driving him to pick her apart, but curiosity. He wore a look sometimes that reminded her of Rozz, always studying, always learning. But Mara wasn't interested in conceding her history to any Dern.

Moons, this one in particular was giving her trouble. Why was it so hard to speak to him and so easy to grind her hips into his? When they tried talking, he only made things more complicated. Like in the hall the other night, when he'd offered no apology for his Empire's actions, and somehow given her something better. Unexpected support. And in doing so, made her question whether she'd been wrong about him. Misunderstood what drove him. Mistaken his natural earnestness for Dern zealotry. In that moment, he hadn't been an entitled prince, nor a blindly committed soldier. He'd been someone else she hadn't gotten to know.

Now it seemed Calvy D'Aldiern was a man who questioned, who listened for the answers, who learned. He was a man who surprised her.

She didn't want that Calvy, sincere and open. She preferred him riled up and hostile. A soldier who volunteered to fight for a cause she abhorred. That detail made things easier, clearer. Even out of uniform, she couldn't let herself separate him from the enemy. He was Dern—royally, despite the crown's opinion.

Queen of dust, that's what my father called her.

Calvy's sire would know all about it. The particles and smog thick in the air. They hadn't only killed her people, they'd destroyed her home. Sucked the beauty from its bones like marrow. Taken all the life Balti had to give.

Except hers.

And despite his pledge, there wasn't anything Calvy D'Aldiern could be or do to fix what had happened on Balti. What had happened to her.

No one could make it better.

Dust. The wind would sweep it away, along with everything else.

Mara didn't hear the footsteps behind her and jumped, feeling someone pull her hood up over her head. She turned, wide eyes finding the woman from the bathroom, her own hood drawn up, covering her hair. That conversation, the two of them doubled in the mirror— every time she remembered it—seemed less and less real. Just as she'd determined that Queen Balticourt's Resurrection was a myth, she'd almost convinced herself the encounter itself had been a dream—the wild hope stirred up in her a storm at sea, leaving no trace. The woman as much a ghost as the queen she claimed to support. But here she was again. Her upturned eyes bright despite the shadow of her hood.

Mara moved to sweep her own head covering back and the woman stopped her. "No, it's too easy to spot, the both of us out here talking."

"Who would spot us?" Mara asked, following the woman's gaze to Dannos, who had wandered to the stone wall lining the hill. He straightened when Mara looked at him but she held up a hand to keep him at bay.

"Your bodyguard, for one, I don't know who he reports to. But there are others."

"Others who would care about two women talking?"

"Nothing more dangerous." The other redhead reached out, tucking back one of Mara's crimson curls. "Together we're quite noticeable. You really don't dye it?"

"Why would I?"

"It's how we spread the message. How we spread hope."

"Hope for what?"

The woman pursed her lips then released a little sigh. "Say you see the glimmer of red across the square and for a moment, it seems possible that maybe it's her. Or at the very least, you know you aren't the only one wishing for change."

"Her? You mean Queen Balticourt?"

"Of course."

Mara shook her head and her hood slipped down. She pulled it back up. "That's not real."

"Not to you. You don't need it to be. Taking your leisurely strolls every day, living in your fancy hotel. A right tourist."

Had the woman followed her? Mara should ask, only she couldn't help defending herself first. "I'm not a tourist."

"And yet you haven't been compelled to work in a factory."

"And you? You're not in a factory."

"I make my own way."

"Doing what?"

"Offering a little bit of peace. I take care of people, and they take care of me."

"You're a Temptress?" Mara almost choked on the words, saying them so quickly.

"I didn't say that," the woman snapped, drawing back, a defensive maneuver of her own. "I provide solace but I don't claim to be a Temptress. There are no Temptresses left." She breathed out. "Except Queen Balticourt."

"Right," Mara said, turning her eyes back to the horizon. It was too far, too much, for her to suspend the facts and believe in fairy tales. As much as she wanted them to be true.

"You have questions. And you must have connections. Maybe we could help each other."

Questions. Mara had them. She doubted the woman had the answers. Nobody did. Nobody could answer the mysteries that plagued her, that had always plagued her. Except… Along with wondering about herself, she'd always imagined others like her. Was there another little girl, as alone and confused as she was?

"What's your name?"

The woman squinted at her. "Iola."

"I'm Mara."

The wind pushed a white cloud over the sun, but Iola's eyes remained narrowed. "I thought you wanted to know about the Resurrection."

"I want to know about you."

"Why?"

"I—" Mara faltered, unwilling to reveal the sentimentality that had precipitated her question. "I just do."

A longer sigh from Iola told her she should have done a better job keeping her feelings to herself. "I was born on Balti, my mother was from Niell. We were there visiting when the poison spread. That's the big moon."

"I know what Niell is."

Iola shrugged. "You're not from here."

"Yes, I am."

"I mean you're not like us. You didn't live it, wherever you came from."

"That's not true." She sounded petulant, a child tugging back her toy and shouting *mine*. Only the toy she was fighting for was pain. She was claiming her own tragedy—it was all she had, and she wouldn't let anyone take it from her. "I lived it. I survived it. Saw it all from a drop shuttle. I was here."

Iola raised a skeptical eyebrow. "Your parents weren't already off planet."

"No. They died in the poison. This is my first time back."

"And?" Iola asked.

The boats knocked together again. Mara wanted to say more. To confess that she found the entire planet unrecognizable, so frustrating she wanted to tug at her hair, pull every red coil from her scalp. That the moments Balti felt like home were fleeting, like she was trying to cup the wind, hold on to something that wasn't there anymore when she opened her hands.

But it was Iola who answered her own question. "I remember how relieved I was, when we finally came back down. I went right to my house, like I was expecting my father to still be there, waiting. The feeling was short-lived."

This was another version of the story. And Mara felt a flare of jealousy for it. What if she had a place to check? A person to miss?

"We all need something returned to us," Iola said quietly. "You don't believe in the cause?"

Mara blinked quickly and cleared her throat. "I would, if it were possible."

"Then you do, for it is."

"The Balticourts are dead. By all accounts—there are pictures—"

Iola rolled her eyes. "Pictures can be doctored. Think about the source, Mara."

Tightening her arms across her chest, Mara shook her head. "That's a reach. Explain the rest: Where would she go? Why hasn't she returned?"

"You've only just returned—haven't you? She's like anybody. Waiting for the right moment. That's our job, to make the moment happen."

There was conviction in the words, reverence. Mara felt it anew as Iola spoke, the hope glowing inside of her. But she didn't trust it.

"Our people were annihilated. And those that witnessed it forced to work." A cold breeze rippled off Iola's hood.

"Why don't they find something else, if they don't like the factory?"

An incredulous look took over the stranger's face. "There are contracts. There are—you don't understand. This isn't your life. Even before Dern, the people down here kept the Balti way to themselves. We weren't at risk of being washed away on the moon, but we had our own struggles, our own ups and downs to combat, yet no Temptress bothered to grant us any rapture."

Mara shifted side to side, Iola's revisions to her narrative making her uncomfortable. She'd never thought about what prejudices might have been present on Balti long before the Dern arrived.

Iola waved the past away, saving it for another time. "What we must do first is rid ourselves of the Dern, that's the only way to be free. To rebuild Balti better than it was. Stop it from becoming some sooty production planet."

How did Iola do it? Make the Resurrection sound real. Possible. Just like Jimma had believed. Maybe Mara was too disconnected, too other to manage that kind of belief.

Iola started down the road, the wind at her back deepening the cave of her hood around her face. "Think about it. Think about what you believe. Think about what you want."

She turned away and Mara was left behind, staring at the boats just as she had been. Another thud. Another clink. But a new sound joined the chorus—the screech of a bird. Above Mara a shoregull hovered in the wind, wings spread, going nowhere.

She'd been searching since she got here. Searching for her place. And so far she'd just been drifting, bobbing idly in the current. Finding nothing.

If it was possible.

It wasn't.

But if it was.

She'd have a purpose. She could be part of something.

Chapter Thirteen

"Damned Virtues, Mara—is there something you like about me standing outside your door every night with a raging hard dick?"

Mara gripped the dresser, as far as she'd gotten on wobbling legs after dismounting Calvy midclimax. "I assumed you gave it a tug yourself before coming to work."

"It's not the same." Calvy fell back on his bed, his fists balled and his eyes squeezed painfully shut.

A creeping guilt wound its way up her spine. The guilt of seeing him differently, and using him the same. Hearing the pragmatism in his tone instead of insults. Reframing all those questions he'd asked not as mockery, but genuine interest she'd mistaken for derision. She forced the guilt back. When she provoked him, he always revealed his true Dern colors. "That's not my problem."

"Is part of being a Temptress making someone hate you as much as they want you?"

He should hate her. Hate the way she used him.

Sometimes she hated him. Hated that she'd started seeking him out even when she wasn't aching for him, when she wanted companionship, wanted to talk. Hated that she had noticed how he'd begun to fill out, his shoulders rounding and widening. She'd seen him running along the boulevard, his army-issued cargo pants tucked into his boots, a white cotton undershirt stark against his newly tanned skin, tucked tight at his waist. Everything pinned down, in place, where it should be.

"Training," he'd huffed as he went by, though she hadn't asked aloud.

"Are you sure you've enough pockets on those pants?" she'd called after him. He'd turned to grin back at her and she hated the flush it'd brought to her cheeks. The reaction she should not have had.

Mara straightened herself and went to the door. "Why don't you confer with Liam, he's due to call tomorrow."

"Fuck Liam."

Calvy's ragged breath filled the room. And she was the cause.

It took all of her effort to smile casually and tell him, "I would. If he were here."

But it wasn't just her tone that felt forced. She'd been with Liam for two years, together daily on board the ship for eight months of it. They'd only been parted for the last three. And she felt it. Time and distance pulling on their connection, stretching it, thinning it. He was expected back in a week, maybe two, and then, she hoped, everything would snap back into place.

It would. It had to. Because this thing with Calvy, and the fact that it wasn't as unpleasant as she'd imagined—not even remotely—it made her feel like she knew less about herself than she had when they'd landed.

Her whole life, she'd used her Balti heritage as a shield. Strengthening it around her. Hiding her missing pieces behind a wall of bold identity. And now it felt thin. It might be easier to let it drop. There was no one here to perform for anyway.

After a fitful night of sleep, Mara sequestered herself in her room. Liam was supposed to screen in. She'd missed the last time he'd tried to make contact and the message he'd recorded for her had not given much detail—other than that he planned to leave Mi-isk in the morning. For some reason he'd been out of range ever since. But it had been enough to know he was heading here, to her. That he was on his way back. Still, it had been too long since she'd seen him and she couldn't risk missing him again. Not now, when it felt like their relationship depended on a clear connection.

The morning passed slowly and Mara roamed the space, her body used to being out. Despite the wide window the room seemed confining. The sun was just angling downwards when the coffee table's chirp registered an incoming call. She could barely see the glow in the sharp shards of light that slanted into the room.

Mara activated the display and Liam appeared.

"One second," she said, transferring crumb-filled plates from an early lunch to a side table.

"What's happening?" He cocked his head to the side, trying to get a better angle on her.

"I'm cleaning."

"Now?"

"I'm almost done. There." She sat on the couch. Liam looked back at her. "Hello."

"Hello."

His pale green eyes were even more subdued in the projection but his gaze was sharp as ever. Mara looked down, shifting on the stiff cushions. "When are you getting in—week end or—"

"Didn't you get my message?"

"Yes, that you'd left Mi-isk weeks ago."

The image flickered as Liam shook his head. "And then we had to go further out."

Her palms pressed flat in her lap. "How much further? Where are you now?"

"The Rim."

"The Rim." She repeated the words, testing them, trying to make sense of them.

"There's an incredible view of the Pebble Belt." He twisted the camera around but Mara saw nothing, a blur of rocks in deep black space. Dust. More dust. "My dove, your face almost makes me regret this decision."

"You were—you were to be here in two weeks—"

"It'll be closer to three months now. To get back."

Three months. Another three months.

Mara stood, pacing the floor between the couch and table. She tried to articulate the problem, but she couldn't. The sphere on the hill winked at her in the noon light. "We were supposed to go to the Pearl—I've been waiting. I told you, didn't I? The Dern won't deal with me. If you were here they'd—"

"I'll call in some favors. See what I can do—there's no need for you to wait. There. Is that all? Mara? How can I fix it?"

But Mara had turned her back on the screen, her eyes filling with tears she would not let fall. "I'm fine," she said, filling her lungs with air. Gulping it down, gasping for breath.

"It's been hard for me too. Why don't you show me what I've been missing?"

Three more months.

Mara swiped at her cheeks. "I've been in all day, waiting for your call."

"And?"

"And I've got to—" Do something. She grabbed for her cloak, hanging on the back of the couch, and jabbed her arms into the sleeves. "Go out."

"I was talking about taking clothes off."

There was an edge to his voice that she ignored. "Cal—Private D'Aldiern thinks the city isn't safe at night."

"Private D'Aldiern sounds like he's doing his job dutifully."

It wasn't a question, so Mara provided no answer.

"According to his reports," Liam finished.

Of course Liam knew. Of course Calvy had reported her visits to his room. The good soldier that he was.

Mara forced herself still as Liam watched her closely for a reaction.

"I'll be back when his contract ends," Liam reassured her.

A tremble shook her hands. She hoped it wasn't something the screen could pick up. That if it were visible, Liam thought it a glitch in the display. She needn't have worried about him focusing on her too long. His eyes shifted off target for a moment and Mara pictured the stone in his hand, glowing red, another distraction. Accusations that would do her no good rose in her throat and she fought them back. She had to get him off the screen so she could calm down.

"I'll let you go," she said, shutting off the display as soon as he nodded.

Then she was pulling the door open. Some urgency compelling her forward. Setting her in flight.

She was in the elevator before she realized she was alone. No one had been outside her room and now she was heading out of her hotel for the first time without anyone shadowing her steps.

The elevator doors opened and Mara was free.

At least from that room. That conversation. And her chaperones.

Inside she still felt trapped. Suffocated by the feeling that had ignited in her hearing Liam's news. The feeling she hated the moment the smoke of it expanded her lungs.

Three months, he'd said.

And it had cracked through her body like lightning, electrifying her. As unexpected as the man who'd caused it. Because the feeling that charged through her when Liam said he wasn't on his way, the one that made her want to fight and flee, was relief.

Chapter Fourteen

"What do you mean she's not in her room?"

Calvy had been expecting the exquisite torture of his nightly wake-up. Mara's nimble fingers pulling back the sheet, curved nails dragging across his hot skin. The creak of the mattress as she climbed over him. Grasping her soft hips until he felt the rigid bone underneath. But it hadn't come. He'd woken ready for her only to find himself in the growing dark alone.

Even an icy shower couldn't numb the thoughts stinging his mind. She hadn't come to talk to him in the hallway last night either. He'd done it again. Lost control and said something stupid.

Fuck Liam.

Even if she wanted an apology, he wouldn't take that back. He'd meant it. But he should have kept it to himself.

If only he didn't always feel so on edge around her—his body responding to her the way it did to enemy fire. Life raging harder in his veins in moments he felt the most danger. Talking to her was trench warfare, he'd shoot blindly just for a reprieve from the grenades she lobbed with the precision of a sniper.

Whatever was between them, it was combustible. And that's what he felt now, realizing she was missing, like he might explode.

Dannos and Harper exchanged a glance. "She left while we were changing shifts."

"Where did she go?"

Harper used her stone to project the hotel security footage. There was Mara—practically flying out of her room, running blindly for the elevator without stopping. She rode it down, her face uncharacteristically tight, and was gone as soon as the doors opened.

"Why was she upset?"

"Upset?"

Calvy motioned to the image, paused on Mara's face in the elevator.

Dannos squinted at the display and scratched his side. "She looks normal to me."

Then Calvy noticed the time stamp on the feed. "This was hours ago."

"I had it under control," Harper said.

Dannos offered an apologetic shrug. "We didn't realize she'd gone until she didn't answer about dinner."

"And then?" Calvy asked, his muscles tensing, readying for—for what? What had happened to her? Where would she go?

"And then we checked her usual haunts, thinking she'd turn up. Which she didn't." Harper sucked her teeth. She was frustrated Mara was missing, had probably hoped to find her before Calvy even knew about it. Reporting the incident to Pent herself, with Calvy out of the loop, would have made a nice point. He knew Harper hated answering to him, but she had no choice.

If she weren't so deep in Pent's corner, he might suspect she'd let Mara wander off. But Harper wouldn't do anything that went against Pent's wishes. And above all else, Pent wanted Mara safe.

With Mara still missing, the situation no longer served Harper's interests. It became a problem for them both. "We were just about to—"

"The docks?" Calvy snapped.

"Not there."

"The Ring, the Royal Park, the—"

"We checked them all."

"Then we'll check them again. Split up." He divided up all her favorite places and the three of them set out. The night was cold and he was glad at least that she'd had her cloak on her when she'd left. But her legs had been bare. Like she hadn't expected to be gone long. So why wasn't she back yet? Worry seized Calvy's chest.

He had to focus. On finding Mara. That was the only thing that mattered. Not because of what Pent would do if he failed, but because she could be hurt. Mara could be hurt. It was his job to protect her.

Every corner he turned, Calvy hoped he'd see the red flash of her hair, the bright glint of her eyes. But he didn't find it. He didn't find her.

It was hours later when he gave up on the park. A fine mist filled the air, dispersing the light of the streetlamps, and he couldn't picture her sitting on a bench in the wet and the cold. He'd accused her of always being comfortable. Looping the Ring instead, the thought entered his mind: maybe they'd crossed paths. Maybe he'd missed her. Maybe she'd gone back to the hotel.

Out of ideas, desperate to be right, he went back to check. Her room was empty.

Calvy leaned against the door. The elevator dinged and he looked up, hoping again to see Mara, safe and sound.

Dannos lifted his hands above his shoulders. "Thought she might have come back this way by now."

Calvy gripped his hair. He couldn't shake that look on her face in the security feed. Something had upset her. Made her run. Pent had warned him that Mara was a handful, subject to moods. He'd operated under that assumption for weeks, waiting for her to pull something like this. And then he'd started to get to know her. She didn't strike him as rash—she was thoughtful, so composed at times it rattled him. He'd stopped anticipating her doing something impulsive. And now she was gone.

Every hour she was missing it was more and more likely that something had happened to her. The people Pent hired to run his factories weren't exactly known for their scruples. And there was a city of abandoned buildings where they could take her—that worry in his chest compressed into white-hot fear.

The elevator doors opened again and his head snapped up, expecting Harper, expecting defeat.

Mara leaned heavily against the metal rail. "Call off the search! Call off the search!" She threw her arms into the air and stumbled towards them. Rain dampened her hair, darkening it, flattening it—wide pupils caused the same effect in her grey eyes.

Relief twisted in him so tightly it disintegrated.

"Where have you been?"

"Out."

"You can't just—"

"I can. I can just. I did and I will and I am."

A wave of spirit-laced air moved with her and Dannos said under his breath, "It's pretty clear where she's been, eh?"

Calvy glared at him. "Get Harper on the stone. Tell her to come back. And then both of you get some rest. I'll deal with this."

"This?" Mara asked, stepping into him and tilting her head up and to the side. "You can deal with me."

Fuck.

Even at his most exhausted, flustered, wrung out, when Mara advanced on him, bold as brass and iron-willed, his nerves woke up. She was—she was—he couldn't think with her this close.

Calvy stepped back. Blinked. Fisted his hands at his sides.

"Inside." He fumbled with the door handle while Mara made a show of waving at Dannos before swaying into the room.

He had handled more complicated situations with much more composure. Where was it now? He forced himself to inhale, exhale, release the spiraling panic that coiled in his gut.

"What were you doing, Mara? We've been looking for you for hours."

She spun around, dropping her cloak on the floor and tossing one shoe onto the couch. The other missed, skidding under the window's long curtain, landing on its side, scuffed and discarded. Calvy was struck by the impracticality of its thin sole. How little protection it offered her. How unprepared she'd been.

"You don't understand the risks here. It isn't safe for you to disappear—"

"I understand the risks." She tapped on one low lamp and shielded her eyes against the light. "There's tension building with the moonclan in the factories, right?"

"How do you—"

"They won't hurt me, Cal."

"It's not them—"

"What is your report going to say about this?" she interrupted him. She always did. Cut him off, cut him down. It was one of her favorite ways to get under his skin. "Liam won't be pleased that you lost me."

"This is backlash? Because Liam told you I'm reporting on you? Fuck, Mara. You had to know that. Two more weeks and he'll be able to watch you himself."

"You haven't heard?" She shut the lamp off and prowled towards him, creeping with the shadows through the room, her voice as dark. "Mr. Pent had business that took him to the Rim. He's staring at the Pebble Belt as we speak." Mara stopped in front of him and pushed Calvy's jacket off his shoulders.

He let her, his mind busied with the news, working through what it meant. For him. For her. The Pebble Belt was months away. She'd gone out and gotten drunk because Liam wasn't coming back yet. And she was left with the man she never wanted. Calvy had thought he was used to the feeling—he was an eleven after all—but this version stuck in his throat, as bitter as her words when she stepped back, her arms wide, and told him, "I'm all yours."

"You're not mine. You're toasted."

"Completely burnt," she agreed, swaying again, this

time towards him. He caught her waist and brought her close, to steady her. "I was *lightly toasted* the first time, too, idinit seem to bother you." Mara rubbed her hand down his chest.

"You were standing up. And your words came out one at a time. It was different."

"Fuck me," she said, enunciation exaggerated for his benefit. She held his chin when he tried to look away. "Fuck. Me. Now."

"And if I don't want to?" He could smell the rain on her skin and wondered if the red of her cheeks was a needy flush or from the cold wind.

"Nobody cares what you want."

His teeth ground together at her honesty. He didn't resist as she led him to the bedroom, tripping backwards as she went, unaware of the work it took him to hold her up. She fell onto the bed, pulling him down onto her. She forced his pants over his hips and maneuvered the hard length she discovered into her cunt. He let her. Because he was so relieved to see her. To feel her back against him. Under him, she was safe. And she was in charge. That was the job. Nobody cared what he wanted.

Nobody cared that he wanted her.

He let her. Because he still fucking wanted her.

Calvy folded over her. When Mara moaned his name into his hair, arching up against him, he released a guttural groan. She was so warm and tight around him, writhing under him for once—a reversal he'd fantasized about every night when she left him wanting. But her cheek was cool against his and her thighs were like ice about his hips as he pushed them wide.

"You're freezing."

"I can't feel it." She bucked against him. "I only feel this."

His lips pressed into her neck, her hair tickling his nose.

"Mara," he whispered. She mumbled a response. Not a mumble of driving ecstasy, something unintelligible, jumbled words from a mind edged with blackness.

Calvy stopped, pulling out of her and rolling over.

"I dinit tell you to stop—" she slurred, reaching for him with an uncoordinated arm.

The ceiling seemed lower in the dark. The walls closer. A small dark cell that he deserved this time. "I'm not doing this. Not tonight."

"I want you to."

"Well, I don't care what you want either."

Frustration drove him to be harsher than he'd intended. He'd been so stupid. She wasn't in control. Not tonight. Tonight she was drunk and sad and lonely.

"Cal, please."

Cal. Every time she said it his stomach flipped like he was suddenly airborne and plummeting fast.

"It's not happening, Mara—go to sleep."

A tear slipped from her eye and into her hair and she wiped at it clumsily, her hand colliding with his. "Don't touch me," she hissed. "Just leave me alone!"

He knew that tone.

Then shut your mouth, she'd ordered him.

The bed shook as he stood. His hands trembled as he fastened his pants. His resolve, however, remained steadfast. This was not what he wanted. Mara drunk and incoherent and longing for Pent. He would take orders from her when she was in the right mind to give them.

Mara let out a sob from the bed, curling into a ball on top of the blankets.

But she was back. She was safe. And the rest of it wasn't supposed to be his concern.

That's what he told himself, as he slid to the ground outside her bedroom door, and listened to her cry herself to sleep.

Chapter Fifteen

She remembered crying.

That Calvy had been concerned for her. It all muddled in her brain—smashed up with memories of Liam
and Rozz and Jimma. The people who had cared for
her. How limited her experience with that feeling was.
How few people had looked at her with anything other
than pity. How desperately she wanted more of it, that
genuine caring, surrounding her and never leaving. And
that made it worse.

Because she also remembered pleading, remembered
when the door opened and closed, remembered when
Calvy was gone.

The thought of him made her nauseous, or maybe
that was the alcohol working its way out of her body one
throb of her head at a time. The mist had turned into a
steady rain and she stayed in her room, suspended in
the grey. The grey darkened to black and black faded
to grey again before she could stand well enough to
hold her head high.

Dannos and Harper were talking in hushed voices
when Mara finally opened the door to the hall a day
after her disappearance.

"Do you need something, miss?" Dannos asked,
stopping short whatever he'd been saying to Harper.

"Yes, breakfast. Please," she added, noting a stiffness in the air. She glanced back and forth between the two guards, registering their combined presence. "Is he making you both stand here now?"

"Your little stunt had consequences for the whole team," Harper said with a yawn.

"That's ridiculous. I'm not—I'm fine. Tell him to let one of you sleep."

Dannos looked nervously down the hall to their room. Even he didn't want to talk to Calvy. Mara didn't blame him.

"You know what, no, I'll tell him."

"He's—" Dannos began but Harper cut him off.

"We appreciate it, Ms. Leanor."

Mara felt something was wrong the moment her hand touched the doorknob. Harper's watchful eyes were hot on her back and she sensed motion from behind the entry, not the normal stillness she met entering the room at dusk.

She pushed the door in anyway.

Light sliced into the hall and she blinked, the scene too bright, too clear.

Calvy was awake. And he wasn't alone.

A woman sat on the dresser, her hands deep in Calvy's hair and her tongue deeper in his mouth. She had dark straight hair, the tanned muscular shoulders of a soldier. Calvy nestled between her legs but they were both fully clothed, down to their matching boots. They had probably passed by Harper and Dannos moments ahead of her. Dannos had tried to warn her and Harper had stopped him. But what would a warning have done? Kept her from seeing it? It wouldn't have stopped it from happening. And that's what Mara's body urged her to do now. Make it stop.

She stepped into the room and let the weighted hotel door swing shut behind her. She heard Dannos groan a protest. He'd have to imagine what happened next.

"Am I interrupting something, Private?"

Calvy twisted his neck, finding her with unfocused eyes. Mara felt the heat in them on her cheeks. The other soldier kissed the side of his open mouth.

"Tell her to stop."

Calvy shook his head, recovering himself. "You're not in charge here, Ms. Leanor. The whole point of this is that I won't have to stop. For once. Whatever you need, Dannos and Harper can—"

"They can't."

His hands cupped the soldier's cheeks and he kissed her before responding to Mara. "Why not?"

"Because—" Mara's chest heaved as the other woman pulled Calvy's shirt loose from his pants. Her breasts swelled and tightened, her cunt grew heavy with lust. "Because I want to fuck."

Calvy pinned her with a look so intense Mara shuddered involuntarily, a tingle zinging across her shoulders.

"Now?"

"Now. That's what you're here for, right?"

"You can't be serious."

"It's fine," the other woman said, mouth dragging up his neck. "Let her join."

"She's not joining," Calvy said. "She's leaving."

"I'm not going anywhere. But she is." Mara crossed her arms to keep him from seeing the tremors that shook her hands. Anger and need—the frustration of them both.

The soldier stared back at her, slipping her hands under Calvy's shirt. Mara tensed but Calvy caught the woman's wrists. "Hold on, just a second." The woman's teeth pulled at his earlobe. "Runa, stop."

Mara gestured to the door. "Runa. Small pleasures to you."

Runa's hands dropped from Calvy's grasp. "Is this happening?" she asked, looking from Calvy to Mara.

"No," Mara told her.

"Yes," said Calvy.

He was unbelievable. "You didn't want me the other night, but you're fine hiring—"

"I didn't hire Runa. I know it hasn't crossed your mind what I prefer, but it's willing partners. Wanting me. Not passed out drunk, thinking about someone else."

Mara wet her lips and put her hand on the doorknob. "Well. I want a cock. And if yours isn't available, I'll just have to go find another one. Good luck explaining that to Liam." She turned and opened the door an inch before Calvy's hand was flat against it, pushing it shut.

The rush of air from his lungs broke over her ear, raising the hairs on her neck. "Explain to Pent that you're a demanding little vixen? I think he's aware."

Mara took a step away, into the room, and waited.

The seconds ticked by.

Calvy opened the door with enough force to test the screws that secured the knob in place. He nodded at Runa and she slid off the dresser.

"Another time?"

"Unlikely," Calvy answered, his dark eyes fixed on Mara.

Mara flashed a smug smile at Runa as she passed.

Calvy was hers. For three more months. She turned back to him as the door closed and he sprung at her, twisting her around, lifting her like nothing, and setting her on the dresser where Runa had been before her. Replacing his damsel, Mara thought, her eyes hardening.

"You think that's funny? That you can throw your fits and do whatever you want whenever you want without any thought for how it affects any of us? The people below you?"

How dare he claim to know her.

"Me? You like to play the honorable soldier but you give up on anything the moment it gets hard for you. What do you have to offer apart from your sad little prince complex?"

"Fuck you, Mara."

"That's all I want you to do," she countered.

"That's it? Fine, I'll fuck you—"

And his hands were on her knees, pushing them apart, revealing the wetness that had coated her while she had watched him with the soldier. He'd been so involved, so engaged—it ignited her memories of him on the ship, his mouth warm and eager, relishing his ability to please her. The last few months she'd been using him had been different, he'd been subdued. By her own will. She'd felt the intensity of his eyes but she craved the force of his touch. Now she was going to get it.

He thrust into her hard, pressing all his frustration into the motion. Her hands went to his back, grasping him closer. This was a different Calvy, unrestrained, claiming her for himself. Taking from her as much as she would give. And then after a few rough jabs, his hips began to roll with more fluidity, a familiar pattern that she recognized. One he'd learned from her.

Queen of Dust

Beneath her. He had been paying attention, when she'd used him. Mara went tense and loose all at once as Calvy moved in her, knowing exactly what she liked and how she liked it.

She felt her climax coming, the first clench of her cunt around him, the signal that she should pull away from him. But he was in front of her, pressing into her, and there was nowhere for her to go. Calvy was in control and she crested, crashing against him at the thought—clawing at his shirt and clinging to him with every muscle in her body. How good it felt, to come around him, with him still hard inside her. To clutch at him, the satisfaction of having her fill of him. The waves rocked through her as he kept moving, lengthening her pleasure, drawing it out. And then he was groaning, knocking into the dresser harder, once, twice. Its front pegs lifted from the floor and held there as he spilled into her.

Time stopped.

She was sure of it.

There was no other way to describe how the moment lasted. They were frozen in the relief of shared gratification, paused in the glow of morning light.

Slowly Mara caught her breath and Calvy eased the dresser back to the ground. He withdrew, turning his back to her and leaning both hands against the windowsill.

Mara looked past him, out to the Balti sky that dominated the room's view. What was she doing? She was supposed to be here with Liam. Getting to know her home again. Trying to understand what had happened in her past. But ever since she'd arrived, she'd felt more lonely than she ever had. The reality that the Balti were truly gone, that she didn't have a home to return to—it was too much. This place was empty.

Except when she was with Calvy.

He pulled at his hair. "I know you don't like me to—"

"It's fine," she assured him. "That was good. That was—what I wanted."

Their conversation stuttered as they navigated around the debris, the fallout of their argument.

"Then all's right in the world. Ms. Leanor got what she wanted."

"Nothing about this is right, Calvy. Obviously."

"Well, we can agree on that at least. Pent sure—"

"I don't want to talk about Liam. Don't talk to me about Liam."

Liam had started this. Started it with *his* damsel—and Mara did not want to think about that. Not when the difference in how she'd felt then and now was too apparent to ignore.

Calvy let his head fall back and set his hands on his hips. "Why don't you make me a list, Mara, of the things you do and don't want me to do. Because I'm having a hard time keeping track."

She should have ignored him. He wasn't being serious. But her response came out in a rush of air, her nails digging into her palms. "I don't want you with anyone but me."

Watching Liam with the damsel on the ship, she hadn't felt a lick of the possessiveness that had flared inside her at the sight of Calvy with someone else. And she didn't want to consider why. She couldn't.

He glanced over his shoulder at her, the sun on his face, highlighting the quirk of his mouth. "You're jealous? You go out and get drunk because Pent's not coming back and you're mad that I want to be with someone who wants to be with me?"

"It must be exhausting being so wrong so much of the time." Her feet found the floor, but she got no further than leaning on the dresser, her knees weak. "I didn't get drunk because I was sad about Liam, you absolute grunt. I did it because I was happy. I was happy and I shouldn't have been. Because it meant I had more time with you." She should stop talking. She had to stop talking. She couldn't stop talking. "—and yes, I was jealous. Seeing you with her because—because you don't *kiss me*."

Calvy crossed the room in two strides, his palms open in front of her. "I'm not allowed to kiss you! You think I don't want to? Ask me, Mara. Please, just ask me. Order me to do it and I will."

But she couldn't. It was bad enough to admit that he mattered to her, that he was turning her world upside down. She needed to drown the feelings rising inside her, not pull them to the surface.

He shook his head. "You know what's truly pathetic? After months of you fucking me thinking about Pent all I wanted to do was fuck her and think about you."

"I don't. Think about Liam. With you. I can't. Because it's you. You under me and you with me and you filling me completely, pushing him out."

"What are you saying, Mara?"

What was she saying? Why couldn't she fucking stop?

"I don't know, okay? I don't know. It's this place, Cal. It's making me crazy—blurring what I know and what I don't. I'm finally home and it's just dust and air.

Sometimes I feel just as trapped as I did on the ship, a million miles from anything, with no way out."

She dropped her face into her hands and Calvy backed away from her, the force of her outburst repelling him. Mara didn't dare look up. She couldn't bear his retreat. It was better to keep it all in than to let someone see the cracks in her foundation. Nobody wanted to stand on weakened ground, waiting for it to give way. Nobody wanted her truth. What little of it she had.

But she couldn't help being honest with Calvy, looking in those big black marble eyes and telling him what she was thinking, instead of hiding it from him like she did the rest of the world.

She should have been used to it. The way he surprised her.

Calvy smoothed back his hair with both hands. "Will you get dressed? Then meet me in the hallway."

"Why?"

"There's something you need to see."

Chapter Sixteen

When Mara emerged from her room, having scarfed down a flatbread with jam while changing her clothes, Calvy wasn't waiting in the hallway for her. Dannos told her to go downstairs, where she found him leaning against a hoverbike instead. He yawned and rubbed his eyes.

"Where did you get that?" Mara asked, looking at the bike, her lips parted in surprise.

"What?" His jaw had gone slack looking at her, but the rest of him had come alert. She felt him take in the tight black leggings that hugged her bottom half like a second gleaming skin, the soft white blouse she'd tied above her navel to provide a tempting contrast. She noticed his fingers twitching, like he wanted to reach out and touch her.

"That's a hoverbike."

"Oh. Right. I liberated it from a shipping container by the base."

"On whose orders?"

Calvy shrugged. Calvy never shrugged.

"Can you get in trouble for that?"

"I'm on loan to the Pent Corporation. The army can take it up with them, if they are so inclined."

"You can tell Liam I asked you to do it. If it comes to that." Mara couldn't look away from the bike. A thrill had gone through her when she'd spotted the relic.

Calvy smiled watching her. "Do you want to drive?"

"I don't know where we're going."

"On the way back then?" he offered and she nodded. He handed her a safety collar—or tried to.

"Is that necessary?"

Calvy held the device out, unwavering.

With a sigh for his benefit, Mara took it and connected it around her neck. He straddled the bike, pushing the round button between the handlebars. The machine began to hum and lifted a few inches off the ground. Drawing up his feet, he checked with Mara. "Ready?"

She put a hesitant foot on the rail and hoisted herself over the seat behind him. Not an hour ago she'd been confessing—what? What had she been going to say to him? Nothing she really meant, surely.

In any case, a joyride on a confiscated hoverbike was a welcome distraction, even if she disagreed with Calvy's assertion that it would somehow help her. Still, by the time her arms were wrapped around Calvy's middle, her legs had begun to tremble with anticipation.

The hoverbike thrummed as Calvy steered them onto the Queen's Road, using the center lane and gliding over the tile. Mara sat up straighter behind him, taking in the city from this new perspective.

"Where did you go—the other night. Which pub?" he asked over his shoulder.

"That little place by the docks that's always empty. I was watching a fire, out on the water, when it started to rain."

"One of the oil rigs had an accident."

"It's such a crude technology," she said, tapping the sides of the hoverbike with her heels. "Dern must know solar power is cleaner, less dangerous?"

"Requires a source," Calvy countered. "Not all planets are as well situated as Balti. Renewable energy is expensive. It's more affordable to ship oil."

"Depends on what you consider valuable."

The hoverbike curved around the Ring. The air had been crisp and cool outside the hotel—yesterday's rain temporarily clearing the pollution—but closer to the canal Mara smelled the factories again. And something else, something new that grew stronger as they neared the flashing lights of a Dern construction crew. This time they weren't digging signposts, they were paving over the colorful mosaics of the road. The scent of tar thickened in around them—black and sticky.

Fresh anger turned her stomach. "Why are they doing that?"

"The tiles break apart, under the weight of the trucks. It looks pretty enough but it isn't functional."

"It's not functional? It works fine for a Balti hoverbike."

"This is a Dern colony now. We use trucks. Normally we'd be digging it up—laying magnetic tracks for trams."

"But there's not enough people to warrant public transit?" Whose fault was that? She loosened her hold on him.

"I don't like it either, Mara. If I—I'd want to see it restored to the way it was."

"I'd rebuild it better." Mara repeated Iola's words

quietly, more to herself than Calvy. Louder she asked, "You're taking me out of the city?"

"Yes," he said, one inadequate answer for both questions. Dern economics.

They passed over the bridge, barges dotting the canal. Up close she could see the Pent logo on the smokestacks that lined the north side of the canal to the east. A soft green *P* slashing through a circle. She hadn't been north of the shuttle station since landing. The rest of the continent was wild—forest and shore and—

"To the cliffs?" she asked.

"Yes," he said again.

A better answer. She pressed tighter against him, the gleaming pants flush against his thighs.

"Can this thing go any faster?"

Calvy leaned into the handlebars, taking her forward with him, and they sped down the black road between the shuttle station and the barracks, soldiers in the yard between the shipping container dorms whooping as they went by.

Her nose at Calvy's neck, even with the rushing wind, Mara couldn't help breathing him in. Bringing that warm, clean scent of his into her lungs, muddling her senses with the sweet coco in his hair. She dipped her face deeper into his collar before she could stop herself. His shoulder pulled up automatically and he laughed. The bike swerved sideways.

"Maybe this was necessary." She used one hand to check her safety collar. "You're sure it'll work?"

"It'll activate. If you need it."

"You skidded across three lanes—I might need it."

"It's just us," Calvy said and Mara was glad he

couldn't see the slow smile that she smothered against his back.

Just us.

The Balti had never built on the upper half of the continent, preferring to leave it untouched and natural, a place of retreat. Calvy slowed the bike under the canopy of trees, and Mara's heart slowed with it. They settled into an unhurried pace as they wound through the forest. The road became a trail, the hoverbike gliding over dark green moss that marked the path. Mara wished she could take off her boots and let her feet drag in the soft, spongy earth.

Hours passed more peacefully than any Mara could remember, but when the trees finally thinned into a meadow filled with the red fringe of wild Balti heather, she was shifting anxiously in her seat. The ground rose up gradually and she couldn't see what was coming, just that the moss trail ended at the top. Calvy pulled the bike sideways at the peak of the hill, stopping for Mara to take in the view.

In front of them the ground sloped down, cutting off in a dramatic cliff. An endless blue ocean stretched before her. The cliffs continued east and west, jagged light grey rocks that blackened and glistened where the waves splashed against them.

Calvy turned off the machine and it lowered to the ground. Mara could still feel the vibrations in her legs. The rush of speed in her ears continued—but now the source was the wind that came off the water, flattening the long rusty strands of heather that covered the ground all the way to the cliff. A sea of bent crimson stalks.

Birds soared above them, wings wide, feathered with grey and brown and white.

"Petrels," Calvy answered before she could ask. "They nest on the cliffs here."

One of the petrels dipped down, out of sight, and Mara was compelled to follow it. She stumbled off the bike, legs stiff and unsteady, and rushed downhill towards the water. Calvy caught her around the waist when she was almost out of land.

"The winds change quickly—one gust can send you over," he said into her ear. On cue the heather rose up and fell in a wave, bending the opposite way. Mara's hair whipped into her face and she felt Calvy brace against the impact of the gale. She swiped at the curls that tangled in her long lashes, but the wind was intent on keeping her blind. She turned instead, to face it, and her hair blew back out of her face. She looked up into Calvy's eyes, gasping at stolen air as the wind left her breathless.

Just as suddenly, the wind changed directions again, blowing from the north, pushing her against him. Her hair was back in her face—but then Calvy was turning them both, setting his back to the wind, to the cliff. A dance at the edge of the world. He blocked the gale, letting Mara breathe in the stillness, in the space between them, the space he created for her.

The wind loosened his hair, the wax he used to hold it back no match for the force of air plowing over them. "I love this place."

"You've been before?"

He nodded, his chin lowering, bringing their faces closer together. "First thing I did. I'd read about it. Dreamed about it. Since I was a boy. I thought I'd never see it. Or that if I did it wouldn't be what I expected. But it is. Do you feel it?"

Feel what? she wanted to ask, to fall back on indifference, mocking his sincerity. But she knew exactly what he meant. There was a charge on the cliff, a raw power that churned in her gut as forcefully as the water around the rocks below.

"Yes," she said. And regretted it, as he took the opening as permission to delve into what had happened earlier.

"You said some things. In the hotel."

"I said I was confused."

"You said more than that."

"If you brought me all the way out here expecting something from me—you should forget it."

"I didn't. I don't expect anything from you. I brought you here because I thought you needed to see it. The wild part of Balti. The free part."

He hesitated and she pushed him to continue. "Why?"

It was a mistake. Pushing him when she knew they were on the verge of saying things they couldn't come back from.

"Because it's you," he said, like it was just that simple. "Red and grey and dangerous. You're the cliff, you're the sea—you're the—"

Her heart dropped. "Stop it, Cal."

His venerations were a taunt. Just like everything else. She could feel the connection to her heritage all around her, surging inside of her, and yet she couldn't claim it. Couldn't name it. Because she was still missing. She had stood with her feet on the black beach, wet sand compressed in her hands, and known she was holding something more, without knowing what or why. Whether she let go or squeezed them tighter in her fist, the grains would slip through, and she'd be left with nothing.

"If you mean I'm selfish and demanding, you're right," she admitted, wanting to whisper, but having to shout over the wind. *It's just us*, he'd said when they crossed into the wild north. Here, on this endless edge, she could say what she was feeling. Where it was just her, protected by his embrace. Where she could breathe. She gripped the sides of his jacket as the wind teetered them back and forth and resumed its push at his back. "I've only thought about myself for so long because I know there's more to me that I haven't figured out yet. And I thought I would find it here. But I don't know this place. I don't know it or me or anything. I'm just as lost on Balti as I was when Rozz found me."

"You're not," he said, his hands knotting behind her. "You're not lost. So you don't remember where you started—doesn't mean you don't know where you are. Who you are doesn't have to be based on where you came from. It's what you choose that matters. It's what you want."

What did she want? Liam, back now, so this moment would be ruined, so she'd have no reason to continue down this path. Queen Balticourt, restored to the throne, so the Dern would leave, so she wouldn't be the last Balti Temptress. Or none of that. And just time and space to be with Calvy.

"What I want is impossible."

She stared up at him, his face bathed in natural light, heather perfuming the air. His eyes weren't black, she realized, they were dark brown, warm and rich as thick Balti coffee.

Kiss me, she could command him. And he'd do it.

Kiss me. It would only take two words.

But she didn't say them. She didn't want to order him. Instead she pulled herself up into him, rising to her toes in her boots. His lips were soft against hers—soft and malleable, parting for her, inviting her to stroke her tongue across his. Calvy opened himself up to her so easily and she dove headfirst into the peace he offered.

A limitless kiss. Natural, heavy as a current dragging against the ocean floor. Slow. Powerful. Building in intensity the further it went. The wind lashed her hair around them again, cocooning their faces in a blur of red. Mara's eyes were long shut, to better accentuate her senses, to heighten the all-consuming grip of their kiss.

Jimma had always told Mara that was the power of physical connection, the way the world would concentrate, narrow to what was good and here and now. What was happening in the moment. "Two halves of a citrin," she'd said, "protected by the rind." Mara had felt it with other partners—she'd felt it with Liam—but not to this degree. Not the way their split seams merged, becoming whole again. She felt his body's reactions as precisely as her own. With Calvy, the world constricted so tightly around them, it closed everything out.

The wind pushed at Calvy's back again and he tripped forward into Mara. His lost balance had Mara opening her eyes, dizzied and disoriented. She stepped back, pressing her fingers to her mouth. Calvy stood, stooped, forgetting to snap back into his rigid soldier's stance. He waited with his shoulders curved, his head bent low enough to kiss her again, should she come back to him.

"Time to go back." She turned, looking down at the long line of their shadows.

He moved behind her and the shadows overlapped, becoming one. She stepped sideways to separate them.

And then Mara walked away from the edge, away from the uncontrollable force that threatened to push her over it.

Chapter Seventeen

"You should slow down," Calvy said from behind her. "I can barely see the trail."

Mara took the next turn faster.

His hands, which he'd kept on his own knees, jumped to hers as he grabbed for something to hold on to. Not that he'd find much purchase on the slick glide of her pants.

"I can see it just fine," Mara lied. The sky had darkened and there wasn't much light filtering through the treetops above them. She flipped the bike's light on and continued without adjusting her pace.

The light helped, but Mara couldn't relax. The heat of Calvy's palms on her legs drew her focus. She ignored it. Or she tried to. She'd thought she'd been working him out of her system, but she'd only been drawing him deeper. She needed space, which was hard to accomplish while sharing a hoverbike. As soon as they were back at the hotel she'd have it. She'd put as many doors and walls between them as she could.

He brushed one thumb back and forth across the glossy material that separated her skin from his. She was so distracted she didn't notice the bike slowing until it began to stutter, splutter, and stop. The bike dropped a few inches with a lurch and settled against the ground.

Mara stared at it, waiting for it to turn back on, charged by the force of her gaze.

Calvy reached around her to tap the display. It flickered on and the bike rose half-heartedly. Then the light faded and it sank again. He rapped his knuckle against it a second time but the craft stayed resolutely earthbound.

"Battery died," he said.

This couldn't be happening.

"It was over half-charged—we used less to get out to the cliffs." Mara listed reasons as if they could change the situation. As if the way it should be could overwrite the way it was.

Calvy, as always, had answers ready for her. "Gauges aren't always accurate. And we didn't use the light on the way out." His eyebrows flicked up and she spoke before he could comment on the reliability of solar power.

"You encouraged me to see the road."

"You could have slowed down."

"Forgive me for wanting to get out of here faster."

"Why was that, Mara? Why were you in such a hurry? What was it you were running from this time?"

"Nothing," she said, biting out the word.

"It wasn't nothing."

"It wasn't something either."

She'd made better arguments.

Calvy got off the bike. He roughed a hand over his face and she noticed how tired he looked, his features downturned and heavy. "Can we go? Or did you want to quarrel with the bike some more?"

He looked dead on his feet. She couldn't fight him

like this. It was hardly fair when he was at his best.
Mara looked around. "Go where?"

"I saw a sign for a pod tower about a mile back."

"A *pod tower*? A glorified stack of coffins?"

"Coffins with power docks." Calvy slid the start circle open and pulled out the battery. "Or we can wait
here for the sun? Charge it up the old-fashioned way.
We can make camp—the ground is still wet. We'll have
to keep each other warm but whatever you prefer—"

In answer, Mara dismounted the bike and started
back the way they'd come, on foot. "Separate pods,"
she said over her shoulder.

"I don't expect they'll be at capacity."

Mara's teeth were chattering by the time they found
the turn, a short rock path that lead to a mossy clearing. She stopped walking to stare at the pods, stacked
in columns and arranged in rows. Maybe twenty years
ago they had looked clean, but now they were the picture of disrepair, rusty and overgrown with vines.

Calvy wiped dirt off the check-in console embedded in the first row. "Doesn't look like it's got—" The
screen lit up.

"You have to love the longevity of solar coils." Mara
satisfied herself with a quick smirk. Gloating properly
would take too much energy.

"So reliable, as evidenced by our current situation.
You really are lucky," he said, navigating through the
screens. "They're almost all marked as occupied. The
system must have glitched out—"

"How am I lucky?"

One metal chip clanged through the chute. And then
another.

"There were two available."

Mara extracted the keys from the slot. She glanced at the markings on the pods and closed her fist around the one she wanted.

"This one's got your name on it," she said, handing him the other.

He looked around for the corresponding unit, finding the number 11 painted on the highest pod of the tower closest to them. "Are you sure? It probably has the better view."

"And the better chance of falling off that rusted ladder."

"And yours?"

"Ground floor." Mara flashed the 32 on her chip.

He followed her to the third tower, hovering better than their transport while she scanned the chip on the grey pad next to peeling numbers.

The metal-framed glass door groaned, opening out halfway.

"I'm going to look around," he said.

"Okay?"

"Do you want to—"

"Stay here? I do. Good night."

Mara pulled the door the rest of the way up and settled herself into the bunk. Alone. Away from Calvy. Where she needed to be.

She exhaled slowly. What she needed was to get herself under control—she might even commit herself to his damn Virtues if it would just stop her from saying whatever she was thinking around him.

Mara rocked from side to side to get comfortable.

It wasn't that bad, actually. The pods in her tower were the larger option, so she had ample room on either side. The ceiling was too low for her to sit up, but it didn't matter—she was here to sleep. She hit the button next to her head and the door stuttered into motion, closing her in.

That was better. Warmer. Only—Mara sighed. She needed to find the bathroom. She pressed the door button and waited. And waited. She pushed it again, harder.

Nothing happened.

Mara slammed her hand against the wall. The button clicked in and out but the door remained motionless. Closed. Closed with her on the inside. Panic swelled in her chest but she tried to fight it back. Calvy would be back in the morning. He wouldn't leave without her.

But the pod didn't seem so big anymore. And it wasn't warm—it was hot and tight and she was trapped. Sweat dampened her shirt and she kicked at the door.

Her feet thudded dully against the glass and still it stayed closed. She hit her fists against the low ceiling.

Mara's breathing came in inconsistent shallow bursts. There was no fighting the panic anymore—it overwhelmed her senses, her vision starting to narrow, to blacken at the edges. She turned herself as best she could and kicked the door again, one foot slamming into the button on the wall while the other pushed the door out. Her sob lanced through the hermetic silence.

Then she heard the hiss of the door's vacuum seal loosening.

She sprang forward, pushing all her weight against the panel. Straining and huffing, she managed to lift it just enough. She squeezed herself through the gap and landed on the knobby earth just as the mechanism tightened again, sealing the pod back up.

Mara was leaning against the chipped exterior, panting, when Calvy rounded the tower. He had two tins of water tucked under one arm and was biting off the end of a condensed nut bar.

"I found a vend," he said. He cocked his head, trying to figure out what she was doing on the ground. "What happened?"

"I'm not going back in there."

"You're not?"

"No, Cal! The thing sealed shut. With me in it. We can't stay here."

"You can have mine. I'll sleep out here."

Mara shivered as a breeze rustled the trees. "You'll freeze."

"Then we'll share."

"I don't want to share."

"Well, Mara." He let out an exasperated sigh. "You're going to have to pick. Pick what you want."

She didn't want to stay here. She wanted to be back at the hotel. She didn't want to know what it felt like to kiss Calvy and have the rest of the world dissolve away—because she'd lost a life once, and she wouldn't give up what little she'd scraped together since. But they weren't going anywhere tonight and she wasn't going to forget Calvy's kiss anytime soon either. And she really didn't want to wake up and find Calvy's cold dead body, pecked to pieces by raptors.

Calvy waited, his shoulders slumped. He looked as drained as the battery, in need of a good night's sleep, a full charge.

"We can share," she said finally.

He nodded and offered the sticky brown bar out to her.

"Not that. That's probably older than I am."

"Probably."

He handed her a tin of water next, and that she took.

"It's citrin. They didn't have the one you like—with the blue lid."

"Gilderberry. This is fine. Thank you." She gulped the water down, which was easy to do as the carbon bubbles had gone flat. Citrin stung her cheeks. "It's all fine. Lucky number eleven, was it?" The sooner she slept the sooner she could get out of here.

Calvy pointed out the bathroom pod and Mara made use of it as quickly as she could before climbing the rickety ladder up to Calvy's bunk.

"I tested it," he called as her boots clanged on the metal platform in front of the unit. "Opens and closes fine. Worst-case scenario I'll break us out the top."

She bent down to see him testing the window panel at the top of the pod. He had been right, 11 did have a better view. It distracted her—momentarily—from noticing he'd stripped down to his underwear.

"What are you doing?"

"What?"

"Where are your clothes?"

"They were dusty. From the road. I put them in the wash."

"What wash?"

"Have you never been in a pod?"

"No, Calvy."

"Then. Let me give you the tour." He lifted a panel behind the pillows. "Shoes and coats, and what we're here for, a charger." He'd already hooked the hoverbike battery into the docket. "Down here is where the science happens." He opened the panel at the opposite end with his foot. "Dirty clothes go in, clean clothes come out."

"Which explains your state of undress."

"Nothing you haven't seen before. Would you like to make use of the amenities?"

Yes and also definitely no. But her pants were tight and dotted with mud where the hoverbike's air jets had splattered puddles upwards. Mara sat on the edge of the bunk to remove her boots and leggings, untying her blouse so that it hung like a nightshirt. That she'd keep on. Not out of some ill-conceived modesty, but as the only barrier available between her and the tantalizing swaths of Calvy's bare skin.

She squeezed in next to him and held her breath as the door lowered shut.

"We can open it again. If you want to be sure."

"You tested it?"

"Many times."

"Then I'm sure it's fine."

Calvy pressed the button anyway. The door opened immediately, even though it shook and groaned, protesting the disturbance. Mara felt better when he closed it the second time. Until he began shifting under the sheet, pushing his underwear down to his feet.

"You can keep those on," she said.

"Not if I want them washed."

"Cal—"

"Mara. If there's an opportunity to wear fresh bloomies in the morning, I'm taking it."

"Bloomies."

"What do you call them? Cunt covers? Take yours off and put them in too. I'm surprised, frankly, that you're even wearing any."

It was reluctantly that she shimmed her panties off her hips. The blouse covered her anyway. Fresh bloomies were worth it.

Finally they were still again, lying with their sides mashed together. Mara's double bed would have been more comfortable. But this one had the advantage of the working door, and the open ceiling. Mara's gaze drifted across the night sky, finding stars above, but no moons. Not yet.

She should sleep. Only she couldn't. Every time she tried to relax, her mind would flash to one of the mortifying things she'd confessed to Calvy in his room, or on the cliff, and she'd shudder, a jolt running from her shoulders to her knees.

"Are you okay?" he asked, probably feeling her body tense.

Mara swallowed. "I'm fine. I just can't—I'm—I'm hungry."

"You should have had some of that nut bar."

"I didn't want it. You'll really eat anything, won't you?"

"Thinking about the night we met?"

"The dinner," she clarified. "I—I remember thinking you ate like a starving man. You were."

"Yes."

"And…that's why you were so focused on me. You probably hadn't seen a woman in—"

"Ever. I hadn't ever seen a woman like you before. I almost thought you couldn't be real. That I wasn't really there. That I hadn't actually made it out."

She held still, her lungs full of air that smelled of him. Warm linen, sweet wax.

Calvy stretched a hand up to brush the ceiling and kept talking. "I had a sergeant turn the lights on during a night vision drill. Nearly blinded me. That's what it felt like when I saw you. So bright it hurt."

Her stomach clenched. And she held her silence, watching the stars slowly drift across the sky. She didn't have it in her to issue the order, to make him keep those things to himself. Besides, it would mean admitting how much it affected her, and she knew if she started talking she wouldn't be able to control what was said. Not with Calvy.

Calvy turned over onto his stomach. An elbow knocked her ribs and she pressed herself against the cold wall to move out of his way.

"Can you stop?"

"I'm almost comfortable."

"Well, now I'm not." He didn't move. "Cal, you can't sleep like that."

"I already am."

"No." She put a hand under him and rolled him up. "This is basic spatial reasoning, we can't both fit flat, we'll have to sleep on our sides." Mara turned onto her shoulder, scooting away from the cold door and towards Calvy's warmth. His arm was wedged between them, stopping her from nestling into the curve of his body.

There. That was better.

Except she was still wide-awake. Through the trees she caught sight of Balti's two moons, full and gleaming. Larger than normal, as moons look at the start of their rise, compared to the horizon. Jimma had told her about moons, the strength of their gravity. The way they seemed to draw people out, of their homes, of themselves. Especially on Balti. There was something in the Balti blood, Jimma said, that rose to the moons' sway, just like the ocean. Moons like this were meant to be felt. Mara closed her eyes.

Do you feel it?

Calvy's voice filled her mind. What she felt was his breath, slow and warm on her back, prickling the skin of her neck. And she felt her own, higher in her chest than it should be. Uneven. Irregular.

And the magnetism she expected to pull her up and out drew her backwards, lower. Her bottom brushed against Calvy's thighs. Mara stopped. And waited.

Tension built in her bent legs, but Calvy seemed entirely unaware—perhaps he was already asleep. She shifted again, under the pretense of trying to get comfortable, again brushing his groin with her round backside. This time, as she waited, his knuckles grazed her back. Once, twice. Then they stopped.

Mara felt she might explode. Couldn't he tell that she wanted him? Couldn't he feel the way connection seemed to pulse between them? On the cliff, when he'd asked her if she felt it—she'd almost thought that's what he was talking about. Not the majesty of that great natural formation, but the strength of what drew her to him. That was where the real danger was.

Or where the danger would be—if this had not already been arranged. It was in her control and under control and completely controlled. If she was the sea, he was the cliff, and she would crash against him until he was gone.

Mara rocked back into him again and Calvy lifted his arm, anticipating her move. She gasped, surprised by his reaction, how quickly she slipped into his embrace.

His lips met the skin behind her ear. "Don't start that," he whispered. "There's nowhere for you to run when you're finished."

"I don't run."

"No, you escape. It's how you survive. Admirable.

But you can't do it here. You can't be done with me to-night."

This was exactly the conversation she had to avoid. She craved him, she ached for him, she didn't want to have to name what else. She couldn't. And if he'd just let her use him the way he always did, she wouldn't have to. But Calvy needed something from her too. He ached to know her mind. They were both trapped by the situation; if she expected him to ease her suffering, she could at least try to do the same.

Her voice was raspy when she spoke. "Why do waves have to break to come back to the sea?"

"What does that mean?"

"I won't be done with you tonight."

In answer, Cal trailed a line of kisses down her neck. She guided his hand under her blouse and closed her eyes as his calloused palms scraped the valley between her breasts. He traced the curve under each, and her nipples puckered tight and hard. She twisted, pulling her shirt up, exposing the ass she'd been using to get his attention and she pushed it firmly against him, flattening the rising cock against his leg.

"You never wait," he scolded her impatience. And he was right. With him she couldn't. She forgot everything she knew about anticipation, that revered part of pleasure. She couldn't stand to wait with Calvy—they didn't have time. And she was overpowered by the force of desire she felt with him, especially then, in the moment just before he eased into her, his hardness finding the soft pink of her cunt from behind.

They moved together with exceptional leisure. It was the antithesis of their previous encounters, private, un-hurried, entirely reciprocal. They matched their pace,

their hips finding a lazy rhythm that took their mutual desire and squeezed it slowly, the juice that much
sweeter, arriving on the tongue drop by drop.

Mara lost herself in sensation, closing her eyes and giving herself over to it. When she opened them again,
tilting her head back, her mouth open in a long moan,
the moons had dipped into their descent. Not that she
could see them—the pod's windows had fogged, their
heat steaming the air inside. The top of Calvy's foot was
soft against the bottom of hers as she braced against
him. Her nails dug into Calvy's butt as she pulled him
into her, the final waves of her release his undoing inside her.

   In three months it would be over. He would leave—
he was already training for it—and there would be nothing she could do to stop it.

   This would all end.

   For the first time, that thought made her feel better.
Gave her some solace. She had felt herself losing control on the cliff. But no matter what she felt, Calvy came
with an expiration date. His contract was set. Liam
would come for her. There was a limit. A safety net
to catch her if she fell. Broken waves collected again.

   Pleasure was good, she reminded herself. And with
Calvy it was very good. There was nothing wrong with
it. As long as she recognized it for what it was: temporary. That's all pleasure ever was. That was the Balti
way and Mara was a Balti Temptress, spending the
moonlight on her own satisfaction.

   That's all anyone could do. Hold on to the good while
it lasted and know when to let it go.

Chapter Eighteen

The fabric of her black leggings gathered awkwardly at her ankles. Mara bent to pinch the material and stretch it up, distributing it more evenly across her calves. She stood when she'd finished, wincing and drawing a hand up to her side.

"What is it?" Calvy asked, dismounting the last rung of the pod tower ladder.

"It's fine."

"It's not—you might be dehydrated—have some water."

Mara swished the tang of citrin around in her mouth and swallowed.

"I can get another—"

"That's not it," she said, passing it back to him. "It's my muscles. They're just sore. I...exerted myself yesterday. Quite a bit."

"You're sore? You're sure?"

"Yes."

"Well. Okay." He tipped the water back into his mouth but Mara caught the self-satisfied smile that lifted his cheeks.

"Please, don't flatter yourself."

He shrugged, light dancing in his eyes. "You said it."

"You're giddy. You're actually delirious."

"I'm tired. I haven't slept much the last few days."

Birdcalls had woken them earlier than Mara'd have liked, impossible to ignore. "You're a soldier—shouldn't you be used to operating without sleep? What happens if you're called to war when you're tired and giddy like this?"

"In a fight? We learn to keep it together. Or people get killed."

He'd said something similar in the shuttle, high above Balti, months ago. She hadn't quite absorbed it. What he'd been through. Who it had made him. She hadn't wanted to ever get this close, close enough for his words to impact her. Close enough to care.

Whether she wanted to or not, she did care. They were in this together, for the next three months. And then it was over. For good.

But for now...

Mara linked her hand in his and tugged Calvy towards the path, ignoring his surprise at the gesture. "We should get you home then, so you can rest. And I'll have to try not to be so hard on you."

Calvy's thumb tapped the back of her hand as they walked, a warning that he was thinking.

"What?"

"How did you end up with Pent?"

She wanted to snap at him, remind him she didn't want to talk about Liam. But why not? Liam was her future. Calvy's bookends. She couldn't ignore it.

"Oh, you know, a pretty little worm like me does a little wiggle and hooks a nice big fish."

Mara's grip relaxed and Calvy tightened his in response, squeezing her hand in his.

"That's not what I—"

"It's not? It's what everyone thinks."

"I meant: How did you meet?"

"Same as us." He turned his head to question her with a look. "On a tram. He was on Støsh for business. His driver was late and he decided to handle it himself. Take transit."

Calvy waited while she sorted through the details of the memory. She could see Liam, sitting across from her on the tram. Legs wide, hands folded together, resting low in his lap. Eyes up, finding her, glinting with interest.

"I always like not having a screen on the tram. Feels like I have a second sight, that nobody else does. As usual, they were all wrapped up in their devices, off somewhere else. Liam got on and he was like me— aware, awake. And we stared at each other, like we were the only ones there. Like we were in on a secret. I know what's been said, but I couldn't have planned it. I recognized him. Of course. And he recognized me— or what I was. We both wanted to know more. So we started seeing each other when he came for business. He makes things easy. Understands what it feels like to be alone, even with people around. After Rozz died, I didn't have any more ties, any more reasons to put it off. I told him I was going to board an Arrow to Balti."

"An Arrow? It would have taken you years to get here. And the relative time passing—"

Balti would have changed, even more than it had now. She'd never have seen the mosaic under the tar. There would probably have been factories reaching all the way north by the time she'd made it.

"I couldn't afford a Fold—and I wasn't leaving anyone behind."

"Except Pent. He didn't want to lose you."

Mara fell silent, thoughts of Liam washing over her. He'd prioritized getting her here, taking time away from the Center and the majority of his business dealings to do so. She could be more understanding that he'd gone to the Rim to make some of it up. She stalled on an image of his sly grin, the one he used just for her. It was hard, to hold him in her mind and Calvy in her palm. But that was the way of it. Calvy was a problem with a built-in solution. Mara wasn't going to worry about it anymore. She only had to remember it was Liam who'd given her everything she wanted. Liam who understood her, who knew what it was to have a questionable past. To want to explore it and embrace it as much as escape it. He'd delivered her here in time to see Balti, almost as it had been—even if it was still unrecognizable to her. Even the parameters he'd put on her when she'd landed—he wasn't playing a game with her, he was ensuring her interests, as he would his own. She wanted Calvy and she wanted control. Liam made sure she had both. It was on her to enforce it. And she could do that.

So there was nothing to fight. No reason to pull away. From either of them. It was all so transparent. Mara's feet stepped lighter and she tugged Calvy along with a small smile, which he returned slowly.

The hoverbike was resting by the road where they'd left it. When Calvy replaced the battery, it lit and lifted with a soft rumbling hum. Mara ignored the cold that bit at her skin without Calvy's hand on hers.

"All fixed," he said. And Mara agreed, their problems growing fewer by the minute.

She mounted the bike and waited for him to take his place behind her. He secured his arm around her middle, as he had done while they slept, and Mara leaned into the handles, setting them on their way.

"Dannos and Harper are probably wondering where we are," she said as the path curved before her.

"Unlikely. You're with me. That's what matters—to them. They know you're safe."

"Right."

And he was. There was no one waiting outside her door when they returned to the hotel. Mara fiddled with the old-fashioned knob. Calvy scuffed the floor with his boot.

"If you're hungry, I can—" He cut himself off with a yawn.

"Go to bed, Cal." She checked the watch on his wrist. "Send Dannos over—he can watch the door. You earned some time off." She didn't know what he was expecting, after their field trip. After all the confusing things she'd confessed. His own confessions still burned in her veins. She wouldn't bring them up again; better to let them fade. But she wanted him to know, that it was settled, at least in her mind. That nothing had to change. "I'll see you tonight."

"Tonight," Calvy repeated.

"Tonight." Her throat closed around the promise.

But he didn't go to his room. His gaze dropped to her mouth. The air grew heavy as he lingered, waited for her to tell him to do what he wanted to do unbidden. Because he was a soldier and she gave the orders.

It was so easy. It was so simple. It was up to her.

"Kiss me, Cal."

Calvy reacted to the command like a shot, a bird startled from its roost. He grasped her face and pulled her lips to his, his fingers tangling in her windblown hair. His tongue crashed against hers, expressing his hunger and relief simultaneously. It almost scared her, the passion he waited to unleash. But he would always wait.

She could tell him to kiss her. And she could tell him to stop.

But she didn't tell him to stop.

She didn't want to. Not yet.

Not quite yet.

Chapter Nineteen

"If you don't want to go, I'll just take Dannos with me."

"I didn't say I don't want to go."

"You didn't have to. It's been all over your face since I told you about it yesterday."

Calvy wasn't like her—when he thought about something, it showed. And he'd been thinking about the hotel's Balti-themed full moons dinner with his jaw tight and his forehead lined.

"I'll take Dannos."

"You're not taking Dannos."

Mara had been closing the bedroom door when he said it. Now she held it ajar, her brow purposefully smooth and even. Calvy had been a captain and she recognized what that meant in moments like this, when his tone slipped into command. But he didn't command her.

"I'll be deciding who accompanies me, Private." A muscle flickered in his jaw and she softened. "And it just happens to be your luck that I prefer a bodyguard who won't partake so thoroughly of the free drink that he forgets to see me home."

"Mara. I need to know if that really happened. Because if—"

"It was hypothetical."

"It better be."

Silence dragged through the moment, lengthening it.

"I want to take you," Calvy said finally, his shoulders stiff, his body rigid. He wouldn't lie, it wasn't in his nature—he could never conceal it. But something about the dinner bothered him. "At least it's in the hotel."

"Cal—what does that mean? What could happen to me here? The city is practically deserted."

He didn't answer and Mara knew instinctively it had something to do with Iola. Iola and the people who believed in the Resurrection. She still hadn't decided if she was one of them.

Now wasn't the time, Mara thought as she closed the door. She needed to get dressed. The hotel wasn't exactly her first choice for celebrating the full moons, but the concierge had promised a traditional Balti meal and she still couldn't bring herself to join a moonclan block party uninvited.

Mara pinned the front of her hair back in a dome, darkened her eyes, paled her lips. She swept through the room into the hall when she was done, already imagining herself upstairs, the moons overhead, so lost in the pull of them that she didn't notice Calvy—not properly—until the elevator doors closed and their reflections stared back at her.

While he was always handsome—that shell of slicked-back hair, that solid brow, and the eyes underneath that always seemed to find some light to reflect back at her—tonight he was arresting.

"What are you wearing?"

"A suit? Couldn't wear my uniform. Not technically army right now. It's not a casual occasion—look at you."

A suit. The word didn't do the garment justice. He

was covered in deep navy, faintly patterned with plaid, a thin silk dyed to match hung from a triangular knot at his neck.

"What, Mara?"

"Nothing."

He considered her and she knew he was taking note of the slight flush at the top of her cheeks. "Oh." He looked down to hide a grin. "Oh."

"Oh what?" Her flush darkened. But he knew what. They both did.

He shrugged. "You like it. You *really* like it. You want me."

"I don't."

"You do. This is your aesthetic, right? A well-mannered civilian."

"Well-mannered is negotiable."

"But you like formal wear. You like a fancy man."

"Have you been sleeping? You're giddy again." She shifted her gaze purposefully up to the corner.

"You know full well how I spend my nights. Go ahead and look if you want to. Maybe we should go back downstairs—"

"Is that your plan to get out of this? Thought you could—" she breathed out, taking him in again "—distract me? Because you can't."

But her tongue pushed automatically over her lips.

He turned towards her and thumbed the hem of her dress, checked with shiny green scales. It was long-sleeved, slightly collared, and extremely short. His knuckles brushed just under her cunt with the motion. "I can't," he agreed.

"Just so we're clear."

The elevator doors opened. And the cool air broke

over Mara. Then Calvy moved a step closer to her and all she felt was his heat.

"Not very much fabric," Calvy said, his neck bent, his mouth closing in on hers. The doors began to shut again and he reached out on instinct to stop them. The motion gave Mara enough space to remember what she was supposed to be doing.

"Are you done trying to persuade me? Can we go now?"

Calvy's grasp tightened around the metal door. "You tell me."

Mara exited the elevator.

As much as she disliked the hotel's Dern style, Mara appreciated the rooftop restaurant. From here she could see all of Balti—the city, the ocean, the sky. And, for their part, the hotel had tried to bring more natural elements to the restaurant's decor: wood tables and chairs, and greenery. Tonight the tables had been rearranged in the communal Balti fashion for celebration. They weren't the first ones on the roof, but none of the hotel guests had taken seats yet.

A waiter passed carrying a tray of sparkling wine, the golden liquid glimmering as he moved. From where the guests milled around the tables, people began to notice Mara. Like heat rising, she could feel them taking her measure, from her long bare legs and her glittering dress to the vibrant red curls that sprang free around her head and danced above her shoulders as she swept two wide-mouthed glasses from the waiter's gilt tray.

Mara went straight to the edge, where an ivy-covered rail lined the roof's perimeter. Calvy followed a step behind her. She offered him one of the glasses.

"I'm working," he protested.

"Not tonight."

Again his face tightened and his forehead lined but he took the wine.

Mara fingered one of the pale tendrils that reached up to her from the thick leaves and found the Pearl glowing in the distance.

"If I could get you in—" Calvy started.

"I know."

A waiter carrying a tray of oesters gleaming in their shells caught Mara's eye.

"Wait here," she told Calvy before trailing after the spoils. She lost her prey, looking back at Calvy to grin, and turned to find herself interrupting a small group: two men and a woman, all clad in long shapeless tunics of pale purple and blue.

The shorter man stammered a greeting.

"Well—um—you must be Mr. Pent's—"

"Ms. Leanor," Mara supplied, allowing herself to compare the way his features were clustered in the center of his head to the faces Jimma used to carve into melons for the summer moondays.

She'd had a few run-ins with Dern prospectors. Some of them were curious. Of course they knew about Liam Pent, and they'd heard he'd put Mara—a nameless commodity belonging to the corporation—up at the hotel. They all wanted to be able to go home and tell their colleagues and friends that they'd been to Balti and seen a real Balti Temptress.

"Yes—well—right—" the man spluttered before the woman came to his rescue.

"Fine evening, Ms. Leanor. I'm Mrs. Rosier. This is Mr. Rosier and Mr. Zhoe."

Mr. Rosier, the melon-faced man, nodded along with the introduction. "Fine evening."

"Fine evening," Mr. Zhoe echoed, saluting her with his glass.

"The moons rise well," Mara replied. The wine sparked in her mouth. She looked around for the oesters.

"Where are you from?" Mr. Zhoe asked, in the disingenuous manner of someone who felt required to engage in polite conversation.

"Balti."

"Yes, but where are you really from?"

Balti, Mara wanted to say. "I was raised on Støsh."

"Støsh!" Mrs. Rosier smiled. "An urban paradise. You know, I've heard people say the skyline is more impressive than Dern itself. Planning was more strategic."

"Lucky you," Mr. Zhoe added.

Yes, it would be lucky to grow up in a place of indescribable beauty—Mara considered reminding them how that opportunity had been taken from her, but she was distracted by the waiter's reemergence. He was coming straight towards them. And his tray was still full.

"What in Virtue's name are those?" Mrs. Rosier exclaimed, looking over the opal shells.

"Oesters," Mara answered.

Mr. Zhoe leaned over them. "They look ghastly."

"No, thank you," Mrs. Rosier said with a laugh, "not for me." Mr. Rosier simply flattened his mouth and shook his head.

Mara picked an oester, tilting her head back to let it slide into her mouth. Salty and cold and brighter than she'd had on the beach—was that citrin? And she liked it. That was new.

"Delicious," she told the others.

The way the Dern looked uneasily at her was less novel an experience. Mrs. Rosier eyed the empty shell Mara replaced on the tray. The waiter hovered, unsure of what to do with the uneaten food.

They would remain untouched, Mara realized, because Dern judgment had been passed, and they had been found too strange, too different.

Mara downed her drink, shooting it back as she had the oester.

"Let me take those," she told the waiter, trading him her empty glass for the tray.

"It may be my overly mannered upbringing talking," Calvy began when she returned to the railing, "but I think even on Mi-isk it's insulting to come to a party, steal food, and leave. Please know I'm all for it."

"We're not leaving."

"And the mollusks?"

"They're oesters," she corrected. "Have one."

He took a grey shell and poured the contents into his mouth. "Mollusks," he insisted after swallowing, "bivalves though, not cephalopods."

"We would need a bigger tray for that, I imagine."

Calvy didn't crack a smile. Instead a fierce look hardened his eyes as he glanced at the taller of the men she'd been speaking to. "Is that what it sounded like? When I called you lucky?"

Mara lifted one shoulder and let it drop. "That's how it always sounds."

She waited for one of his automatic apologies. It didn't come. Instead Calvy reached for her hip, a gesture of understanding, an offer of warmth.

Suddenly Mara could see, clear as a cloudless sky,

how different he was than these people. How he didn't
quite belong with them. He was not blindly dedicated to
Virtue but guided by some internal drive to do good, to
do better. She was vaguely aware that more people had
joined them. But she couldn't look away from Calvy any
more than she could let go of her new understanding.

"D'Aldiern?" someone said with cruel enthusiasm.

"Attention, Soldier," another voice added.

"It's occupied," Calvy responded without breaking
eye contact with Mara.

"There's a general present," the second voice repeated.

A nerve in Calvy's jaw quivered. He was caught, she
realized, between his present and his future. But the
present was temporary—if he wanted back in the army,
he had to show that dedication now. Mara nodded, taking his still-full glass from him so he could clasp his
hands behind his back. He widened his feet and picked
a spot across the roof to set his eyes on.

Mara spun around. "Oester?"

"I didn't realize the hotel had retained Balti servers
for the evening."

Mara regarded the man who had spoken, from the
sagging belt of his uniform, so different from the clean
lines Calvy adhered to, to the stiff cap above a square
face. Block-headed, Mara thought, because she did not
like the way he'd emphasized *server* and she really did
not like the way he regarded her captain. As though
faced with rubbish he'd already binned.

The man was flanked by three soldiers, the one on
his right laughed at the comment, the other two main-
tained their steely composure—Mara recognized Runa.

Calvy swayed behind her, like something had urged

him forward and he'd had to hold himself back. A quiet anger burned in Mara's veins, hot coals dangerously close to a nuclear reactor.

"General D'Mont," the right-hand soldier provided.

"Mara Leanor." She was capable of contributing her own name.

The general didn't bother with a greeting. "I work with Mr. Pent. Shame he couldn't join you."

"He's away on business."

"And so you've come with—"

"D'Aldiern is acting as a security liaison, for the Pent Corporation." Mara aimed the explanation at the general. "A temporary position until he is reinstated with the Dern Forces."

"Hmph," the general replied. "We'll see."

A waiter skirted around the soldiers to collect the oester tray. "Dinner is about to begin. Would you like to be seated together?"

"No," Mara and the general answered as one, finding common ground after all. She started for the furthest end of the table, looking back when she realized Calvy wasn't behind her.

The general had gone in the other direction, but Runa had dropped away from him and was whispering to Calvy, her mouth close enough to his ear that should he bend to hear her better, her lips would graze the lobe. Heat continued to simmer just under Mara's skin.

"What did Runa say to you?" she asked when Calvy reached her.

"That I'm an idiot. I didn't stay to hear her list of reasons. I'm sure yours is more comprehensive."

Her rising jealousy flattened, a wave losing power and

failing to crest. She had to remember: he did what she wanted. And she'd told him not to be with anyone else.

Calvy pulled out a chair and settled Mara into it. He started for the other side of the table but she caught his elbow.

"Sit next to me."

"Then I can't see the elevator door."

"For tonight, Cal."

His thigh was warm against hers as he sat. She stilled the fingers tapping his knee, covering his hand with hers.

"D'Mont gave you the order. The one you disobeyed." He didn't respond. "Cal."

"What? You're not asking me. You've already put it together."

The salad was served and Mara experienced another jarring flashback to the night they'd first met. When he'd been a stranger. A toy Liam had found for them to play with.

Above them the moons glowed—so much had changed since then. But not enough.

Calvy frowned at her. Mara lifted her cheeks, adjusting the face she'd let slip. This was supposed to be a good night. She'd been excited to share it with Calvy. He was good, they were here, this was now. But they were both floundering for some reason, failing to find the pleasure in it.

"Sorry, sorry, my apologies." The table shook as a man thumped his side into it, attempting to reduce his lateness by taking the seat across from Mara as quickly as possible. "I didn't think you'd be here so early, I—oh—uh, my apologies. Again. I thought you were someone else."

"I'm not," Mara said.

The man rose up halfway, looking down at the full table. He shook his head. "Do you mind if I—"

"The seat is yours."

"Thank you. The moons rise well." He smiled at her and Calvy, and despite his Dern clothing and constant apologies, Mara found herself smiling back, not likening his features to any unkind shapes.

"Very well," she said. His light brown eyes twinkled back at her and he lowered his voice conspiratorially. Mara leaned in to hear him.

"*Fine evening*, such a drab greeting. I'm Arin—uh, Dr. Protaris, for propriety."

"Ms. Leanor."

Calvy stretched an arm over the back of her chair but did not offer his name.

Mrs. Rosier's voice carried down the table as she complimented the salad, and recounted how the oesters had not been to her liking. She'd been excited to try the local flavors, you know, but she never imagined anyone could eat something so *goopy*!

"I missed oesters?" Dr. Protaris lamented.

"You like them?" Mara asked.

"Of course!"

"Me too," Calvy said. "What's not to like? Soft, wet, a little salty."

Mara nearly choked on a small purple radiche.

The general, seated in the middle of the long table, heard him. "After a diet of stewed yarrow I'm sure anything is palatable."

Calvy stopped chewing. He took a deep breath through his nose and then reached for his wineglass, finally taking a sip.

Mara glared at the general until Mr. Zhoe captured

his attention, discussing his afternoon tour of the rig off the coast. The security had been *very* impressive. Another incident appeared highly unlikely. Wasn't that a load of worry off their shoulders? Mr. Rosier nodded, this could really be a…a…a *sound* investment.

The general agreed: "progress" was being made.

Mara's tongue found the roof of her mouth. Couldn't they see? Couldn't any of them see? Not only had they destroyed the people of Balti, but their continued interference would destroy the planet itself.

The truth, she knew, was that they did see. And they did not care.

"The storms aren't the problem," the general told a rapt Mr. Zhoe. "It's the waves. We've had to reinforce the platforms, raise them higher than normal regulations. Up to forty-five meters now."

"That's not enough." Calvy pulled his arm from behind her and leaned his elbows on the table. "Forty-five meters won't be enough. You should build them higher."

The general laughed. "A prince, a soldier, and an engineer now?"

"No. But I know Balti. And the waves will—"

"Last season the waves didn't get above forty. We expect—"

Calvy's voice rose, civility ebbing away. "You can't expect anything here. It doesn't matter what happened last season. Don't you understand this planet? The Balti's entire belief system teaches acceptance in the face of what you cannot control. Because they lived here long enough to know: it's ocean. It's unpredictable. They prepared themselves for the worst. And they didn't think it was us."

Us.

Had she ever heard him align himself so distinctly with the Dern? But he was one of them. It was Calvy's people who had washed hers out quicker than any wave. But she knew there was no use arguing with them. She put her hand on his knee again under the table and Calvy sat back.

Mr. Zhoe cleared his throat. "Is this it, then? A simple dinner outside? Not much of a tradition."

Mara's grip stiffened. They didn't understand any of it. These people, expecting pleasure to appear for them, out of thin air, they didn't know you had to work for it. Make it yourself. Look up at the satin sky spread above you and drink in the grandness of it. To see two moons shining like pale suns in the night and feel the curious tingle of excitement in your gut. The way those moons found a rhythm in your own blood, linking you to something bigger, something more.

How could they? They weren't Balti.

"What's served for the third?" Mrs. Rosier asked, steering the conversation back to food.

"Fish," Dr. Protaris answered. "Such lovely fish here."

The general scoffed. "Fish, fish. I've tired of fish!" An appreciative murmur came from the Dern around him. "I long for fowl. That would be a service. They've taken down more drones than I'd care to admit."

Mara stirred her soup and spoke without looking up. "Have they? The Pent Corporation doesn't have that problem."

Mr. Rosier sighed. "They also took my cat."

At that Mara laughed. "You'll find our planet is no place for pets."

"Tell that to Mr. Pent," the general murmured.

"You don't want me telling him anything," Mara warned, her gaze narrowing on D'Mont.

"Let's go back downstairs," Calvy whispered in her ear.

But Mara had never had a Balti feast under the full moons. Liam would be here before the next—and she knew him, he wouldn't want to stay on Balti long. Not when the deals here had already been made. She might not have another opportunity to do this.

Recommitting to her determination to find pleasure in the evening, she returned her attention to Dr. Protaris and tried to ignore the others. They weren't worth her limited time.

"You've an interest in Balti?"

"I do. I've studied it for many years."

"So has Private D'Aldiern." Mara nodded at him. "Thus his apparent affinity for mollusks."

Calvy ripped a flatbread to pieces as Dr. Protaris spoke.

"I've focused more on the history and the politics—not so much the wildlife."

"I'd be fascinated to hear more. It's my first time back on planet since—since leaving."

Warmth flooded the doctor's eyes—not the usual discomfort she found when speaking to a Dern about Balti. "Has it been a hard adjustment for you?"

"Yes," Mara answered, setting her spoon against the rim of the bowl.

"It isn't easy to think about. What happened here. Part of my interest is in preservation, so nothing more is lost. Like this." He used his stone to project an image for her: a thin gold disc next to a measuring ticker for scale.

"Is that a coin?"

"A chip. Or it would be. If it weren't such old tech.

A very early prototype. Extremely early. Maybe even from the settler ship. It has no receptors, can't connect to any mainframe, or link to our current systems."

"Why? What's it for?"

Dr. Protaris shrugged. "Honestly? I don't know."

"You can't make it work?"

"I think it's coded. To the royal family. I'd need Balticourt DNA to activate it. I've got a few searches flagged in the regulator database. Anyone who gets one is sequenced and cataloged. I might be able to make a match, even if a distant relative—"

"Where did you find it?"

"Where I work. At the Pearl—I'm the curator."

Mara knocked into her bowl, splashing soup over the edge.

"The Pearl—Doctor, I—"

"Oh—there she is. Excuse me." The doctor stood, jolting the table again. He was up and moving before Mara could make her request. She spun in her seat, craning to see where he went—a flash of red disappeared with him behind the elevator tower.

Calvy sopped up soup with a bit of bread. Bread, she thought, that did not belong at an authentic Balti meal. But the Dern had to have their comforts. "Why don't you follow him? I'm sure you can find a way to convince him to let you in."

"I'm sure I could."

It must have been the chill in her tone that made his eyes close with remorse.

"Pent says you can't—"

Or maybe not.

"Moons, Cal, really?" She couldn't decide what pissed her off more, that he'd remind her of Liam's rules or that he was actually worried she'd track Dr. Protaris down and suck his cock in exchange for a tour of the Pearl.

The third course arrived while Mara sat with her arms crossed.

"Fish it is," complained the general.

The joy she'd been hoping to find not on the evening's menu either, Mara snapped. "Well, there is an abundance of it. When there were people here—they needed to eat."

D'Mont's smile was half grimace. "I can think of better ways to fill a Balti mouth."

Calvy rose from his seat, a cold, detached look in his eyes she'd never seen before. "We're leaving."

"No, we're not."

"Pity," the general said.

Mara trained her eyes on him. "You're as closed-minded as you are rude."

He pushed back in his chair. "Me? I've heard about you, girl. Were you not spread on a table like this once, acting as the entertainment? Is that not rude?"

"It was a simple expression of pleasure—no more offensive than Mr. Rosier moaning over that soup." She stood, dropping her napkin over her plate. "Do you install a chip at birth that limits Dern cognitive ability or is it a natural display of inferiority that you cannot manage any thinking that requires a shift in perspective?"

"If you think so poorly of us why do you keep one on staff?"

Mara opened her mouth but couldn't respond. The fact was: she didn't consider Calvy one of them anymore. "It's Liam's business," she said finally.

The general laughed. "That's how we felt about him too, Ms. Leanor—best to pass him off and hope someone else takes the blame for him."

"It was my understanding that Private D'Aldiern had a stellar record prior to his demotion."

Calvy took hold of her arm and tried to pull her from the table. "I believe the intent of Ms. Leanor's flattery is to ensure you continue to hold Mr. Pent's business prowess in high esteem."

Mara turned her glare on him. "The intent of Ms. Leanor's flattery is to issue recognition where it is due."

She shook him off and headed for the elevator. Now she'd had enough. None of them should even be here. Celebrating something that wasn't theirs—judging it, corrupting it.

Calvy pushed their floor number. She stepped forward to jam her thumb into the button for street level.

Of course he followed her out into the night.

Mara's heart hammered in her chest as loud as her feet on the pavement. Her eyes stung and she told herself it was irritation from the wind generated by her quick pace. An army truck rattled behind them but she refused to move aside, to give up the road. The truck honked.

"Let them pass, Mara."

"No."

The engine revved, drawing nearer—much nearer by the sound of it—and a moment later Calvy had yanked her into a narrow pass between buildings. Her hair snagged on the rough wall as his body pressed her against it. She shoved him back but he couldn't go far before he hit the opposite wall.

His chest heaved. "They were going to plow through you."

"So let them. It feels like they already did most of the time."

"I would *never* let them."

"You wouldn't? That's why you had my back up there? That's why you called for a retreat?"

"You were making a scene."

She angled her head. "You've gone along with it before."

His jaw jutted out. "You don't want to be linked with me, Mara. You *know* who that was. General D'Mont gave me the order to leave my people on Theos. They were going to rot in that zoo even though he gave them counterfeit weapons—*army-issued.* It wasn't their fault. But he has protection. And they didn't. So I stepped in, and he fucking loved it. That was torture for me, Mara, sitting there with him, biting my tongue instead of ripping out his throat. I'd have spent an extra month on Theos to have avoided that table. Avoided how useless it made me feel. So, thanks for that."

"My pleasure."

"It always is. Whatever you want."

"I wanted some support up there—if Liam were here—"

"The general wouldn't have dared treat you that way. You think I don't know that? But Pent wasn't there. You just had me. And I couldn't do anything. Not if I want to go back." He looked up at the sliver of sky revealed in the gap between the two buildings. Then he turned to the side, away from her. "No matter what I do. Born a fucking eleven."

She pulled at his elbow. "You're not an eleven."

It was his turn to try to shake her off. "Right. I have no title. No number."

She persisted, ducking under his arm as he twisted away from her again. She took hold of his jacket.

"You've got a number. Oh dash two six one one dash one four two three two seven."

"You've memorized my military ID number."

She put her hand on his chest over the tattoo. "I've seen it a few times."

"And? You're trying to remind me I might have no rank as well?"

"I'm trying to remind you that you made them give you something they didn't want to give you. That you can take more from them than you think." He didn't answer. He didn't consider the Dern his enemy like she did. They were on opposite sides. They always would be. "You don't believe me. But I see your power too, Cal. I wanted to be with you tonight. I wanted you to be my date."

He held up his hands, bracketing his face. "I can't be your date!" He pulled at his tie. "That's not me!"

Mara straightened her neck. "Who are you then? What do *you* want?"

Calvy squeezed his eyes shut, his dark lashes crushed into his cheeks.

"You can't tell me? Or you don't know?" She wanted to push him again. Shake him, shove him, make him see. But this was exactly the kind of conversation that would make what had become easy too complicated to bear. "Kiss me, Cal."

"Mara—you don't want me to kiss you. You're pissed at me."

"I am. And you're going to fix it. By making me feel better."

Then she did push him, following him into the wall, pinning him against it. Hard as it was, she waited. For him to do as he was told. To end the conversation before they reached more dangerous waters.

When he kissed her, his mouth was hot and angry—like he was trying to continue the argument, but without words. They battled with teeth and tongues, heads pitching one way and then the other. They slammed into the walls on either side of them, bumping along the surface as they moved further between the buildings. Mara was breathless when Calvy finally shifted down a gear, slowing them into a rhythm of desire instead of vexation. Without the storm of his mouth clouding her mind, she could focus on what came next. Hands that had gripped his jacket, holding on through the onslaught of his kiss, could now drift lower. She found him already there, unfastening his pants. And then he was hoisting her up, and driving his cock into her waiting cunt, stretching her to make room for himself inside her.

The moment they connected, Mara groaned, dropping her forehead to Calvy's. He rocked his brow against hers.

"I should have—the way he spoke to you—"

"Just kiss me, Cal."

Again he obeyed, his lips caressing hers as she gripped his neck. She held tight as he jounced her up, bringing her down hard on his cock.

Her fingers cramped and her grasp slipped to his shoulders, his jacket dusty from scraping against the sand plaster. His knees buckled and together they slid down to the ground, legs bending. Mara straddled Calvy, her dress peeling up. His hands at the top of her thighs kept them connected through the fall. And it didn't stop him. He lifted his hips, pumping into her, hitting that spot inside of her that made her throw her head back and moan. Calvy braced his back on one wall and Mara found leverage with her shoulders against the other. She angled her hips, matching his thrusts, her abdomen tightening each time they moved up.

For once his eyes weren't on hers, but trained on her cunt, spread wide in his lap, his cock plunging in and out of her depths.

She was exposed, to him, to the moons. A moan stuttered in her throat as everything squeezed shut— her eyes, her knees, and her cunt closing around the sensation that was Calvy beneath her, inside her, with her. Like she could keep him there, if she just held tight enough.

Pleasure overwhelmed her as he continued to delve in and out of her warmth. Pressure blocked her ears. Calvy sounded fuzzy and far away. But he was right there. Another thrust and then another and then his straining pelvis was lifting her up and it was his turn to crush a groan behind his gritted teeth.

Calvy lowered his hips back down, his chest rising and falling from the exertion. With his cock still deep inside her, he ran both thumbs along the sides of the slippery pink skin that was open to him, to the night.

"I was right," he said finally.

"Unlikely," she managed.

A satisfied smile pulled at his cheeks. "You wanted me."

Chapter Twenty

Mara couldn't shake the thought she'd had during the full moons. That she wouldn't experience them again.

And definitely not like that.

Not with Calvy.

She'd spent nearly six months on Balti—getting to know it, getting to love it—and she still hadn't found a single trace of who she used to be. Time was rubbing against her heels, blistering her skin worse with every movement, every moment.

And Liam's bright face from the projector did little to ease the sting. "I don't know what to tell you, you're right. You know you are."

She'd asked him to confirm what she suspected, that he wasn't planning an extended stop on Balti. "But what if I'm not ready to go."

"Mara. You'll have had six months. It'll be time to move on."

"But—"

"We won't be staying long after I get there."

She pushed back. "Why is there a rush? I might need more time. To find out where I lived—where I came from."

He threaded his hands together and leaned in.

"There's no record of Leanors owning property or business on the planet."

"Balti didn't keep the same meticulous records that Dern do. People knew each other—there was no need to catalog every little thing."

"However—"

"Don't say it, Liam."

"*However.* There is a possibility that your name could be wrong."

Her eyes shut and her shoulders sagged forward. She knew that too. But she wasn't ready to face the possibility yet. It would mean stripping away one of the few things she had left.

"It's a small planet, my dove. You must have looked everywhere by now. What else is there to see?"

"The Pearl."

He tsked at the reminder. "Oh—I was meant to—I forgot. I'll do it when I arrive. We'll go together. I should have done it sooner. I'm sor—"

Her eyes flashed open. "Don't. Just. Just fix it. Okay?"

"Okay." Those soft green eyes hardened, reflecting his resolve. "See you in a few weeks."

A few weeks.

In a few weeks she'd be raw and aching.

In a few weeks she'd have to admit that she'd failed. That it was over. That she was no one.

She couldn't ignore the awful constriction of time. Even now, as she walked hand in hand with Calvy around the Ring, she was plagued by the gaps in her past. She'd done everything she could think to shake loose some memory, but all she found were whispers of familiar tastes, smells, feelings. Nothing concrete, nothing she could hold on to. Nothing she could take with her.

Calvy squeezed her hand, reading the tightness in her face. "There's still time."

The night was clear and the stars were bright. She felt the pull of the moons in her veins, her Balti blood responding to it like the ocean. He'd been right, saying they should get some fresh air. It helped. She tried to focus on the night. Before it was gone.

The square was bustling with late-night business. Men and women from the factory, looking weary from the day yet energized by the night. Like her. That moon magic that came alive inside all of them, connecting them to the planet and the sky they shared, connecting them to each other. And was it her imagination? Or had she caught a few glimpses of red hair in the crowd? She'd noticed an increase lately—Iola converting more followers to her cause while Mara had been cut loose, found wanting.

Think about what you believe.

Think about what you want.

She looked down where her fingers were linked with Calvy's. His knuckles grazed her thigh and she used the connection to tug herself up, bring him closer, and take a bite of the rice cake in his other hand.

"No. I don't think so. You said you didn't want one." He extended his arm, moving the cake out of her range, and she caught his wrist to pull it back, taking hold of the dessert.

"I changed my mind."

He was reaching out to wipe the powdered sugar from the corner of her mouth when someone hit them from behind, slamming into her shoulder. The rice cake dropped. Mara's wrist bent painfully trying to hold on, but Calvy let go.

He turned on the assailant, a hand reflexively going for his sidearm. Mara stepped back as the man rushed forward again, tackling Calvy about the waist and lifting him into the air. Calvy clapped his hands on the man's back, his face twisted in—a grin? Then he laughed. And Mara's brow furrowed. What? She wasn't used to hearing him laugh like that. He'd quip with her often enough, but Calvy wasn't prone to such easy displays of humor. He wasn't loose, he was always so buttoned-up. She found herself grinning at him, despite the strangeness of the situation. That laugh. There was so much more to him under the surface.

The attacker set Calvy down and the assault transformed into an embrace.

"I thought they'd sent you back to that palace of yours," the man said.

"They tried."

"You never do as you're told, do you?" The man crushed him in another hug.

When they pulled back, Calvy blocked the glinting chevrons on the man's uniform. "What's this? I'm blind."

"You're the one with the story—what are you doing here?"

Calvy glanced at Mara. "Private detail—this is Ms. Leanor. Ms. Leanor, Shef. *Lieutenant* in the Third."

"You served with Private D'Aldiern?" Mara asked.

"Captain. I serve under him."

"Not anymore. You outrank me," Calvy said.

"What a crock of—" Shef spat on the ground. "Sorry, miss."

"No need to apologize. It's white, runny shit, Lieu-tenant."

Shef looked Mara over before raising his eyebrows at Calvy. "Private detail, eh?"

"Temporary. Until I can get back in the service. Back in a grunt ditch with you lot, where I belong."

Where I belong. At least one of them knew. And why would he trade that? A Dern king hadn't traded his kingdom for a Balti queen's. Why would a prince trade his rank for a nobody? Why would she want that? Knowing the man who'd made him a prince was the same man who'd made her an orphan. Except he hadn't made Calvy a prince. And she didn't see the link be-tween them as clearly as she once had. What Calvy represented now was...something else.

Mara tapped her foot to release some of the anxious confusion that swelled in her.

Calvy cleared his throat. "We've got to be—"

"Yeah, yeah, always on task—but a bunch of us just arrived. Waiting orders here. The squad would love to see you. After what you did. They didn't get a chance to thank you. Meet us out for a drink?"

Mara watched Calvy struggle for an answer. But why shouldn't he go?

"He's free tomorrow. Lunchtime," she answered for him.

"Stellar." Shef smiled at her and after exchanging a few more bits of news with Calvy, he left.

"Mara," Calvy said when they were alone, "why did you do that?"

"You were going to say no."

"Yes. I was."

"You shouldn't say no. You should see them."

This was the start of it. The start of the end. They had to remember what was waiting for them. When this was over. Calvy had found his place.

"I don't know if I—I don't know how to—"

"That squad knows you, believes in you. Don't you miss that? Don't you miss them?"

"Yes."

"Then go have a drink."

He lifted his hand to finish wiping the sugar from her lips. "Small pleasures?"

"May there be many."

There, that was the smile she associated with Calvy. Slow and steady, paired with a deadly smolder from his black-brown eyes.

A warning pricked her neck and she turned away, her gaze fixing on Iola, standing in the narrow slip between the buildings. Hood up, face half-covered, she nodded Mara over.

Calvy turned to see what had distracted Mara and she caught his arm.

"Shame about the rice cake," she said with a pout. The fried ball had smashed into the ground at his feet, the sticky filling exposed. "Get us another?"

He looked around, gauging the crowd. Would he refuse to leave her?

"I'll wait right over there." She pointed to the wall near where Iola was hiding out of sight. "Okay? Out of harm's way."

He waited a moment, two, and then nodded, heading back to the vendor's stand.

When Mara settled against the rough wall, Iola's voice teased out of the alley.

"Mara. Mara *Leanor*. Yes, I looked you up. Grew up on Støsh. No wonder you stayed away so long."

The other redhead had a talent for poking Mara right where she'd flinch hardest. "I stayed away because I couldn't afford to make it back."

"But you've got the means now. And I'd say, by the way you've got Liam Pent wrapped around your finger, you've got plenty of them."

Mara's shoulders threatened to rise and she forced them back down, leaning one into the wall as she turned to find Iola in the dim light of the alley. "That's not Liam Pent."

"I know. But if you're doing all that under his nose, you must be confident in your ability to soothe the wound."

"It's not— What do you want, Iola?"

Iola clasped her hands and held them low. "This is a serendipitous development. It turns out you have access I need."

"If I want to help you."

Iola's eyes were dark in the shadows, solid and set. "You want to. You want to blow through this city, decimate the Dern before they can take anything else from us. I see it in your face like looking in a mirror." She gestured to Calvy, who was making his way back over to them, a fresh rice cake in his hand. "I don't see how you can stand it—he's pretty, sure enough, but underneath he's just another Dern. Another oppressor."

Heart racing at Calvy's approach, Mara rushed Iola to her point. "Were you here to ask for my help or insult me? You'll need to pick one and forget the other."

"Meet me tomorrow morning, by the docks. If you

can pull yourself away from your Dern." Iola sank back into the shadows.

"Let's try this again," Calvy said, and Mara jumped. The rice cake he pressed into her hand was hot and sweet and he looked at her expectantly. Waiting for her to say something.

What's good and here and now.

Only her thoughts whirred, spun up by Iola as they always were.

What did she believe? What did she want?

She wasn't ready to let go yet, of any possibility Balti offered. And maybe this was a way for her to finish what she'd started here, without waiting for Liam. He'd excluded himself from the rest of the experience anyway. She wanted to keep the planet to herself. Let Balti be hers.

"I want to head back," she said, recovering herself. "I've got plans in the morning. I should sleep."

"What plans?" Calvy asked.

"I'm sure Harper will give you the full report."

That made him laugh again—seeing Shef had made him light as air. His burden was almost lifted. His penance nearly complete. It was better for both of them, to start now, getting back on their own paths.

Mara risked a glance into the alley. She could sense that Iola was still close by, listening.

"I have something I need to do," Mara said.

Chapter Twenty-One

Harper rapped on the door. Dawn lit the sky outside Mara's window. Calvy's shift was over.

"Be right there—" Calvy nipped the side of her cunt and Mara cut herself off with a yelp. "A few more minutes," she called instead.

He stopped to grin up at her.

She let her head fall back. "I've got places to be, you know."

"Do you want me to stop?"

"I want you to get on with it."

"No patience whatsoever," he lamented. "And I know you hate to be told you're wrong," he stroked a finger over the top of her thighs, ruffling the red curls, calling her nerves to attention, "but I maintain that this is no cunt. This is a pussy—you want to be pet and fondled and caressed."

"Do I," she attempted to drone but he finally brought his mouth down on her and the words were overtaken by her moan. Further argument would just interrupt the tight pressure of his sucking, and that would be a tragedy. He finished her off a few minutes later and she lay trembling and unfocused.

"You do," he said, standing up, trying to claim the

last word. Mara let him, for once, her mind hazy and slow. She propped herself on her elbows and looked him over. His hands flexed at his sides and she imagined what would happen next, under different circumstances. How he'd take her behind the knees and pull her to the edge of the bed, sink himself into her—but things weren't different. And if she wanted him to do that she'd have to ask.

"Anything else, Ms. Leanor?" Calvy said, following a step behind her.

"Does it look like I need anything else?"

"I'm just trying to make sure I do my job well."

Right. That's all it was. The pleasure that still shuddered through her body in shock waves, squeezing her cunt tight. His job.

She forced a smile. "That work ethic, how lucky for me. But your shift is over. You need to get some rest. You're meeting Shef this afternoon, remember?"

"How is it that you can give me orders even when I'm off duty?"

"I'm a powerful woman."

He waited for her to dress and they left the room together, Harper stepping out of the doorway as they came through.

"Private," Mara dismissed him. He offered a sideways salute before heading for his room.

Harper kept her stony silence all the way to the docks. She didn't have to say anything. Mara knew what she thought.

The ocean was churning, crashing into the land in white arcs. Iola waited under a stone arch, her hood pulled up. From a distance, Mara secured her own. The spray beaded in the patterns shaved in Harper's short hair.

Iola disappeared, moving deeper under the masonry that covered the path down to the docks. She was right to be more concerned about Harper noticing their interaction than Dannos. Harper noticed everything.

Mara stood at the stone wall for a minute before moving slowly towards the covered section where Iola had gone. She drifted successfully under the arch without Harper following and stopped. The path curved out of Harper's sight but Mara stayed where she was, visible to Harper and Iola both.

The other redhead nodded at Harper, waiting in the distance. "Why seduce the Dern when your other bodyguard looks like that?"

"It wasn't a choice."

"She wasn't interested?"

"What's your point?" Mara wasn't sure if meeting with Iola would be worth her time, but she knew she didn't have long to find out.

"I looked you up."

"Yes, and decided I'd be useful to you. That's why we're here."

Iola tried to keep her tone casual, but Mara heard the effort it took to conceal her interest. "They say you're the last Balti Temptress." She couldn't control the eager quake in her voice as she asked, "Who taught you? Could she teach others?"

A lump threatened to close Mara's throat but she managed to answer. "She's dead."

Iola dipped her head down to avoid a spray of seawater that scattered through the stone opening in front of them. "So they're right. You are the last." She lifted her chin. "And you waste it on a Dern grunt. If you are inclined to slop a Balti Kiss on the enemy, why not one with more sway? The city could be under our control already."

Wind pushed Mara's hood across her face and she took it off. Droplets in the air stung her skin like a cold rain. "You don't know what you're talking about. That's not how it works at all. It's power in the moment. Not absolute. Is that what you think I can do for you? Because it isn't happening."

"Maybe you didn't learn it right."

"I assure you I did."

"And yet you waste your training on—"

"I waste nothing. Is that what it feels like to you—when you seek a moment of pleasure? A waste?"

If Harper hadn't been there, Mara was sure Iola would have forced herself forward. "It feels like I could be doing so much more. If only I'd had the chance to learn. And that is a waste, a waste for all of us."

"So dedicate yourself to it now. Practice the mindset."

"The mindset?" Iola balked.

"That's what I was taught—the truest pleasure comes from within. Is it not the same on the moon?"

"No. Everything was static there. I think they forgot—why we needed the philosophy of temperament. And here—when we returned—the Dern have tried to stamp out every trace of our culture. They pave our streets and cut us off from what's rightfully ours. They took our history and they crumbled it to dust." The rant brought Iola back to the point. "We need you to help us make some noise. Let the queen know there is support here, that we're readying for her return."

"I told you I don't believe in that."

"But you're here. You believe in Balti?"

Mara nodded.

"And there's something you want. For helping us?"

Mara nodded again.

"Then it doesn't matter if you believe in the Resurrection. Even if she isn't out there. We have to rally support for the fight anyway. Because we can do better than this. Forced to drain and wreck ourselves, our home, for their benefit."

Every time Iola spoke with such passion Mara felt the fire of it catch in her blood, warming her from within. With or without Queen Balticourt, this was what Jimma had wanted for them both. Not the chance to return to Balti, but to return Balti to itself.

She was glad that dream was alive, that someone would work on it even after she was gone. For now, she'd do what she could.

"What do you want me to do?"

"Nothing hard. Just make an appearance. At the Pent arms factory this afternoon."

Well, so much for keeping the dream alive. Mara turned back to Harper. It was time to go. "I'm not spying on Liam."

"Who said anything about spying? I haven't asked you to steal anything. I don't care what you do once you're inside. Just get in."

Mara glanced over her shoulder at Iola. "Why?"

"Call it a test. I need to know that you'll do what I ask."

Mara rubbed the roof of her mouth with the tip of her tongue.

"Unless it's not worth it to you? You've only just returned, how much could this place mean to you?"

Mara should be used to the way it felt, when Iola

used that particular jab. She should be over it by now. Instead Mara thought back to the full moons dinner—watching their traditions mocked, remembering how it had felt to defend them.

"It means everything to me."

"Then you'll do it—and I'll owe you one. Proof of my own. A show of good faith. You can get in, can't you?"

"I could try."

How would she—why would she—

"Are you with us, Mara?"

The water splashed against the rock and she thought of the cliffs—*This is you*, Calvy had said. She was Balti—it was the only thing she knew. It was why she'd committed herself to Jimma's training. Why she'd traveled through the Black.

She'd come here to prove it. And now she had her chance.

"Yes."

"Then don't try. Do it."

Chapter Twenty-Two

But how? Liam was in and out of the Black—he wouldn't be able to arrange it. And what would she say to explain it anyway? That she'd developed a sudden interest in arms production?

Mara felt Harper's silence like a weight all morning. At least she was free of that dark-eyed scrutiny in the afternoon. She stood in the bathroom, working up the courage to ask Dannos for help. He might know someone. Dannos always knew someone.

A look of doubt met her in the mirror. But she wasn't doing anything wrong. She wasn't doing anything that could cause harm. Yet she was letting Iola test her. And she wanted to pass.

Calvy leaned unsteadily against the doorframe.

"Hi," he said, his eyes heavy. He stumbled into the room, planting his hands on her waist.

"You smell like you bathed in lighter fluid."

"Military-grade vodka. Standard issue. Do you need me for anything?"

"I wouldn't dare—the friction alone would set you aflame."

"I'd burn for you," he mumbled into her neck, hands still roaming, one reaching up under her dress.

Mara fumbled the earring she'd been trying to string through her ear and the end dangled at her neck. "I didn't initiate this," she warned him.

He wrestled with the clasp on his pants. "But you want it, we both do—that's what matters. Not what Pent—"

"Cal."

He stopped and Mara felt her heart beating unreliably in her throat.

"Kiss me, Mara."

Whether it was a command or a plea, it didn't matter.

"No. It doesn't work like that."

There were rules. There were boundaries they'd both agreed to. Mara stood stiff, waiting for Calvy to recover himself. She exhaled as he released her. He backed away until he hit the matching vanity behind her and sank onto the counter.

"Fuck," he said, wiping a hand across his face. Mara slowed her breathing, picking up a powder brush, resuming her routine. An endless line of Calvys and Maras stretched behind them both, trapped, untouching, between the two mirrors.

Calvy fell back against the glass. He watched her for a moment, sitting still, his spread legs opening his pants wider. Then he reached down to free his cock from the layers, sliding his hand along the solid length of it.

"What are you doing?" Mara froze, the brush at her cheek.

"I can't have you, but no one ordered me to keep my hands off myself." He stroked himself up and down, tugging in a way that seemed both rough and tender. Intimate. Mara's cheeks flushed pink, the brush in her hand forgotten, useless—now that her blush was natural.

"I can do this somewhere else. If it makes you uncomfortable. But it doesn't. Does it, Mara?" She loved
the way he talked, stringing fragments of understanding together like bulbs on a wire, lighting Mara up with
each one. He leaned his head back and groaned, his
cock swelling in his hand. "You like this. You like everything that feels good." He didn't wait for her to respond, but stood and made his way back to her. Mara
drew a shaky line of kohl under one eye and he smiled
a lazy, personal grin. "That first time I saw you. Your
hand working deep between your legs. I felt the same
way. Dumb with lust. Talking like an idiot because I
liked it so much I didn't know what to do. All I wanted
was to pull those fingers out of you and into my mouth."

Mara set her hands on the counter to steady herself. Drunk Calvy was not someone she was prepared
to contend with. And he knew it. His words caressed
her mind, drawing a response from her body the same
as if his hands had made contact with her skin. Calvy
stroked his cock again, a bead of white squeezing from
the tip of its smooth head. He wiped it onto his thumb
and brought his arm around her, offering the taste. She
found his eyes in the mirror and opened her mouth,
sucking his finger clean. Calvy groaned again and
pressed his head into her shoulder. He drew his finger
from her mouth and lifted the back of her dress, revealing the round curves of her ass. He took one cheek in
his hand and gripped it firmly, all the while stroking
his cock with the other.

He angled his hips and pushed the head of his cock
gently against the seam between her cheeks, lifting his
eyebrows in the mirror. *Okay?* That would be tight,
slow, excruciatingly good. But she didn't have time for

it. Mara shook her head and the pressure decreased. Still she could feel him dripping that white liquid onto her skin, warm and slick and uncontainable as his arousal grew. Her mouth dropped open as his finger spread it up and down the fold, lightning striking inside her at his touch. Then he was raising his eyes to hers again, looking to her for confirmation. This time Mara responded with a resolute nod and Cal smiled, pressing his wet finger deep into her crease. Mara's grasp on the counter tightened. Her wet cunt swelled with a sudden contraction, though his attention remained further behind.

"I need more hands," Calvy complained, biting the taut tendon of her neck as her head fell back into him.

Mara was already releasing the counter to engage the ache between her legs. Their gazes locked, both of them determined to work together, to keep pace with each other and stay connected until the end. As Mara rounded her middle finger over her grateful clit, Calvy pressed the finger in her ass higher. She felt her insides grind together, the mechanics of her orgasm clicking into gear. And the rest came to her in fragments of sensation: her name on his lips, tangled in her hair. The hip he'd overlapped with hers, pushing her harder against the counter's sharp edge until it dug into her bone. And then: white lines of come jetting past her like ribbons in a breeze.

Calvy eased his finger out of her and wrapped his arm tight around her shoulders. He pulled her into him, his nose at her neck taking and releasing deep breaths that tingled across her skin.

What was she doing?

"I've got to get dressed," she said.

Her knees shook as he let go of her and she leaned

into the counter for support. Mara couldn't tell if it was her pulse or her cunt throbbing harder. She tried to steady them both.

"Right." He blinked, looking around the bathroom to orient himself.

Mara looked at herself in the mirror, her face misted with sweat, her eye makeup lopsided and smudged.

"Are you leaving?"

"Exploring some more," Mara said, attempting to even out the kohl sketched around her eyes with trembling hands. She was lucky that drink slowed his mind and he didn't pick up on the deception.

"I'll come," he offered.

"Like this? You need to sleep it off—"

"I need a cup of coffee."

"Dannos has it covered."

He stumbled backwards as she passed him, leaving the bathroom. She pushed him onto the bed and he fell like dead weight.

"Mara?"

"Yes, Cal?"

The blankets muffled his response, but she caught three words clear and undistorted—"lie to me."

Behind her ribs, Mara's lungs compressed. How did he know that she—

"Will you lie to me? When it's time? Tell me you're with him for the power or the money. I could understand that. I could take it—I can't offer you either of those things. Just don't tell me it's him." He stopped rambling and she thought maybe he'd passed out. She was at the door when he spoke again, desperation clear as the words. "Lie to me, Mara."

Her heart pounded and it took effort to peel her lips apart, sticky with manufactured coating.

"Sleep, Cal."

Outside the bedroom she stalled, needing to collect herself.

Everything was fine. Calvy was drunk, talking like that because his brain was addled and loose. That hadn't broken the rules. It had come close but—no, it hadn't. There was nothing to worry about.

She pulled her attention back to the factory, what she would say to Dannos. But it was Harper who snapped to attention when she entered the hall.

"Where is Dannos?"

"Indisposed. As is your private, judging by the state he was in upon entry."

Mara huffed air out of her nose as Harper studied her.

"Were you going somewhere? Another hour or two staring at the docks? I confess I had my fill this morning."

Could she know? Had she somehow seen Iola? Or was she just...being Harper?

Moons, Mara needed to get a hold of herself and stop being so paranoid.

"No. I—Dannos was going to—I've developed a sudden interest in arms production." She'd had all day to work out an excuse and that's what she managed to say under pressure. But she hadn't been expecting Harper's shrewd consideration. She'd been prepared for a shrug and a nod from Dannos.

"Huh," was Harper's reply.

"I want to go to the Pent factory. Across the canal. I thought Dannos could get me in."

Harper uncrossed her arms. "You thought wrong. He can't do it."

"Look, Harper—"

"But I can." Her stone was already in hand, her mouth moving to compose a message.

Mara's face creased with surprise before she smoothed it flat. "You can?"

"I know one of the foremen."

"You do."

"I handle many things for Mr. Pent." Then Harper clamped her mouth shut and raised her eyebrows.

Mara sighed impatiently. "Oh, just say it."

"You're digging a hole you won't be able to get out of. You can't manage the damage you've done with D'Aldiern by showing an interest in Mr. Pent's business. He's going to bury you."

"I guess I asked for that."

"You did."

"Then can we get going?"

"Yes. It's a long walk."

"We're not walking. I've a hoverbike," Mara said. Harper blinked at her. "I asked the private to—"

"Sure you did."

They stood side by side in the elevator. Harper was capable of eviscerating Mara in an argument. But she was loyal to Pent above everything else. Knowing she had Liam's protection was the only reason Mara was confident enough to ask, "What do you have against Private D'Aldiern?"

"It's better for a woman to know when to—"

"It's better for a woman to speak her mind. Instead of stewing like—like prison yarrow."

"Prison yarrow? Because I'm from Theos?"

Mara coughed. "No—I didn't realize—"

Anger tightened Harper's eyes and loosened her tongue. "We may not be known as a natural paradise—but we are as proud on Theos as you Balti pleasure seekers. Your private confessed to procuring counterfeit weapons. The only thing worse would be if he made them himself."

The doors opened and they exited. "He was lying—to protect his soldiers."

"Then he should have stayed out of it. Let us find the real culprit."

"It was the Dern army who supplied them."

"So a Dern prince could have paid the price. He still robbed us of justice." Harper stopped walking. "What does it matter to you—what I think of D'Aldiern?"

"It doesn't," Mara said.

"You'll remember, won't you? When Mr. Pent stands above you with the shovel, that I tried to throw you a rope."

"I'll remember that I didn't need it."

Because Harper had it all wrong. Liam knew about Calvy. Calvy had been Liam's idea. So why did Mara feel her heart sinking like a rock tossed into the sea?

On the hoverbike, Harper leaned away from Mara. Her hand on Mara's waist ghostlike, barely there. Mara huffed out another breath. *Really.* It wasn't like she was contagious, like Dern-sympathy was catching. Mara turned to throw a look over her shoulder, but Harper wouldn't have seen. Her eyes were closed. Her head back. Her free hand twisting this way and that in the wind like a leaf. She looked like she was flying—she looked like she was enjoying herself. Mara almost missed the turn after the bridge, focused on Harper's reaction to the hoverbike.

A planet dedicated to small pleasures. Shared pleasures. That's what she was trying to protect, she reminded herself as they pulled to a stop. And she wasn't betraying anyone.

"I can ask Calvy where he got the bike—"

"When I want something I get it myself."

Me too, Mara thought, but she didn't say it, because a man was approaching them. He was lanky in a too-short jumpsuit—brown, not the grey kind she'd seen on the weary workers as they made their way to and from the factory each dawn and dusk. His face was lined, sporting a patchy stubble and a scowl.

"Her? Can't do it, Harper."

Harper walked forward as though she hadn't heard him. "Gibbs, Ms. Leanor; Ms. Leanor, Gibbs."

Mara offered a nod that Gibbs ignored.

"It isn't happening. Why would you even bring one here? Do you know how much trouble they're causing? That fire on the rig was just the start of it."

Harper kept going. "Ms. Leanor is—"

"I don't care who the dyejob is—"

"—Mr. Pent's personal companion. She's recently developed an interest in the details of the business and I know he'd appreciate you letting her take a look. She won't be any trouble. Mr. Pent trusts her implicitly."

Even if I don't. Mara read the rest in Harper's eyes.

Gibbs crossed his arms, his head shaking.

"My hair? That's the issue?"

A nod from Harper and a grumble from Gibbs confirmed it.

Mara pulled up the hood of her cloak, as she'd been

doing each time she met with Iola. What had her people done on the oil rig? As long as it was bad for the Dern, Mara didn't care. If Iola could run the Dern off their planet, Mara was all for it. But Iola had only tasked her with getting into the factory. She wasn't leaving until she'd done it.

"Will this do, Mr. Gibbs?"

Harper scoffed at her formality, but Gibbs offered a gruff reply and nodded towards the wide door he'd come out of.

The stench of chemical waste and hot metal made Mara's eyes burn when they stepped inside the factory. But she smiled at Harper's foreman friend and took the hand he offered her, helping her onto the walkway above the factory floor.

"Grinder, crowning, rifling, finish." He rattled off the stations, shouting above the clang of machinery. "Ratchets, down there." He pointed across the area. "All the finesse work. You know, Harper."

Mara took her time on the walkway, trailing behind the other two. She didn't know exactly what she was supposed to be doing. Iola must have people outside the factory, people who'd report that she'd gotten in. That she'd passed the test.

"Does that do it? Enough to satisfy her curiosity?" Gibbs leaned on the railing, looking back at Mara, but directing his question to Harper. At the end of the walkway was a closed door and a set of stairs leading down to the left.

Harper was already at the bottom, turning a finished firearm over in her hands, inspecting it with her Theos-born commitment to detail. "Yes, Ms. Leanor can now report to Mr. Pent that she's shown an interest in his work."

The foreman barked a laugh, beginning his descent. Let them laugh, they didn't need to understand what she was doing here. Mara reached the door at the top of the stairs and paused, looking through the window to the other side.

"Can't take you next door. It's where we make the rods," Gibbs said.

Mara decided to flex a little of her knowledge; she hadn't picked up nothing from Liam. "And the ore—do you import it from Mi-isk?"

"Some," the foreman said with a hard look. He wasn't laughing now. "But heating the raw stuff—that's the nasty part. Mr. Pent wouldn't want me taking you in there, miss."

"I'm sure he wouldn't mind." Mara smiled. But the man wasn't looking at her, he was leaning over the railing, shouting at the workers to get back to work. They'd been looking up at where she stood. Free of watching eyes, Mara tested the panel with her palm and the door slid open.

She didn't need to go any further. She'd passed Iola's test. But what if Iola wanted more before completing their deal? Maybe, maybe Mara could find something small. Something she could use to ensure that Iola held up her end of the exchange.

Mara stepped through, into an office between the buildings. The foreman's desk was covered in papers, some with the seal of Theos, others stamped by Mi-isk and Dern. Production schedules, graphs, schematics.

Mara crossed the room to the door at the other side and pressed that panel too. A blast of heat met her and she coughed in the smoke and metal dust that filled the air. Mara had only managed a step when the foreman caught her arm. Her hood fell back as she turned. She yelped in surprise and men and women in face masks looked up to see the foreman dragging her back into his office, the red glow of fire reflected in their safety visors. The door panel hissed shut as she wrenched her arm away from him.

"I told you not to go in there," he spat.

But Mara had her own concerns. "There's too much dust in the air—"

He waved a hand dismissively. "Vents broke this morning."

"So why didn't you send everyone home?"

"Mr. Pent wouldn't appreciate losing a day of production—"

"Mr. Pent wouldn't appreciate losing a factory to a preventable explosion."

"The building is built to withhold blasts, all Pent factories are. It would be contained—"

"But the people working in there—"

"We have quotas to meet—"

"You have lives to protect."

The foreman grabbed her arm again, his fingers digging into the bone. But then Harper was behind him, twisting his other arm around his back so he was forced to let go of Mara.

Mara's breath came quick and hard. "Shut it down."

"I don't take orders from you. You don't tickle my prick."

Harper increased pressure and the foreman dropped to his knees. "Take it up with Pent," he gasped.

"I will."

Harper released him. She kept close to Mara, ushering her from the building as quickly as she could.

"What were you doing in there, Mara?"

"Nothing."

"That was not nothing. What did you drag me into?"

But Mara couldn't answer, her throat was too tight.

"You know that rope I offered you?" Harper said, settling behind Mara's seething form on the hoverbike. "It's not long enough to reach how deep you are. Which is fine with me. It's not my grave."

Chapter Twenty-Three

A groggy Calvy sat with his head bent between his knees while Dannos relayed the news. Something had happened. At the Pent factory across the canal. His head throbbed. Whose idea had it been for him to go drinking with Shef? Right, Mara's. She was full of good ideas. She was—his balls tightened thinking about her, like her hand had just gripped his sack.

She was devastating.

She'd do something, like scrunch up her nose in response to some inane thing he'd managed to say to her, and his lungs would empty of air the way sponges empty of water when wrung out. He'd be fine and then he'd look at her and be breathless. Useless. Devastated.

He had to remember that it was almost over. That he wouldn't be the one to press his mouth to that soft skin, to have his fingers slip through those silky curls. He tried to remind himself that it wasn't for him. She was trained to lure someone in, he wasn't special for falling for it. He was a fool. And he was acting like it—he'd been a jealous idiot during the full moons. If there was someone he should be jealous of, it wasn't that doctor who'd smiled and laughed with Mara. It was

Liam Pent. But Mara had confessed she wasn't thinking of Pent when she was with him.

He was a fool.

Because the thing he'd felt hearing that was hope.

He had to remember. He had to remember that it
was almost over.

"You said you wanted to know, if the climate seemed
charged."

Calvy sat up and nodded. He gulped at the scald-
ing coffee Dannos had provided with the news. "When
was this?"

"Half an hour ago. The news is moving fast."

"And Ms. Leanor?"

"Out with Harper."

Where? Calvy was about to ask—but the hotel room
door opened inwards and the couple in question came
into the room. Mara had a fierce look about her—fiercer
than normal, he amended. And both of them reeked
of soot.

A chill shuddered through his body.

"What are you two doing in here? Don't you have
your own quarters?" Mara said, seeing him with Dannos in her room. Calvy eyed her closely, watching for
the moment she relaxed the tension in her face, tried to
hide the agitation that ran under her skin like a current.

Her eyes lingered on his for a moment and—there.
She'd done it.

"There was a disturbance," Calvy said slowly, fitting the pieces together. He had access to the daily security briefings, littered with words like *Resurrection*
and *dyejob*. But she couldn't be one of them, could she?
He couldn't have been so distracted that he'd miss some-

thing that big? Her hair was loose and wild, dancing over her shoulders as she unbuttoned the clasp at her neck and flung the smoky cloak over the couch. He was suddenly alert, adrenaline and understanding making him rise to his feet.

"A disturbance?" She didn't meet his eyes, smoothing the cloak where it lay.

"At one of the factories. Something set the workers off—sparked a riot. The mid crew refused to go in." He stared at her and Mara lifted her chin. "Where were you, Mara?"

"Sounds like you already know."

"You went to the factory?" His head swung to Harper. "And you took her?"

Harper crossed her arms. "I did what I was told. You should try it."

"I—"

"Cal—"

His nickname rebounded through the room.

Mara glanced at Harper. At Dannos. But there was no use in pretending. Everyone in this room knew what was going on. At least as far as he and Mara were concerned. Mara seemed to draw the same conclusion, continuing despite their audience. "Cal. It's not her fault. And what's the problem? I wanted to see what Liam's built here. Where's the harm in that?"

Her face was drawn in a careful, easy calm, but her eyes—those two grey moons that haunted his nights— her eyes gave her away. They refused to dull.

All he needed to know now was whether it had been an accident—or if she'd done it on purpose.

"You didn't do anything?"

"What could I have done?"

"You tell me."

"I'll tell you why they refused to work—the conditions today were terrible."

"The conditions are always terrible. Something set them off *today.* Something made them think it was worth it to fight back." Calvy's fingers drummed against his thigh. She was lying. She was lying to him. "Why are you pretending you don't know what's going on here, Mara?"

"That's my business, Cal."

"Your business? It's all of our business." He swept his hand around the room. "We all report to Pent. What are we supposed to say? What will happen to us if we don't tell him about it? You think he's going to sign my papers if I cross him?"

"A little late for that," Harper muttered.

Mara's eyes burned. "Report what, Cal? What exactly goes into your reports? How many times I come?"

Dannos choked, coughing a mouthful of coffee back into his cup.

Calvy pressed on, refusing to let her derail him. "He's going to know you were at the factory—he's going to hear there was a riot." Liam Pent was no fool. He'd catch on faster than Calvy had. He wouldn't be distracted. "He knows you better."

"What does that—"

"Mara. What did you do?"

"Nothing." She drew out each syllable, as he had emphasized the last four of his.

"Nothing? More nothing?" He turned away from her, one hand on his hip, the other gripping his jaw.

"He shouldn't have left you here. It would be safer on the outskirts."

"He didn't know—"

Calvy spun back around. "Mara. I doubt there is anything Liam Pent doesn't know. He knew my contract was up for grabs before my own father—the leader of the Dern Empire."

"Yes, and he secured it with me in mind—installed you here to make sure I was safe. So do your job—"

"—and you'll do yours and we'll both keep him happy?"

She stomped forward. "Being with Liam isn't my job. I'm not an employee. He doesn't own me. He owns you. I'm with him because I want him. A Balti Temptress cannot—"

"I'm not talking about a Balti Temptress—I'm talking about Mara Leanor—can she be bought?"

"Get out."

Calvy didn't move. His heart pounded in his ears. His face felt hot. He shouldn't have—

"I told you to go, your grace."

Her words cut but not as deeply as his own regret. He'd done it again, let frustration push him over the line. The apology caught in his throat. Because Mara didn't want it. No apology he'd ever offered had appeased her. She only wanted better—and he couldn't give her that either, apparently. Couldn't contain the impulse to push back at her, to lash out against the situation that she controlled. Couldn't carve away the part of him she'd always hate.

There wasn't anything else to say. He crossed to the door with purposeful strides, stopping to address Dannos and Harper. "This conversation doesn't leave this room. And neither does she."

"You can't do that," Mara protested.

"I can't do a lot of things, Ms. Leanor. But this is my decision. You stay here. Until the factory situation is resolved. Who knows what other chaos the sight of you might inspire."

Chapter Twenty-Four

Mara pulled two pins from her pocket, holding them in her mouth while gathering the mess of curls the breeze had tumbled into her face. She dug one pin through her hair at the top of her head and secured it with the other, the metal scraping her scalp, pulling it tight.

Dannos had brought news that Calvy had lifted her hotel arrest with lunch, under the condition that she stay away from the factory. So she'd finished eating and marched straight there, standing directly across from it at the canal's edge. Dannos shifted in place a few paces away, like he was worried she might jump in and swim across, just to prove a point. She might.

But she didn't. She wasn't sure what the point was. Nothing Calvy wanted mattered. Liam had docked on nearby Lita. He'd be back in four days, he'd said on his latest message. All Mara had to do was wait. She might as well do it here, watching smoke drift up out of the stacks and into the blue sky, dirt tossed into water, muddying everything.

"Are you planning on making more waves?"

Mara glanced back long enough to register Iola's presence, then returned to staring at the factory. The other woman came to stand at her side.

"We should get going, miss," Dannos called.

"Tell him to give us a minute," Iola said.

"Why? We have nothing else to discuss."

"We don't?"

"Not if you're going to lie to me. You said it was a test. But you wanted disorder, and you used me to make it for you."

Iola's brows arched. "Worried how Pent's going to react? You should be celebrating. We're starting a rebellion—"

"You don't need a rebellion. You need a labor dispute. You need industrial reform."

"Is that what we need?"

"You're outnumbered. You have no weapons. You have no leader. You have no claim." Mara turned to face Iola. "You don't need red hair and symbols of the past. You need Liam Pent. And he'll be here soon."

"Liam Pent? Is going to personally reform the conditions in one factory out by the rim?"

"You don't know him. He's considerate, he cares—"

"He cares about himself. And his earnings. That's why we're here. To work for him. He helped displace us, gave us no choice but to leave another home, evacuate—"

"That was the Dern—"

"It was them both. Both of your men. They lengthen their fathers' shadows. While you do nothing."

Dannos shifted restlessly and Mara sighed. "What would you have me do? I will talk to Liam. He will understand. That is how things will get better. The Dern will not leave this planet without a Balticourt on the throne and you and I both know the rumors are just that. They're enough to drum up civil unrest—not enough to sway political action. We can't go back to how it was.

This planet needs real change, not ghost stories—not the queen of dust."

"Talk—that's how the Balti Temptress persuades a man?" Iola taunted her but this time Mara didn't take the bait.

"Yes. Iola. That is how. You don't understand what Balti was at all, do you?"

"No. I don't. There was no one left here to teach us. And now you're the last and you've picked your side."

Mara bit back a laugh. "You want to be the last Balti Temptress? That'll solve all your problems—so by all means, let me tell you how to do it. But know this: it isn't about what to lick and where to squeeze—it's you. It's your own power—your understanding of what this place was built on. The Balti devotion to the moment. Our respect for the fleeting. And you can't do that if you're stuck in the past."

"Miss," Dannos said more insistently, his eyes on the downward slope of the sun, which raged in a red ball behind Mara.

"We're not finished," Iola said. "I'm not going to have a favor hanging over my head. What do you want from me? In exchange for helping us?"

Mara had almost forgotten why she'd agreed. It seemed silly now. But she didn't want it any less.

"I want to get into the Pearl. Soon."

"What makes you think I can help with that?"

"You know Dr. Protaris."

"Why don't you just persuade him yourself?"

Mara couldn't help her mocking tone as she countered, "Can you do it?"

"I'll try," Iola offered dryly.

"And I will talk to Liam," Mara promised before

joining Dannos on the path. Balti was an industry planet now, and the only person who could make things better was a man of resources. Liam Pent would help. She was sure of it.

"I could learn it," Iola called after her. "If there were someone to teach me. I could learn it." Mara looked back to see Iola's face distorted with longing. So much had been taken from them—their families, their homes— but maybe they could get a little back, by sharing, preserving their culture.

What could I have done? she'd asked Calvy, her flippancy at the time hiding a truth, a very real compulsion behind her question. What could one lost little girl on borrowed time do to create a better Balti than she'd found? Than she'd left?

"Find me at the hotel," Mara said.

Iola nodded.

Mara couldn't get the strangled look out of her mind as she made her way back. Darkness filled the gaps between the buildings as she and Dannos walked side by side.

She didn't notice the men until they were close enough to smell, the sweat and the soot.

She didn't notice the way the big one sneered and pointed to her.

She did hear them laugh, and felt the hand close over her mouth.

But by then it was too late.

Chapter Twenty-Five

The room seemed loud—it was hard to differentiate the hum of the appliances from the rush of blood in her ears. Mara found herself pulling a tin of water out of the cooler under the sideboard. When she stood she was surprised by how pale she looked in the mirror that hung above it. She should have been flushed red—stained by the fury that had pulsed through her. The fury that still vibrated under her skin. She fumbled with the tin until Harper eased it out of her hands and peeled back the lid. But Mara's hands wouldn't work to take it back.

She turned towards the windows, the rushing sound so loud it overwhelmed her senses. Around again, she faced the door where Harper stood waiting. Her eyes couldn't seem to focus. She spun to the windows again, heard the door open, her name, muffled and far away. She bumped into the couch and leaned against the back of it.

And then Calvy was in front of her, and the rushing subsided, withdrew, stopped. She fixed on his face, an anchor for her disquieted gaze, as he tilted her chin up with gentle fingertips, angling her cheek so he could see the abrasions from the wall.

The wall.

She closed her eyes.

She opened them.

Calvy. The last time she'd seen him, he'd been storming away from her. Now he was here, and so calm. Her earring had come loose from the top loops and his touch was easy, his hands steady as he began untangling the delicate chain, freeing it from her curly hair and then her ear.

"Harper, damp towel, warm water," he commanded. This was Calvy as he was meant to be: a captain taking control. Collected, determined. "Dannos says you were attacked. I need to know who it was—who did this to you."

The answer came from behind him. "It was those factory bastards—I don't know if they recognized her—I heard dyejobs are getting jumped all over town—I shouldn't have taken her—"

"Dannos, there's a tube of tomate paste in my ruck. Get it."

"Tomate paste?" She didn't have the energy to keep her forehead from wrinkling.

"Red clay. In the army everything important has a nickname. Did I forget to tell you that, Millie?"

Harper brought the towel and then took up her post by the door.

"Can you tell me what happened?" Calvy pressed the towel to Mara's cheek and she was vaguely aware that it stung, but the pain was muted, inconsequential in comparison to the dull ache of fury that rolled through her.

Her voice shook as she told him. "We were walking home. Dannos wanted to head back west but I was tired—I said it was out of the way. We'd be fine." The door opened again—Dannos with the healing clay. "We had just passed that pub—where there are always people smoking—"

"The Crown, miss—Cap, I've seen these toughs there before—"

Calvy tossed Dannos the wet towel. "What happened next?" he said to Mara, twisting off the cap of the red tube, the lid embossed with a logo signifying Pent production. He squeezed some onto his finger and began to dab it over the scratches on her face.

"There were men. Three men, walking the opposite way. Two took Dannos, the other twisted my arm, pushed me against the wall." Mara stopped, remembering the hand that groped its way across her chest. Her breath quickened. She looked up at the ceiling. Calvy's hand stayed light on her cheek but she could feel him vibrating with contained energy, charging everything around him.

Dannos took over the story. "Dern soldiers showed up—a patrol unit—or I would have—"

"You said your wrist?" Calvy's attention was hers and hers alone. Mara lifted her right hand and he grasped it with his own. He threaded the fingers of his left hand through hers, palm to palm. Slowly he twisted it, testing one side and then the other. He let go of her wrist but kept their fingers tangled together, resting at her side. "No sprain."

Calvy's eyes met Mara's again and she locked onto them, so glossy and round, so solid, like marbles she could keep in her pocket.

"Anything else?" he asked. "Does anything else hurt?"

She opened her mouth to tell him she was fine—to tell him that barely anything had happened. That she was angry, because they'd made her feel weak and taken her control. She would have told Liam that and he would have raged with her, burned this city down on her behalf. But there was something about the way Calvy was looking at her, his eyes black and intense, but his face calm. She felt shielded, as she had on the cliffs, his body blocking her from the torrent of wind that threatened to unbalance her. He created shelter, stillness just for her.

"I was scared," she whispered. And he squeezed her hand in his.

"You're safe now, Mara. You got through it." He brought his free hand against her neck, swiping his thumb just under the drying clay that tightened the skin of her cheek. Mara lifted her chin, raising her mouth to his at the same moment he let go of her and stepped back.

"Harper, do not move from that spot. Dannos, let's go."

Mara slid to her feet. "Go where?" But one look at Calvy said enough. He was electric, his hands twitching at his sides. He was going to find them.

"You—"

"You don't 'you' me," she bit back.

"Just stay here. Please." He said each word slowly, pleading with her, vulnerability peeking out behind the response he was working desperately to keep in check. What could she do but nod?

Dannos sprung off the wall ready for round two. With the way Calvy moved, the purpose that drove him, it did seem like a promising fight.

"Are they going to get themselves killed?" Mara said to Harper when they left.

"I don't think so, Ms. Leanor. More likely Mr. Pent would kill them for doing nothing."

Mara woke on the couch, something wet rubbing against her cheek.

"Go back to sleep," Calvy said. "I'm just getting this

off. It'll pucker. If you leave it on too long." He scrubbed at the dried clay with a towel. She felt his lips, warm and smooth, against the clean skin. "Good as new."

Mara looked around the room, her eyes adjusting to the dark.

"I told Harper to go, it's my shift."

"Your shift," she repeated.

"You know though, I think I've done enough for today." And before she knew it he was lying down on the couch, wedging himself under her.

"Cal—"

"Mara."

He tried wrapping his arms around her, but Mara had pushed herself up. She caught his hand and turned it over. His knuckles had been slathered in red clay.

Calvy watched her inspection. "I took care of it."

"You took care of it. You went down there and showed them what happens when they fuck with Pent Corporation property?"

"I went down there and showed them what happens when they fuck with you."

An unexpected flutter in her stomach caused Mara's toes to curl. "And Dannos?"

"A couple of bumps. Nothing he hasn't felt before."

"You should have taken Harper. She's better in a fight."

"That's why she stayed here. With you."

"Because that's the job. You probably earned a bonus for your trouble."

He'd picked Mara's protection over his own—and she knew it wasn't because of the job. That toasty warmth of his drew her down like gravity. Mara let her head rest on his chest, her eyes on the window, the too-few lights scattered in the city's night.

Calvy's hand traced the line of her arm. "I didn't do it for Pent, Mara. He didn't make me and he couldn't stop me. I did it for you. And I did it for me. I did it for us."

He had to know what saying things like that could do. Had to know she couldn't respond in kind. Slowly, quietly, she reminded him why. "There is no us—you know that, right?"

"I know."

It had been days since they'd been together like this. She'd become resigned to the idea that it wouldn't happen again. Not after their fight about the factory. The things he'd said to her then.

"There can't be. Not when you think I'm some damsel. That's one thing and it's fine—but it's not what I am."

"I don't think that. I know the difference."

"You said it again. When we fought."

"I didn't."

"You implied it."

"Can we consider that progress?"

"You're a hothead, Cal—it's no wonder you can't follow orders."

He sighed, and she bobbed up and down with the motion. "I'm not a hothead. But I spent months in prison for a crime I didn't commit. And the one thing I want is being dangled in front of me. Just out of my reach." The thing, he'd said. Not the person. She needed the reminder: he wanted his rank back. His position. "I enlisted at seventeen. Against the wishes of my parents and sovereign. And I wasn't half as nervous then as I am talking to you. And it's not like you give quarter. You go right up to the edge—"

"You go over it."

"I know."

She lifted her gaze to his, drawn in by that overwrought sincerity. The frustration he couldn't conceal. That he didn't try to. It was impossible to ignore that she responded to it, a blossom turning up to the sun for more.

"So do better," she told him.

Mara expected Calvy to ease out from under her, to take up his position on the other side of the door. But he didn't get up. She nestled into him. Just for a little longer. And they lay there together until the sun rose, another day closer to the end of them.

Chapter Twenty-Six

"You said you'd teach me." Iola crossed her arms, a scowl twisting her mouth as she pierced Mara with her sharp eyes.

"I'm trying to. You seem to expect choreography. But that's not what makes a Balti Kiss powerful."

"What does, then, oh great Temptress. Tell me how to harness my inner moon power."

It took most of Mara's strength to ignore Iola's sarcasm, to follow Jimma's patient example. "You have to make yourself a conduit for the pleasure of another—letting your own passion charge through you, into them. And your reward is absorbing the power released from them."

"Is that a metaphor?"

Mara sighed. "Yes." She paused, considering before amending, "But it's also an instruction."

"To lick clean the mess you make of the plate?"

"If you aren't going to take this seriously, I can't help you."

Iola's folded arms tightened across her chest. Her mouth flattened as she pressed her lips together.

Mara continued. "Don't fixate on the details. In this case, pleasure is about the bigger picture. They have to know that you are capable of doing more for them than anyone ever has before—and for them to know that, you have to believe it."

"I would believe I could do it—if you would only just tell me how."

"The process itself is mostly intuitive."

Iola shook her head in disbelief. "You're not going to teach me anything. You're going to keep it for yourself—"

"I don't *want* to be the last Balti Temptress, Iola. I'm trying to explain it to you—if you would listen patiently—"

"Patient? Like your Dern soldier—how does he reconcile his Virtues when you're applying that Balti Kiss to his big, occupational cock?"

"He doesn't have to."

"Why not?"

"Because I'm not allowed to give it to him!"

Mara closed her eyes, breathing in through her nose. This wasn't how it had been learning from Jimma. She was meant to be calm, she was meant to be open and giving.

Iola's mouth had softened by the time Mara's eyes opened, but curiosity lit her gaze. "I'm listening," Iola said.

"The power comes from—"

"No." Iola held up a hand to stop her. "Tell me about the Dern. And what you're *allowed* to do to him."

"That's really not—"

"Pent knows, doesn't he? Did he arrange it? As some sort of punishment?"

"It's not a punishment."

"A gift then?" Iola's eyes gleamed with the excitement of discovery. "He put you up to it. But he doesn't know what it's become."

"It hasn't become *anything*," Mara insisted. "There's nothing else he needs to know because there's nothing else going on." *Nothing, nothing, nothing.* She'd said it so many times, the word had started to lose meaning.

There was nothing between her and Calvy.

Except air.

Charged air. Blistering air. Life-threatening air.

There were moments when she admitted that something was different with Calvy. That the pleasure she'd wrung from him was more intense, more explosive than she'd experienced with others. But that was typical of a new flavor, wasn't it? The way it could light up your tongue—surprise you. Make you crave more. Only it had been six months, and the novelty of Calvy's cock had not worn off. With Calvy her desire swelled, her pleasure wrapped around him growing more and more, better and better. And now that she'd had a taste of him—

That's all it could be. A taste. Lingering and unwanted, sharp and sour as citrin.

A gift, Iola had called it. Him. Calvy. Reduced again to a toy soldier Liam had given her to play with.

"It isn't fair," Mara said quietly, her eyes unfocused. All she'd ever done was take from him. She wished she'd had the chance to seduce him. To know what it would be like to overpower him with her pleasure—without Liam's interference.

Iola was waiting for Mara to continue, but Mara was caught in the hurricane of her thoughts. Spinning around and around, with no way out.

"Well," Iola said, startling her. "It looks like you need something from me, as much as I need it from you."

"What's that?"

"I can help you make it even."

Mara waited until she heard Dannos's heavy footsteps fade.

The elevator dinged. A shadow moved under the door. She put her hand on the knob.

Liam would be back in two days. If they were going to do this, it had to be now.

The air seemed thin. Her head light.

"Open the door, Mara," Iola said.

A twist, a click, a pull, and there he was. Waiting for her, too, his eyes alive with one of his unbearably eager looks.

Mara widened the gap between the door and its frame, and Calvy moved smoothly into the room. By the time she'd turned and closed the door his hand was on his weapon, his jacket pushed back at his side.

"Cal," Mara said, once, twice. Because his attention had left her as soon as he'd spotted Iola on the couch. The potential threat. His dark brows drew together with a crease. Apprehension tightened his mouth as he took in the red-gold hair fanned around the other woman's head. They had teased it out and pinned it up to look like Mara's.

"Calm down, Cal." Mara eased his hand off his side-arm.

"Mara—" He shook his head, as if to clear his vision, but they'd intended for him to see double. "If this is another rebellion stunt—"

"It's not." She took his hand and led him to the couch. "We want to try something."

"Who's we?"

"Iola," the second Balti introduced herself.

"Try what. Another fire? Another riot?"

"Will you sit down?" Mara asked.

"Unlikely. She can't be here—"

"Sit, Cal."

And he did.

"Mara," Calvy repeated, confusion limiting his vocabulary. "Why is she here?"

"For you."

Calvy started when Iola laid a hand on his thigh. He glanced down at it and shot back up. "You can't be serious."

Mara pushed his coat off his shoulders, folding it over her arms, hugging his leftover heat to her stomach. "Cal. Sit down. Let us do this for you."

"Do what, exactly?"

"Make you feel good."

"You're not allowed to—"

"I'm not going to." Mara nodded at Iola, who looked up at him, her upturned eyes alight with calculated daring.

"I can't—"

"You can. If you want to do this, so do we." Outwardly, Mara tried to emulate that calm command of his—the one he'd had the night she'd been attacked, when what she'd needed, more than anything, was his confident presence. Inside, she was torn between wanting him to give in and hoping he'd refuse.

I took care of it, he'd told her.

It was her turn. To take care of him. To give something back.

Mara reached to his waist and he let her unbutton his pants, push the layers down to his ankles. Those black eyes collected the dim glow of the lamp above them, reflecting twin orbs of light back at her. She scratched at the coarse hair above his cock and felt it beginning to come to attention between them.

He wouldn't refuse. He never refused her. She wished he would for once, for her own good. But this wasn't for her. Still. He was resisting. And there were rules to pleasure.

She held his wrist and brushed his knuckles against Iola's cheek. "Do you want to?"

His eyes were on his fingertips, catching in the red curls of Iola's hair. After a long moment his lips parted, showing the tip of his tongue between his teeth. He nodded, quick and clear. *Yes.* And that settled it.

Mara swallowed the lump in her throat as Calvy sat. She backed away, taking the chair next to the folded blinds of the open window.

"Close your eyes, Cal."

His fists clenched as Iola shifted off the couch. She knelt on the floor in front of him and Mara's tongue threatened to break through the back of her top teeth.

This was for Calvy.

She loosed a shaky breath, setting her hands professionally in her lap.

"The most important part of this, Iola, is that you want it too. That you both dò. But to make it good… better…*exceptional* for your partner—for Cal. *You* have to want it as much as he does. It isn't a Balti Kiss if you don't feel that pull, that rush of need. To make whoever you're with feel everything you feel. That's what makes it better with us—our commitment to the pleasure of it. Knowing that their desire is your desire. Make sure you feel it. Don't start until you do."

Mara willed her body to relax by imagining she was in Iola's place. What would she feel, staring up at Calvy? He'd have his eyes open if she knelt before him. He wouldn't miss a second of her. The thought tightened Mara's chest, a rope pulled taut. Warmth spread between her legs. She inched to the edge of her chair.

"Do you feel it?" she asked Iola. The other woman nodded, looking back, her pupils dark and wide.

"Good. Pleasure is magic that erases the rest of the world. It's up to you to cast the spell—to feel the buzz of it inside yourself, to draw your partner into it, hypnotize them with the thought…the *promise* that you will deliver them into indulgence, free them for a time from what is harsh and cold. Wrap them in your power."

Calvy's eyes had opened to watch her, and Mara could feel the weight of his gaze, the pull of that blackness. His cock swelled as she spoke—straining against his very skin, demanding to be touched. She motioned for him to look at Iola and he shook his head. Her mouth frowned but her eyes burned with understanding.

He wanted it to be her as much as she did.

Mara's instruction was for Iola, but she spoke to Calvy, connecting to him the only way she could: her voice caressing his mind. He was a man who listened, she remembered thinking.

"The Balti experience is unique because we invest ourselves in our partner's pleasure. We get under their skin, make it unforgettable, unlike anything else they've had before. Every touch, every taste, everything they

could want, we give them. And with this Kiss, all they
have to do is receive."

Mara traced the circle of her lips with her tongue.
She was drawing this out. Because anticipation made
it better—and to put off what was coming.

Anticipation. That's what she'd thought had made
their first time together so powerful. She knew better
now. She knew it was magic. She knew it was Calvy.

"Your partner's attention, it's a force of nature." She
wanted to close her eyes in preparation for the next part.
Iola would have to touch him. That was the point of
this. Mara longed to do it herself. To run her hands up
his legs, feeling the authority of his form, the strength
of the tight muscles that corded his thighs. She'd paint
his cock, using her tongue as the brush. She'd drag her
teeth over his sensitive skin. She'd make him beg her
for more and she'd give it to him willingly. But she'd
tease him first, watching him through her lashes, telling him without words: *purity through patience, clarity
through compliance, deliverance through dedication.*
How those Dern Virtues applied well to this lesson in
pleasure. If you considered desire pure. If you considered peace clarity. If you considered bliss deliverance.
And she did.

"Start with your hands. When you touch him, mar-
vel at the feel of it—smooth and hard. And then with
your mouth, the luxury against your tongue. Don't ignore the low-hanging fruit, nor the space just behind it."

A growl or something like it rumbled out of Calvy
as Iola obeyed the instruction.

Mara pressed her knees together. "Take your time—
ease down the length of him. Then relax your throat and

take him all the way in. The depth and the tightness—
it's what he wants to feel—connected, held close."

Iola followed her directions until her face was buried
in Calvy's lap, her cheeks against his thighs. Calvy's
mouth parted and Mara rocked her hips.

She couldn't stop thinking about that first night. On
the ship. When it had been Calvy kneeling in front of
her. She'd been meant to connect with Liam, but Calvy
claimed her attention, drove everything else out of her
mind. Liam had wanted to play—but with Calvy there
was no game.

Calvy jerked forward and Mara feared he'd read the
panic on her face. Because she felt it gripping her—a
vise pinching her airways shut, panic that this was the
end of it. The end of them. Even though Liam knew and
Harper knew and Iola and Dannos and everyone knew.
What they'd shared had been secret, private, sheltered.
And now it was over.

But it was Iola's attentions that had him on a tether.
He sank his fingers into her hair, twisting it up off her
neck. All Mara could do now was watch, hold his gaze
for as long as he could keep his eyes open, before release forced them closed. And when he finally came,
deep into the back of Iola's ready throat, Mara exhaled,
feeling the tension leave her body. *There. Let it be done.*

Calvy relaxed into the couch. His legs trembled. He
brought his hands up, pressing the heels of his palms
into his eyes. A gesture she knew all too well.

When his eyes met hers again she attempted a watery smile, one he didn't return. She wished that he were
tired, giddy, and loose. The silent ardor with which he
regarded her was too much. Too heartfelt. Too real.

It was over now. Didn't he know? They couldn't go

back and there was no way forward. She'd ended it with a Kiss.

Mara stood and Calvy followed suit, pulling up his pants and tucking his shirt in about the waist. Her hands shook and she didn't know why. She'd done nothing. Nothing but sit and watch. It should not have affected her so. He should not have affected her. Not like this.

Iola wiped at her mouth, looking between Calvy and Mara.

He nodded at her, a silent thanks and she shrugged, a satisfied look on her face. Then he regarded Mara, her hands clutched together.

Say something. One of them had to say something.

There was only silence. Neither of them able to break it.

Liam was coming back. And Calvy would leave. She'd done this one last thing. To fix the balance between them. This had to be it. They'd come as close as they could to the line Liam had drawn for them. Anything more would push them over.

Mara went to the cooler, keeping her back purposefully to him. Tears stung her eyes and she willed the pain away. The door opened and she took a deep breath—to speak, to tell him—

Then the door closed and she exhaled empty air. It took all of her strength to stand, hand Iola a tin of water, and cloak her face in indifference.

Iola tapped the metal with the white of her nail before opening it.

Click click click. Fizz. Air rushed up, trying to escape the pressure.

"Arin can meet you tomorrow afternoon."

Mara's voice sounded far away to her own ears. "How'd you manage that?"

"How do you think?" Iola dared her to make another assumption. "I asked him. He's a little like your Dern. Not so bad as the others." She paused. "I find myself wanting to thank you. I've never had an experience like that—"

Mara cleared her throat. "Yes, well, the Balti Kiss, performed properly, can be transformative."

"Sure. The Balti Kiss."

"That's what it was, Iola. That's what you asked me to show you."

"But—that's not all this was. You have to know that—"

"It's powerful, I've been trying to tell you." Mara dared Iola now, to say more. She knew—she knew what the other woman was getting at. Oh, she'd fucking felt it. That there had been something intense, something palpable in the air. Some extra element that charged the molecules between her and Calvy. Something unnameable, not because it didn't exist—but because it wasn't supposed to.

"Well, I feel like I understand it better—the way Balti must have been." Iola judged Mara's silence. "So, thank you. I hope you got what you wanted from it too."

Mara released a sob as a sharp laugh. What she wanted? It was the only thing she'd considered since leaving for Balti.

Until now. When she'd tried to do something for Calvy.

And realized she wanted more.

She wanted a Dern. Who had made her rethink it all.

Chapter Twenty-Seven

The wall didn't seem strong enough to support the weight Calvy leaned against it. His chest was too heavy, his head spinning with a gravity shift that accompanied that apparent fluctuation of mass.

Mara's voice, low and intoxicating, dictating what should be done to him, ran in a loop in his head. She'd wanted him to close his eyes, imagine it was her—so she could spin her magic, make him believe that she'd found a way around the impossible. But he'd needed to see. See what was real. He was already under her spell, whether or not his eyes were open. She'd mesmerized him from the first moment.

And this one felt like the last. He knew what she was doing. Clearing the table. Iola had provided the tip, gratuity on services rendered. He shouldn't have accepted it—but he'd wanted to. Badly. Wanted to take what she had offered him. Any scrap of Mara he could get his hands on.

The door swung open and shut and Iola appeared in the hallway. Calvy flattened his shoulder blades against the wall. She looked like she had something to say— she looked like Mara. Calvy dropped his gaze to the floor, his neck hot.

"It was my idea," Iola said as she waited for the elevator, her back to him.

"The factory too?" He looked up for confirmation, watching her sift through her hair for pins, letting it fall into place, obscuring her neck.

"Yes. She and I want the same thing. A Balti free of Dern. You don't belong here."

"I'll let Mara tell me what she wants."

The elevator doors opened and Iola stepped in, filling the space. "I think she just did."

Anger licked his spine, pulling him straight. Anger that he'd been dismissed. Without a word. Anger that somehow Mara had maneuvered him into making another mistake. Into accepting something she would never forget, never forgive him for taking.

A familiar ache contracted his lungs. He'd burned through all the moments, all the chances he had. Chances to be with her. And he wasn't done. He hadn't had enough.

And then he was knocking on the door, his chest constricted. He barely gave her time to answer before raising his hand to knock again. And again.

"Go away, Calvy," she said, her voice close, as though she were leaning just on the other side of the barrier.

"No. We're not finished."

"Yes. We are."

He resisted the urge to slam his fist into the door. *Words*, he told himself, *use your words. Make them good. Make them better.*

Do better.

"I'm not."

Silence from the other side.

"Mara. I'm not done." He rolled his forehead against the panel.

"What do you want, Cal?" The question was a whisper but he heard it. He imagined her face pressed to the door, directly opposite his own.

"I'm thinking."

"Before speaking?"

"I'm trying something new."

Did she laugh? Or was she crying? He'd be damned if he'd listen outside while she did that again.

"Come out with me."

"I don't want to. I can't sit in the hall and—"

"Not the hall. We'll go out. We'll walk."

The moments ticked by. He tapped them out gently on the knob, jerking back when the door opened. A crack. But it opened.

She'd opened it. "You aren't worried it's dark?"

He gripped the frame. "You'll be with me."

"It's almost morning. You'll be going to bed soon."

"We have twenty-seven hours, Mara, I'm not going to waste them sleeping."

"You'll get giddy."

"You'll understand."

He couldn't keep the distress from his voice any more than he could contain the honesty that made him so vulnerable around her. He should have tried harder, because she withdrew. He moved his foot out of the way and the door closed with a soft click. Calvy slumped against it.

That was it. She'd made her choice.

When the door opened again, he scrambled to hide his surprise, to regain his balance.

Mara stepped across the threshold, her cloak over her shoulders. She held his coat out to him.

"You'll need this."

He had another chance. *Lucky number eleven.* He took it, pulling the coat over his arms. He'd be grateful for it. Out of the hotel, there was a strong wind, saturating the city with cool ocean air while they walked.

Calvy wet his lips, tasting salt. He was jittery, shivering under his coat. "Are you hungry? We could go to the Ring and—"

"No." Conviction, that was one of the things he would remember best about her. "The pavers were almost there yesterday. I can't take it. It's like ink blotting out a page I haven't finished."

"There's still time," he said. He'd said it before. To soothe her worries. It sounded false now.

Mara agreed. "No, there isn't."

Mara turned south, away from the Ring. She looked up as they walked, staring at the moons. This place was still a mystery to her. She'd come here looking for answers, full of hope, and he'd watched it all drain away, wishing he could do more.

Calvy stopped in front of a building, a thick branch of ivy growing across the door. "Maybe it was this one?"

"What?" Mara looked around.

"I could see you here."

Her throat bobbed as she swallowed. "Why are you doing this?"

"You wanted to—"

"I know what I wanted. I'm confident it isn't going to happen. It's been six months. I've been everywhere

I can on this continent. I'm not going to remember anything. I'd have done it by now."

He hated to hear her defeated. "These houses are all wrong—you'd have somewhere with more space—"

"Cal."

"—a view of water—"

"Cal, stop!"

He did. He always would. Whatever she said. He would do it. One look from her was all it took and he was at her mercy. Willing to do anything she asked. Especially when she looked like that, fierce and willful.

"You said it didn't matter. Where I came from. You said I didn't need it."

"It doesn't matter," he repeated. He still believed that. She wasn't lost. She was right where she needed to be. With him. Home. "You don't need the details. This place created you—that raw Balti power, it's inside you either way. Whether or not you know which street, which house you came from. Because this place is enough. You're enough, Mara. But if you want to know—"

"Just stop. Stop worrying about what I want. It isn't your job anymore, okay?"

"It wasn't a job."

He'd known it for months. He hadn't been standing outside the room of some high-profile client. He was guarding his own heart.

His purpose was here. He'd found it. He hadn't been lucky for this chance. He'd never strayed off his path. Every step was a step towards her.

"It was—if you want him to sign your papers, if you want your rank back—"

"What if I didn't? What if I wanted something more?"

Her throat bobbed again and he hated that burdened

look on her face. He hated any pain of hers caused by him. He was the burden. The thing that was making this harder for her. He resolved to stop. He wouldn't say any more.

Then shut your mouth.

"What could you want more than your life back?" Even though he refused to speak, she must have seen the answer in his face. She squeezed her eyes tight and dropped her chin. He couldn't hold anything back from her. "Don't be stupid, Cal."

What was he meant to be? Sensible? Compromising? No. He'd rather be stupid. Stupid for hoping, stupid for believing, stupid for telling her now: "I want you."

"Moons, Cal, can't you keep it to yourself? For once?"

"Why should I? We've always been honest—why not about this? Drop your guard and—"

"I can't drop my guard! I have to protect myself. What little of me I have, I'm keeping, okay? You'd understand if you'd ever had to hide anything. But you haven't. Because nobody's ever paid any attention to you."

Except her.

The urge to lash back was so strong Calvy had to bite his tongue. Mara was so good at setting up the opposing parts of him—the would-be prince and the struggling soldier, the man who wanted to do so much and the one who'd been deemed worthless. So good at setting him up, so good at knocking him down. Provoking him into making a mistake so she could gain ground. But it wasn't going to work this time. This time there was no opposition in him—he'd picked a side and he wasn't going to fight anymore. Not against her, not against himself.

Now he was fighting for them.

"I want you," he said again. Together, here or anywhere. If she wanted to stay, he'd stay. If she wanted a revolution, he'd start with D'Mont and work his way up. He'd apply whatever lingering Virtue he had to her— patience, compliance, above all dedication. Whatever it took to earn her, to be hers.

"You can't have me. It wasn't part of the deal."

"Fuck the deal. Let my father have my contract. Let him tear it up. And you never had one. You had a choice. You still have a choice."

"What choice? Liam is coming back in two days. And then we're gone."

The words were like bricks dropped on his heart, crushing him. He barely managed to respond. "There's still—"

"There is no more time!" Her voice echoed off the buildings that lined the quiet street. But she was wrong. For once, he knew better than her. He had time, he only needed a moment. To tell her it would never be over for him.

She started to walk away and he caught her elbow. He pulled her face to his and kissed her.

Mara pushed at his chest and he stopped. "Liam said I have to—"

"I don't care what Pent says. I care what you say. And you can tell me to stop. Or you can kiss me back." He warmed her cold cheeks with his palms. His nose grazed against hers as he waited for her answer, waited as the shore awaits the wave. Knowing that it would come.

And it did—her lips drawn to his by some force from

above that neither of them could control. Something cosmic and wild and powerful, just like her.

Relief washed over him, the sensation saturating his mind as he pulled her into his mouth. She moaned against him, the sound vibrating through him, bringing every inch of him to attention.

"He's good to me," she insisted between kisses.

"I'm better."

Her tongue collided with his, her teeth pulled at his lip—

Calvy jerked back, a man on each of his arms, tearing him from her. He twisted reflexively, intent on freeing himself before they tightened their hold. The impulse to get back to Mara flooded him, and he kicked out at a third man, hard enough to send him to the ground. Then he wrestled out of his jacket, shaking the other two off with it.

Mara rushed towards him and he fought the instinct to meet her. The three men were regrouping. He'd keep them busy until she got away.

"Mara—go!"

But a fourth attacker appeared from the dark, grabbing Mara from behind, one big hand covering her mouth. Calvy lunged forward too late. The men formed a blockade between them. No matter how he thrashed and fought to get to her, he couldn't break through.

When he fell, his head hit the tiled street with an ugly thud. And maybe Mara screamed? But his ears were ringing and he wasn't sure what was real. The last thing he saw before the blackness claimed him was Mara's eyes wide with fear, her feet kicking off the ground as she fought to get to him too. Something—someone holding her back.

Calvy reached for her, his limbs heavy and immovable as cooled metal.

Mara.

His vision blurred and the world darkened.

Mara.

He was already on the ground but he felt himself falling.

Mara.

There was nothing else.

Chapter Twenty-Eight

Mara woke in the dark. The metal floor was cold and bumpy, textured with skid-resistant mounds, uneven under Mara's hand as she pushed herself into a sitting position. Her head throbbed and her vision dimmed, internally this time. She dropped her head between her knees and fought the blackness back.

What had happened?

One minute she'd been kissing Calvy, the next he'd been dragged away from her. Arms had held her back when she'd tried to get to him—when he'd been curled on the ground, his eyes unfocused, his hand reaching out for her.

She couldn't get to him. And she'd never forget that feeling. How she'd emptied her lungs screaming for him. How she'd hollowed herself out, leaving room for that sound—his head cracking against the pavement—to echo through her.

Nausea swept over her, but Mara forced her head up. Her eyes had adjusted and she nearly choked when she saw him, or the shadow of him, on the far wall. Even in the low light, she knew, she recognized the shape of him. How many dusks had she watched the sun fade over his chest, until only his bright eyes glowed back at her in the dark?

Mara scrambled towards Calvy, half crawling, palming the ridged floor for balance, zigzagging across the room as fast as she could.

"Calvy," she said. "Cal!"

He didn't answer. He slumped forward, on his knees, his arms stretched up behind him. A magnetic cuff on each wrist secured him to the metal wall at his back.

"Cal." Mara cradled his face between her palms. Was he breathing? Her thumb found his pulse, a soft flicker under his chin. She pushed his hair off his forehead, the ends stiff with dried blood from a gash above his eye. "Wake up, Cal, come on," she said, smoothing his hair back again.

What if he fell too hard? What if he didn't—

His head bobbed up and he blinked heavily.

"Mara?"

A strangled sound escaped her throat.

He tried to reach for her but his wrists caught in the cuffs. He pushed unsteadily to his feet, bracing himself against the wall. Mara stood with him, wrapping her arms around his neck as soon as they were both upright.

"Are you okay?" he asked. "Where are we?"

"I don't know," she said. It hadn't mattered. Calvy mattered. "I came to and I saw you and you weren't waking up—" Her body leaned into his as she grasped his cheeks again. His bottom lip was busted, she noticed, just before pressing her mouth to his.

That taste, that warmth.

The cuffs jangled as he tried futilely to hold her to him.

"Are you hurt?" he asked again when she pulled away.

Mara shook her head. "No—but you are." Stepping back, she reviewed the rest of him—his jacket was missing, the collar of his crisp white shirt had been stretched and hung loose and thin about his neck. He was disheveled. He was never disheveled.

She moved to retuck the shirt at his waist, and he winced.

"What is it?"

"Feels like ribs."

"What can I do?"

"Don't worry about it."

She leaned her forehead into his.

"Who were they?"

"Someone who saw me with Iola?" she wondered. "Thought I was part of the Resurrection?"

They stood breathing each other in. Just for a minute, she let herself relax, and then she started considering their options.

"I'll try the walls, one of them must be a door." Mara walked around the room's perimeter, corner to corner, testing the walls for any give. "This one," she said. She pushed it again and a crack of light appeared underneath.

"Okay." Calvy nodded. "When you get out—"

"I'm not leaving you here."

"Of course you are."

"Calvy, I'm your best chance of escaping whatever— wherever—this is."

"How's that?"

"Liam will find me." She didn't intend the words to wound him, and maybe they hadn't—maybe his grimace was coincidental. "You only need to be close by when he does." Calvy started to protest. "I can't get the door open anyway. What we need to do is get your cuffs off."

She came back to where he stood, pulling at the thick silver links that held him to the wall.

"You're not going to budge those," he told her.

"Then we'll just have to wait for Liam to get here."

Calvy tapped his teeth together and closed his eyes. He snapped them open as Mara groped around his waist and into his pockets. "Not the time, Millie—"

"Hilarious. Your sidearm is gone. And they took the knife in your pocket."

"What about the knife in my boot?"

"You really have a knife in your boot."

"I'd like to find out."

Mara knelt, investigating one foot and then the other. She looked up at him and shook her head. "Liam will come for me. He'll find us."

Behind her, the door she'd found rattled open. Glaring sunlight backlit a figure and Mara surged to her feet. She felt Calvy try to straighten behind her.

"Right as usual, my dove. And just where I thought you'd be."

She shaded her eyes against the glare. "Liam?"

It had only been hours—and Liam wouldn't arrive on Balti for another day. Unless—she'd done the math wrong, calculated his return on Balti time, instead of the standard twenty-four-hour unit. He was here—he'd found them.

"Aren't you happy to see me?"

She had been, at first, but the relief rushed out of her as quickly as it came. On the long wall between them, visible in the new light, was the Pent logo, painted in that signature pale green, the same color as Liam's eyes. Sky tinged with warning of a storm. They were in a shipping container. A Pent-owned shipping container.

"*You* had us brought here?"

All she could make out was his outline, those broad shoulders blocking the Balti sun. "A miscommunication. I requested his majesty's presence. When the men I hired saw you—your hair, they said—they assumed I'd want you as well. It seems there's been some…compliance issues while I was out on the Rim."

"You set those toughs on us?" Calvy ground out. "They could have—do you even—you're supposed to protect her!"

"No. That was your job. And you weren't very good at it. As it turns out."

Mara centered herself between them as the air began to churn. She could see Liam better now, the sharp cut of his suit, the crisp white of his shirt. "Cal doesn't have anything to do with what happened at the factory—"

"The factory?"

"The compliance issues. I wanted to talk to you about—"

"You'll have to wait your turn, Mara," Liam snapped. "Private D'Aldiern—"

"Captain," Mara corrected.

"Not when he's reinstated. Which will happen as soon as I sign off on his service."

Calvy's low voice rumbled down Mara's spine. "But you're not going to do that."

"Well, *Cal*, we have some things to discuss first." Liam used his stone to project a set of moving photos, the light catching the dust in the air. Drone surveillance. Of Mara's hotel room. The intrusion was—it was—she was having a hard time getting air again.

"Why—why would you—"

Liam didn't look at her, his eyes focused on the next

image, Calvy and Mara asleep on her couch after her assault outside the Crown. "Harper insisted. Why do you think I left her here? I needed someone I could trust." He glanced at Calvy. "I warned you, I told you she'd be hard to say no to. I thought we understood each other."

"But you know all this," Calvy said. "It's in my reports."

His reports. How much detail had he shared—and how much of her had he kept for himself? Hopefully nothing. Because if Liam found out...

"Is it? Is everything in those reports? You made them seem very dry, very tedious indeed."

"You told me to fuck her, you told me to tell you—I did it. I *did* it. I did all of it," Calvy fumed.

Shots fired, from both sides, with no regard for her standing in the middle, taking the hits.

"Heated, are we, D'Aldiern? Where's that captain's composure? Can't you see you're upsetting our girl?" But it was Liam's neck splotched with red. His veins raised and tight at his temples.

"I'm not upset," Mara said, though she had to release the inside of her cheek from the teeth that had clamped into it to do so. "He's telling you the truth. He fucked me. When I wanted. When I said. Just like we agreed."

It had been a job. Liam was back. And that's all it could be. That's all it was.

She'd imagined what it would be like, to be in the same room with both of them. She'd imagined it flat and awkward—the tension hers and hers alone. They were proving her wrong. She could feel Liam's anger, Calvy's judgment. *And what did he do to earn you?*

Fuck being earned. A Balti—a woman—should give herself freely, as it pleased her.

"We agreed to limits. And there was a distinct... failure...to comply." Liam flipped through more photos as he emphasized each word, landing on a shot of Iola's face hidden between Calvy's legs. Her red hair was crushed in his hands and even Mara had to do a double take to remember it was not her mouth that had wrapped around Calvy's cock last night.

Mara laughed and Liam finally looked at her.

"That's not me, Liam." She'd wanted it to be her. That was the joke. But he didn't have evidence of that. She pushed it down inside of herself where no one could find it. She'd hold it there, until it sank of its own accord. "Look," she said, walking to meet Liam in the middle of the room, "that tattoo at the back of her neck." She lifted her hair to show him her own and he thumbed the blank skin. She was close enough to smell the zyngroot on his breath and she pulled the familiar scent into her lungs as gooseflesh rose under his touch. He settled the weight of his hand against her throat.

Mara willed her body to remember him. He thought he'd caught her, a little boat adrift on the ocean. He didn't know that she wasn't the boat. *You're the sea*, Calvy had told her. And they were two moons, dragging her one way and then the other.

"He wanted it to be you."

"Of course he did," she said, her lashes low, her mouth conspiring. She let herself slip into the Mara Liam expected. It felt good, safe. Like she knew who she was trying to be, if not who she was. "Wasn't that your game? Get the Dern where we want them. Show them what we can do?"

"Let's show him now. I've been his audience. He'll be mine."

That old persona slipped. Mara lost her footing, like stepping on wet rocks. "No, Liam."

"You don't want him to see us together? Why is that, Mara? What would it matter?"

"If you force her," Calvy warned, his arms pulled straight behind him, like a wave on a collision course with a rock wall, but without enough power to reach it. The muscles in his neck and shoulder strained and she worried he'd rip his arms off at the wrists. The numbers tattooed on his chest peeked out of the loose neck of his collar. Mara knew them by heart, how they felt under her fingers, under her tongue. Barely there yet unmistakably part of him, etched beneath his skin. She felt the pull back to Calvy. A tug at her gut telling her that her place was at his side.

It would be a mistake. For them both.

"No one is forcing me to do anything."

She was the one about to rip in half. And Calvy was the reason. He was just like Iola, filling her head with impossible things. Their termination date had been stamped in bloodred ink since the start. It was time to let go. If he would just shut his mouth she could focus, she could manage Liam. Instead the room was narrowing as Liam inched closer to where Calvy was restrained, with her only her keeping them apart.

"I did force her—to be with you, D'Aldiern. You should be thanking me."

Calvy's quiet fury pulsed into the room and Liam laughed, pulling Mara against him with one arm.

"What is it, D'Aldiern—did you think it was more? Do you think it's love when her cunt wraps around you? Certainly feels like it. But it isn't. That's as close as Mara gets, to be sure. But she's too afraid of love to even let herself remember what it felt like to have a family. She doesn't love me, and she doesn't love you. She only longs to feel wanted."

"Mara—" Calvy started.

"Tell him." Liam's arm tightened around her waist and Mara brought her hand to his chest to push him back. The sweet coco smell of Calvy's hair wax clung to her fingers, poisoning the air between her and Liam. "Tell him it was nothing. Tell him you're just that good."

Maybe it was the pressure of Liam's arm on her abdomen, or the enclosed space, but Mara could barely gather enough breath to speak. She turned slowly to Calvy, still banded by Liam's tight hold.

"She already told me," Calvy said. His eyes were wide and marble round, black and glossy in the glare of sunlight that streaked across the floor. Mara remembered the way they'd looked up close at the cliffs— brown and rich and able to see through her.

She'd told him it was nothing.

But that wasn't what he meant. His confidence gave him away. He meant the kiss she'd used to claim him. The kiss he waited for, the kiss that told him she wanted everything he did.

Liam pushed at her back, curling around her, the way the sky curved around the planet, protecting it from the cold and the dark and the unknown.

She was caught. Twisted in a net of wills. As she had been since the first moment they'd come together. Liam and Calvy, they both wanted her—they didn't care if it left her in pieces.

Her heartbeat quivered in her ears, the loudest force in the room. The strongest force in the room. She didn't want to be the sea, tugged this way and that, weighed down by unknowable depth.

Better to be the wind.

"Let me go." She pulled away from Liam. "Let him go, too, and sign his fucking papers. I'm done with this. All of this."

She took Liam's place in the door, blocking the sun again, and those eyes that always found a light went dark.

She was no one's girl. They were little boys—fighting over what? Her allegiance, her body? She could push the storm, she could push the waves. She could flatten the grass in whichever way she pleased.

And she had somewhere to be. She had her own truth to fight for. It didn't involve either of them.

"Mara," Liam tried.

"Now. I've had enough."

His chest heaved, but Liam swiped his thumb across the stone that had been forgotten in his balled fist. Mara heard Calvy stumble forward as the cuffs demagnetized, releasing him. But she didn't look back. Her shadow covered them both.

Chapter Twenty-Nine

It was Runa who gave her a ride back to the hotel. The soldier recognized Mara trying to make her way out of the maze of shipping containers at the edge of the Dern barracks.

"You lost? Looking for your—"

"No," Mara said. "I'm not lost." She had swayed then and Runa had popped open the passenger-side door of her supply truck.

"I'll take you home anyway."

Home. That's what this place was supposed to be, she thought, as the smooth paved road turned to uneven mosaic, setting the truck rattling with her inside.

Harper was standing outside her door, like it was any other morning. Her eyes went round as Mara approached. Mara seethed at the sight of the woman who had spent months violating her privacy, spying on her every move. She blew forward, Dannos catching her before impact. She hadn't even noticed him in the hall, focused solely on Harper, and she fought his hold as she spoke.

"Surprised to see me, you snake? Thought you had me? Thought you could twist that rope of yours right around my neck. Is that why you spied on me?"

The slightest flinch showed on Harper's face as Mara unleashed her anger. "I did what I was told. Doesn't seem to have had much effect. If he's giving you another chance."

"I don't need another chance. I did what I was told too."

Harper scoffed. "Mr. Pent told you to mess around with the cap—with D'Aldiern?"

"Yes! He did!" Mara's voice rose to a shout, shocking all three of them into silence, surprised by the raw emotion she displayed.

Harper's chin drew slow arcs in the air. And Mara stopped fighting. She pushed out of Dannos's grasp and hauled in a few ragged breaths, trying to compose herself.

Dannos whistled. "The boss may know business but he has no head for love."

"Liam and I aren't in love."

"He didn't say you were."

Mara rounded on Harper again. "You should stop worrying about me and start working out why Liam didn't take you with him to Theos. Why he had you here, reporting what he already knew?" She advanced on the door and Harper stepped aside, chewing her bottom lip. "He wanted you occupied. And you called that trust."

Inside her room, Mara couldn't calm down. She'd last seen this place projected on Liam's stone. How many private moments had been exposed? She drew the window shades down and retreated to the bathroom. Her face and clothes were stained with dirt and blood.

Calvy's blood.

She couldn't think about him.

Without waiting for the shower to warm, she stripped the soiled clothes and stepped under the stream of water, relishing its chill. She needed to cool off, to collect herself. Thinking about Calvy had been her mistake. It had made her vulnerable. If she wanted anything from Liam, for herself or what she'd promised Iola, she had to put Calvy out of her mind.

But of course he was knocking—like he had last night. Impatiently, urgently. She should never have opened the door for him. But he'd knocked and knocked and pushed everything over. With his persistence, he'd demolished every wall she'd built between them.

She was still in her towel when she flung open the door, prepared to tell Calvy just how frustrating and stubborn and—

Liam stood in the hall.

She smoothed over the flash of disappointment she felt, glad she could still conceal something from someone. "What do you want?"

Liam walked past her into the room and sat unbothered on the couch. He patted the seat next to him. After some deliberation, Mara sat opposite, in the chair. He rested his ankle on his knee, considering her.

"I see I've done some damage."

"You kidnapped me."

Liam moved to sit on the coffee table in front of her, leaning forward.

"Unintentionally. I was upset. I wanted D'Aldiern to know what happens to people who cross me. I shouldn't have forgotten to stipulate that I didn't want you to suffer the same treatment." He reached for her knee, brushing his thumb up her thigh.

"You shouldn't be treating anyone that way." She

crossed her legs, tucking them to the side. "I went to your factory. The conditions are—"

He straightened, bringing his hands together between his legs. "Yes. You went to my factory. And then a riot broke out. D'Aldiern left it out of his reports. They've been decidedly short of late. Which does make me wonder what else he kept to himself. Very sweet, isn't it? His trying to protect you from me. As if that were necessary. But Harper was quite detailed about the event. What were you trying to do, Mara?"

It was a conversation they had to have, she knew, if they were to move forward. And it was easier than talking about Calvy.

"Nothing. I didn't know what would happen."

"Someone put you up to it?"

Mara nodded.

"Tell me who."

"No."

He sat back further on the table. Mara flashed to all the memories she had of him from the last six months—exactly like that. Projected into the room because he'd left her here. Made her do this alone. Made her do this with Calvy. Created the distance between them. She touched his leg—just to make sure he was really here.

Liam covered her hand with his. "I should have stayed with you."

"Yes," Mara agreed.

"I have to ask: Are you part of the Resurrection?"

"No, but I've talked with them. And I don't disagree that Balti needs change."

Liam sighed. "That isn't something you can accomplish, my dove."

Mara bristled at the comment, pulling her hand from

under his. "They told me you forced the moonclan to come down to the planet. Forced them from their homes. Forced them to work."

"Did they? And did your revolutionaries mention that they were living under rock. Rationing power. That the Pent Corporation offered them passage to the planet, to a better life?"

She knew Liam, that he offered nothing for free. "In exchange for what?"

"There were some contracts involved, as we fronted them passage, lodging upon arrival."

"Lodging? The city is empty."

"And yet the Dern require rent."

Mara stood. "But they don't own any of this!"

"No, the Balticourts did." Liam rose to his feet with her, their faces close in the narrow gap between chair and table. "And the Balticourts are gone. I did what I could for the people who were left. Gave them opportunities to work off their debt."

"And how long will that take?"

"What's your point, Mara?"

"You *indentured* them." She spat the word.

Liam held out a finger to correct her. "I offered them a deal. They took it."

"And what option did they have?"

"I run a business." His shoulder rose and he turned away from her. "And it hasn't been—it's not a charity."

Following Liam to the drink cooler, Mara continued to press him. "But they didn't need to move at all—they had food—" She cut herself off. Liam had grown silent, and she felt his anticipation of her discovery. "What else is under the rock?"

He handed her a blue-lidded tin. "Raw ore. Mountains of it."

The cold metal sent a shiver up her arm. "You and Dern. You moved the people, so you could mine?"

Liam leaned against the sideboard, his ankles crossed. "Yes. But we didn't mine, Mara. The risk was too great. If the moon fractured, it would cause catastrophic damage to the oceans. The planet would be lost. Balti is essentially an island. A tidal wave would wash everything away. So I stopped it, Mara. Just like I fixed the vents in the factory, as soon as I heard. At some cost, I'll tell you. It was damn expensive and everything is—it would have made things easier if we could mine that damn moon. We still haven't. So don't make me out to be some monster, Mara. I'm not. A prolonged circulation issue at a factory? That's nothing. Nothing compared to—" He stopped himself.

"Compared to what."

"Nothing. I'm tired. I misspoke." He did look tired. His eyes rimmed with red, his shoulders curled forward by whatever weight he carried, the long hours of work and travel. He hooked an arm around her waist and she let him pull her against him. "Am I going to be able to convince you to go to bed with me?"

"Unlikely," Mara said automatically, sounding just like Calvy. Her heart tumbled through the next beat, but Liam couldn't tell. He didn't know how her gut twisted, following her thoughts back to the Dern soldier.

Calvy had been bloodied, chained, and baited by Liam. And she'd walked out. She'd walked away.

Liam laughed and Mara looked up at him. There was a glint of arrogance in his eyes that she recognized, that she'd missed. The way he looked at her with a sense of pure collaboration, like he knew her, knew himself, knew how they fit. It was so different from Calvy, who had spent his six months on Balti studying her like he was trying to figure her out. She got enough of that from the mirror.

"Let's go to Lita. Spend a few weeks completely relaxed. Just us."

"There's one more thing I need to do." She leaned her head on Liam's shoulder and felt him stiffen.

"Mara. We're done with D'Aldiern. Both of us. I don't want him near you again."

Mara flashed back to the moment she had opened the door, expecting Calvy, readying herself for another argument, another bout of conflicting emotions. What if he'd shown up and stared at her with those bright-star-in-the-Black eyes and asked her for more?

She couldn't do it. Couldn't give him more of herself—not when she had so little to begin with.

"It's not about him. It's about me."

"Good," Liam said, smoothing a hand over her hair and kissing the side of her head.

Mara closed her eyes—they were in agreement about Calvy once again. They were done with him.

Chapter Thirty

The Pearl.

The Pearl of Balti.

Mara stood staring up at it. Her eyes swept over the rolls and plateaus of the hill and back to the spherical building. Its opal shimmer had faded with time, but it still stood proud and high on the edge of the continent. On the other side, Mara had read, the Balticourt home was built into the cliff, with open balconies and stairs leading down to the water below. She couldn't see the ocean from the bottom of the hill. But she could feel it. Hear it. The wind had picked up and the tide was alive with motion.

The electric fence sparked and she jumped back.

"Sorry," Liam said, a rock dropping from his hand to the ground. They'd been waiting an hour and he'd grown impatient, making a game of tossing rocks between the fence's slits. "You're sure you can get in?"

Mara turned back to the Pearl. She'd been waiting six months; let him throw rocks a while longer. "I arranged it yesterday."

Still, a sigh of relief left her when Dr. Protaris emerged from the curved wall. He loped down the wide-stepped walkway of soft green moss.

Mara rose to her toes as he approached them.

"Glad to see you again, Ms. Leanor."

"Dr. Protaris."

"Arin, please." He pulled a stone from his pocket and deactivated the fence with the swipe of his thumb. The red lines disappeared. The buzzing stopped. "All clear."

"Stellar," Liam said. "Have fun."

Mara turned, flaring the white in her eyes. "You aren't coming?"

"We've been here an age already. And I've got to get down to that factory you're so concerned about." Liam kissed her mouth. She breathed in zyng-root. "More soon."

Harper moved to follow him and he shook his head. "Stay with Mara. I'll take Dannos."

Mara exhaled. It didn't matter that she was left with the snake. It didn't matter that Liam was leaving. She'd wanted this for herself too long to care about any of them.

Mara focused on the Pearl again as Arin watched Liam go. "He's more…shoulder-y in person. Guess that's how he busts through doors that would otherwise be closed."

"He doesn't have to bust through doors," Mara said, stepping past one of the fence posts. "People open them for him when they see him coming."

Harper shrugged, and Mara expected her normal disagreeable retort. "This one opened for you."

Arin reactivated the fence and started backwards up the slope. Mara followed after him, ignoring Harper's comment.

"Did you have any questions for me?"

"Yes, you mentioned that chip?"

"Ah."

"But not where you found it."

He stopped walking, speaking solemnly. "It was found in the gathering room. Embedded in Queen Balticourt's wrist, here." He pressed warm fingers into Mara's skin but she went cold, bumps raising on her arm.

"That's wrong," she said. "A Temptress can't have a chip. Of any sort."

The man shook his head. "I'm afraid you're mistaken. She had it, under her skin."

The world slanted as they continued up the hill. That wasn't right. Queen Balticourt didn't have a chip. She couldn't. It wasn't allowed. Jimma had said it. Jimma had told her. Mara's breath came in frustrated bursts, exacerbated by the slope. The wind swelled in her ears, an indistinguishable roar, and it was Iola's voice she heard in her mind.

Think about what you believe.

These people, these Dern didn't know—they couldn't be trusted to tell her the truth. Not about her own history. She knew better.

The moss gave just slightly under her feet, springing up with her as she stepped forward, buoying her towards the building. Towards something that had been waiting for her too. The moment she entered into the quiet shade of the Pearl's interior, she knew. She knew that she'd been here before.

The air went static, in anticipation of a lightning strike.

Mara forced her wobbly legs to steady and stepped down two worn steps onto the polished stone floor. Inside was a Balti gathering room: curved walls lined with built-in couches. More cushioned benches filled the area, arranged in concentric circles. Two glowing orbs hung from the cavernous space above them, one small and one large, representing the moons. Behind them, a net of vines wove across the open ceiling, blue sky peeking between the red leaves. Sunlight broke into beams, illuminating the circling benches from above.

"I've got to get the storm shutter up soon," Arin told them. "But I thought you'd want to experience it open. This is where the queen held court—you can see, she would have sat on the same level as her people, moved from couch to couch, shared with them. Less formal than Dern in every way."

Was Mara just picturing it? Or was it a memory? A woman floated by her, red-gold hair set with a crown of feathers. She moved throughout the room. But she preferred that bench, over by the wall, where her family sat. Mara stared at it, glowing so bright under the shard of sun that it almost disappeared in the glare.

Her heartbeat drummed in her ears, drowning out whatever Arin said next.

"Ms. Leanor?" he repeated.

Heavy footsteps took her forward. She felt like she was walking underwater, her feet dragging, her vision warped.

Arin stood next to her. "Have you seen the pictures?" he asked quietly, sensing that she was overcome with… something.

Something that was wrong.

Deeply, deeply wrong.

Mara managed to shake her head.

"That's the couch. Where they were found, the family. I thought maybe you recognized it." He paused before continuing, caught between his paling audience and his historian's desire to relate what had occurred. What he knew. "They were all here. The queen, of course, sat just there, the others around her—all together, which is a comfort. She had the youngest on her lap. Poor girl, her clothes were too small and she was barefoot."

"Barefoot?" The word snagged in her mind, hooking itself to a memory that she pulled to the surface.

Down to the last toe, Calvy had said. Mara felt the ground shift, as though the Pearl had dislodged from the hill and begun to roll down it.

"Yes—she had no shoes. It's possible they had fallen on hard times because of the Dern embargoes. Or perhaps it was her age. At six, children are hard to tame."

No, he was wrong. But historians only had so much to work with. They weren't there.

"What was her name?" Mara asked, though in her pounding blood she heard the answer humming to life.

"Naara. Naara Lunoir Balticourt."

The queen's youngest. The one who'd been secretly whisked to the kitchen at the last moment, who'd stood there, grey eyes round as full moons, as she was told to change clothes. To trade places with her friend Fina, the cook's daughter. The girls had thought it was a game at first. But the way the adults had rushed them, the way Naara was hurried from the room before saying goodbye—it hadn't been a game. It had been a decision, to sacrifice Fina, for Naara's survival.

Mara's survival.

Mara backed away from the couch, knocking into Harper, who reached out to steady her.

No.

It was impossible. It was impossible that she was even thinking it. It was impossible for her to remember the warm kitchen tiles on her bare feet as she took off her shoes and replaced them with Fina's too-big slippers.

Looking down, it was like she could see them now: those oversized slippers. That floor. The tiles red and worn and—

Stop.

She was Mara Leanor. She knew that. It was the only thing she knew.

But.

She had been six. Of course it was possible that Rozz misheard her. Because the rest of it had come flooding back—the guilt and the shame of what she'd pushed down, deep inside of herself.

There was one way to know if she was wrong.

Mara turned, bumping into one couch, then another, winding her way out of the circles to the back of the room. She fumbled through a panel of fabric draped over the opening to the stairs. Down she went, using the wall for support. She could feel Harper pursuing her, but she didn't slow. If the floor were blue, or wood, or something else. That would prove she was confused. Prove she was mistaken. That this was some elaborate fantasy she'd concocted as a lonely little girl trying to make sense of what made her special enough to survive.

Mara took a left at the second landing and rushed to the kitchen—ignoring the voice in her head asking her how she knew the way. She stopped in the doorway, refusing to step onto the tile.

The dusty red tile.

The last time she'd been here the air had smelled of freshly ground pepper. It caught in her throat, now, almost two decades later.

"Ms. Leanor," Arin said behind her, "are you all right?"

"She just needs some air," Harper answered.

"Of course, through here." He led them back to the

stairs and then out through a metal-rimmed arch onto a stone balcony, cut into the cliffs behind the Pearl. Not a balcony really, but a ledge of natural rock. When the storm surged, she knew, all the doors that faced the water would be sealed, metal clamshells brought down and secured from the inside. The royal family—her family—safe inside.

The water churned, frothy and white, as Mara stepped to the edge.

"You couldn't have just opened a window?" Harper asked.

"I didn't think—she's not going to—"

"No," Harper said. "She won't jump. Right, Mara? You're just taking in the view."

"Mara?" the doctor repeated. "Mara. Leanor."

"Can you give us a minute, Doctor?" Harper said.

"Of course," came a nervous reply.

Harper waited for Arin to leave them then slowly eased closer. "What happened in there, Mara?"

"I can't—I don't—"

"Then let's go back inside."

"No."

They stood in silence, Mara transfixed by the ocean. It looked as she felt, tossing and swirling, depths dragged up by the current and smashed against the rock. She waited for her hands to shake, for a tremble of shock, but her body was still, steady as the ledge.

"I'm going to message Mr. Pent," Harper said.

"Don't."

"Why not?"

"I don't want him to know. I don't want anyone to know what I—what I did."

"What you did? Mara, you survived. Mr. Pent will admire that. This information can help him—"

"I said no, Harper."

They were cut short by footsteps approaching. Arin tripped off the last stair in the carved archway, towing Calvy behind him.

"I found D'Aldiern outside. I thought he might be able to help."

Harper swore. "You shouldn't be here. Mr. Pent specifically said to—"

Calvy ignored her. "Mara—"

"I've got it under control, D'Aldiern," Harper said, putting herself between them. "Now isn't the time."

"Why? What's going on?" His gaze fixed on Mara at the end of the rock. "Did he do something to you?"

Mara wiped at the tears on her cheeks and laughed. So wrong. He was always so wrong. They were wrong. Everything was wrong. "Liam? He didn't do anything." The world spun when she looked away from the water. "I can handle Liam Pent. I don't need you to save me. People need to stop saving me."

Her family—*her family*—had been murdered. All of them. Except her. Someone had made a choice and picked her life over another little girl's.

"She died," Mara said. "Died saving me."

"Who died?" Calvy asked.

Faces blurred in her mind. She'd had sisters. They'd laughed together, swam, played, fought. "Everyone. They died and I didn't. And no one can fix it."

"I think she had a shock, upstairs," Arin supplied.

A shock. That was an understatement. She'd been electrified.

Calvy inched forward, and Harper gave way. "You're right. Nobody can fix it. Not me, not you. Not Pent."

"Should I try his stone?" Arin asked.

"No," Harper and Calvy said together. Harper glared

at the soldier. "She does not need him now. But she will. When she brings herself back from the edge."

Calvy was almost at Mara's side. Close enough that she could reach out and touch him. Close enough that she could push him away. Like she wanted to push away the thoughts.

Jimma. Jimma had to have known. That's why she'd told Mara not to get a chip—that it was forbidden. She hadn't wanted Mara's DNA in the regulator database. To protect her. To protect them all. It felt suddenly like a betrayal. Weren't Jimma's omissions lies? But in their wake was certainty. She'd found Mara and prepared her because it was Mara's birthright. Mara would always have been chosen.

Harper's voice was thin. "Enough of this. Mara, it's time to go. We'll discuss it with Mr. Pent."

"Discuss what? Mara, will you tell me what's going on?" Calvy touched her sleeve.

She couldn't. She could barely stomach the thoughts—saying them out loud was impossible. She turned back to the water. The edge stopped and the rest was ocean. She couldn't escape this—there could be no peace—especially with her bodyguards bickering behind her.

"It's not your concern, D'Aldiern."

"I'm not asking you, Harper."

"No. *I'm* not asking. I'm telling you to go."

Mara glanced back and saw Harper grab at Calvy's shoulders. He dodged to the side and Mara backed out of the way. But she'd been standing so close, too close to the edge. Her arms spun in the air as she tried to regain her balance. Calvy scrambled towards her, forgetting about Harper.

The same mistake they'd already made: not watching out for Harper.

Because Harper was coming for her too.

Stop, Mara tried to say, *stop saving me*.

She balanced herself. But it was too late. Her two bodyguards collided and Calvy flew sideways. He was there. And then he was falling. Off the ledge. Down through the air. Crashing into the waves. His body disappeared under the water surging below.

"Cal!" Mara screamed.

"Don't," Harper tried, but Mara was already gone, her body in free fall from a leap that took her over the cliff after him.

The water rushed up to meet her and she broke through it feetfirst. Harper hit the water next and they both bobbed to the surface.

"Get off of me," Mara cried as Harper wrapped her arm around Mara's shoulder.

"Stop fighting me, I'm trying to help you."

Mara coughed and went under again. The salt water stung her eyes as she tried to look for Calvy. The cold numbed her limbs, slowing her frantic search.

Harper pulled her back to the surface.

"If you want to help me, help Calvy!" She had to shout over the crash of water around them. "He can't swim!"

Mara took a breath and dove under again, this time when she looked around, she saw Harper, eyes open, underwater at her side, both of them trying to find the Dern.

They spotted him at the same time, grabbing futilely for the surface, too far down to reach it and sinking fast. It took both of them to haul him up. Once they did, Mara clamped her arm around him and swam backwards away from the rock.

"This way," she called to Harper. They kicked

against the current around to a cove on the other side
of the ledge, where the waves were calmer and stone
steps led up out of the water. Arin was waiting for them.
They dragged Calvy out by the elbows. He gasped and
coughed as the three of them sprawled over the flat
rock.

"You could have drowned!" Mara shouted at him.

He could have died. She could have lost him. Hadn't
she lost enough? Hadn't Dern taken enough from her?
Couldn't she keep this one good thing? That's what
Calvy was: good and here and now. And she couldn't
care about the rest of it—not when he was plunging
off the cliff, not when he was asking her to kiss him,
choose him.

Drenched and heavy, he leaned into the rock. "Oh.
It's my fault. Of course. For falling in. Not yours for
always standing right up at the edge, not hers for pushing me."

"I was trying to get to Mara," Harper said, sitting up.

"So was I."

"I was fine," Mara said.

Those black eyes found her, shining like glass. But
he shook his head. Because he hated it when she pre-
tended. He hadn't asked her to lie about this.

"I wasn't going to jump. I needed to think."

Mara shivered, her eyes locked on Calvy's. His hair
was plastered to his forehead, his lashes wet and spiked.
His neat shirt rumpled, waterlogged and sticking to him.
She would have lurched towards him, pulled his stupid
face to hers, kissed the salt from his lips, but Harper
staggered to her feet, blocking him from view.

She offered Mara a hand. "Let's get back to the
hotel." Mara didn't take it. Harper knelt in front of her,
dropping her voice to keep the conversation between

them. "If you leave with me now, I won't tell Mr. Pent about any of this. *Any* of it. Leave with me now or it will be my head if Pent finds out D'Aldiern was involved. Mine and Calvy's."

"Calvy doesn't care if Liam signs the papers or not. He cares about me. He——"

"Theos still requires justice."

Mara sat up. What was she saying? That Calvy would go back to prison? Liam wouldn't do that—he couldn't. But another shiver rocked Mara's body. Because Liam Pent could do anything he wanted.

"Get rid of him, Mara. Make sure he doesn't come back. Tell him whatever you need to tell him."

It was too much, all of it. Mara's voice broke. "He won't believe me."

"Convince him."

Harper stood and offered her hand to Mara again. This time, Mara let Harper pull her up.

And there was Calvy. Bruised and in peril. Again. Because of her. The wind finally managed to cover the blue sky with clouds and the direct sun that had lit the rock greyed.

"How did you know about these steps?" Calvy pushed back his hair. "What did you find up there, Mara?"

But she wasn't Mara—that last bit of herself had been taken now too.

"Just dust," she said.

His face clouded with confusion. He was too earnest, too open to her. Too willing. Too giving. And all she'd done was take. He said he was better than Liam and he was. But someone had taken her place—someone had chosen her friend to die for her. And Mara hadn't even been brave enough to remember it. In what world did she deserve better?

Harper waited at her side, watching, listening. Mara was to dismiss him. How could she, when he saw through her? But convincing someone of something was a lot like seduction. Something she had practiced. She only needed an anchor of truth.

Lie to me, Mara.

"Thanks to the Dern. To your father. To you. That's all that's left." She boiled it down to the simplest conflict between them, even though it no longer mattered. She didn't need Calvy to be any less Dern, only more hers.

That wasn't an option now.

Pain wrote itself along the lines of Calvy's brow and Mara blinked the sting from her eyes. "I've taken all I will from you."

His shoulders sank. "Then it was nothing."

Mara turned to walk away, hoping her wet cheeks disguised the final tear that slipped past the wall she was rebuilding around herself.

"You took nothing," Calvy repeated, calling after her. "Because I gave it all willingly."

Chapter Thirty-One

"Mara? Is the power working? Did it go out already? The Dern are in way over their heads with this one. Some of the waves are already coming in at thirty meters. It hasn't even started yet. Gibbs showed me some of the drone footage or I wouldn't believe it. And I ran into General D'Mont—he was spinning, absolutely mad dash. Capping all the outputs, shutting everything down. It'll put them behind schedule but it's worth it. I know, you'll say he's just worried about losing product—but it's good for the people too, they're clearing the rigs, bringing everyone to shore. Ah, there's the light. It's still working. Mara? Why were you sitting in the dark?"

She hadn't moved.

Not since Liam had come through the door, pouring out the details of his afternoon.

Not since Harper had walked her in, sat her on the couch, placed an open tin of water in front of her. The escaping carbon had long since gone quiet. The water as still as Mara.

She hadn't noticed the dark. The steel-grey clouds that had rolled over the city. Over the Pearl. Even the light Liam activated couldn't compete with the shadows pooling outside.

Liam braced his hands on the back of the couch, his voice rough as he asked her, "Did he come here?"

She was right to leave them both in the shipping container that morning. Here she was, reeling, having uncovered the mystery of her past, and both of them—both of these obtuse men—had blamed the other.

"No," Mara said. And it was true. Calvy hadn't come. He hadn't followed her again.

"Good. Good." Liam rounded the couch to sit next to her. "I think he's dangerous, Mara, I think he's un-hinged."

Her mouth puckered. She had to give Calvy some credit—he'd realized sooner than Liam that what was bothering her wasn't related to whose cock she wanted most.

Liam tucked her hair behind her ear. "Anyone who would hire a damsel just to pretend it was you."

"She wasn't a damsel."

"Who was she?"

"It doesn't matter."

"It does. Because we need to find her." He sighed. "That's the price, Mara."

Mara broke her gaze away from the horizon to look at him. "What price?"

Liam moved to the table, sitting with his elbows on his knees, his fingers threaded together. "I have Dern investors. A red-haired Balti woman started a riot at my place of business. I can negotiate, as long as I have something they want. And they want someone to blame. We can tell them someone walked in there pretending to be you—"

"That's not what happened—"

"It is. If you want to stay out of a Dern cell. Give me a name, Mara."

He waited for an answer that wouldn't come. She wouldn't do it. Not even if it were Harper. She had known so few people in this life. She wouldn't give another one up.

He exhaled, sitting straight when she didn't respond. "This is my business, Mara. There will be a consequence for someone. I won't let it be you."

"But I did it!" She wouldn't let someone else take the fall for her. Not again. "It isn't right."

Liam palmed the air, gesturing for her to settle. "It isn't right? Nothing right happens here—not after what my father did."

"The Dern."

"What?"

She blinked. "You said what your father did. You meant the Dern."

Now Liam held his answer back.

Mara tilted her head. "The P bomb—it was the Dern, Liam. Unless you know something I don't."

His hands came up, bridging over his nose.

She released the air that tightened her lungs. "Tell me, Liam. No lies between us."

He nodded, raising his eyes to hers. "It was my father. The Dern only wanted to kill the royal family, thought that would be enough. But the projections showed otherwise. Even without the Balticourts, there would have been resistance, legal battles, protests, roadblocks, wasted time and money, dragging out decades."

Mara felt sick. "So he vented the whole planet with poison gas."

"Production could start as soon as the gas cleared—

a ten-year delay. Models showed it was the more profit-able option. I found the projections. When I took over the company. And then I destroyed the evidence."

They lengthen their father's shadows. More darkness settled over Mara, blackness that chilled her to the bone. "I can't believe you kept this from me."

"I couldn't tell *anyone*, Mara. Telling wouldn't undo it. It wouldn't change anything."

She recoiled from the hand he held out to her. "Of course it changes things! Your legacy is the destruction of my people for profit."

"It's not *my* legacy. I'm not my father. As D'Aldiern isn't his. That's how you justified it with him, isn't it? How you moved past thinking it was his legacy."

"No, I didn't. I never forgave Calvy."

"Yes, you did. That's why you're not with him. It scares you too much to embrace the grey of your his-tory, to admit that you can accept it."

Calvy aside, Mara had plenty of grey to contend with. And Liam was right, she was scared. Scared to accept all of the dark choices that had gotten her here. Scared to accept what it meant. Their pasts, all three of them, were braided together—a tangle, a knot, that she'd never get out of.

"I'm not him, my dove," Liam reassured her. He was talking about his father, but Mara thought only of Calvy, the differences between the two men. "It's not like I'll do it again."

Her eyes rolled at the preposterous reasoning. "Wipe the planet clean with a P bomb?" Disgust laced her words. "No, you certainly aren't like your father. You couldn't afford a ten-year delay."

Liam's face clouded over. "The P2 clears in six months."

She hadn't felt the drop, when she'd rushed off the cliff after Calvy. It had happened too fast. She hadn't had time to think—only to jump. Now she felt it: a flip of her gut that told her she was plummeting, slipping straight through ground that had once been solid.

"The what?"

She wished he'd retreat again, cover his face and look ashamed. She wished he would take it back. Say it was a mistake. Instead he sat eerily still, an unyielding stare from his pale eyes.

"That's impossible. Dern regulations—they stopped all production after the first 'accident.'"

"And yet the Pent Corporation established a research lab right here on Balti. Under their noses. No place better to develop the next level, where we can study the effects of the first."

She'd known all along: Liam Pent was capable of anything. The lying and spying hadn't bothered her when they'd shared an enemy, when he'd been a shark circling someone else. Maybe it should have, maybe she wouldn't feel as vulnerable as she did now with this inconceivable monster rising from Liam's depths, teeth bared to draw her blood.

"Why would you do that, Liam?"

"Someone else would have. No good being behind on tech. I've said I'm not going to use it."

"Not going to use it here, or ever? Liam. Liam! Promise me you won't."

"You want a promise from me?" His eyes dared her.

"You can't—"

"Is that a yes?"

Mara nodded, slowly, her teeth clenched in her jaw. Though she didn't want him to promise her anything, she needed him to do it.

"Then what do I get?"

She glared at him. But the chill had subsided, her blood thawed. Heat spread from her gut, burning her veins like acid. "What do you want?"

"I want us. Back how it used to be. Before Balti, before D'Aldiern. Whatever happened here. I want to forget it. I want us to take care of each other. And be together. I want you. I'll give you your promise in exchange."

He brought his face close and she caught another whiff of zyng-root, spicy and nauseatingly sweet. Her nose wrinkled in response and her lips flattened, sealing her mouth from breathing in the cloying smell. Why did he smell of edibles in the middle of the day? Unless he'd wound himself so tight, twisted himself up in his work and his schemes, that he'd started taking them throughout the day to relax. Unless business wasn't going well at all. Unless he'd had his own reasons for leaving the Center and it had been a mistake to separate because they could have helped each other. The proof was in the way they'd filled the void. Each with bad habits.

She'd wanted him back. Familiar and safe. Now she didn't recognize the man in front of her, the one who thought he had her on the hook. "Why are you in such a rush, Liam?" But he'd been the same when they'd left Støsh and—she hadn't cared then. Mara's heart pounded. Liam had never hidden what he was about, his whole world was the *P* inside a pale green circle. Her perspective had changed, but his stamp on the universe hadn't. It remained everywhere. Even stitched into the tongue of Calvy's army-issued boots. "That wasn't the first time you crossed Theos, was it?"

"I've worked it out. You give this up, we leave, it'll all be taken care of. Every loose thread tied in a tight, forgotten knot."

"Those Dern investors—"

"Not your concern!" He sucked harshly at the air, and blew it out slowly. His fist closed between them, pumping once. "I am promising you protection from all of it."

"Do you even know what a promise means here? You're offering me marriage."

"I know you. I know tradition is important to you. We'll leave tomorrow, I'm done here. And when I'm gone, you won't be safe. They will come for you. Since you refuse to help yourself."

"I refuse to give up my friend."

"She's your friend now? Did you arrange it for him, Mara? You did, didn't you. It doesn't matter. You want to protect these people. And you don't trust me to do it. Do it yourself. Make me promise."

That was Liam's perspective on her options: him or nothing. *I know you*, he'd claimed. Maybe once he had. She wasn't who he'd left behind—she'd escaped, survived, been chosen—and no matter how much it scared her, she couldn't forget it. As she couldn't forget Calvy's disbelief, ricocheting off the darkened sea rocks.

Then it was nothing. I gave it all willingly.

"I need to think about it."

Liam taunted her. "You need to think about keeping these people safe?"

"I need to think about how I'd stomach seeing your face every day for the rest of my life."

He touched his tongue to his bottom lip as if she'd bit

him. His mouth opened wide and snapped shut. Then he nodded.

"You have the night. In the morning we go to the shuttle port and you can decide if you want to come with me or try to outpace the Dern on your own. Who knows how far you'll get. You won't be able to come back here. So you decide, Mara. What you can live with and what you can't. Decide what—or, let's be honest and say who—to let go."

Chapter Thirty-Two

If the sun had risen, Mara couldn't tell. The sky was thick with layered storm clouds. She was forced to squint against the stab of hard rain when the elevator doors opened and she stepped through for the last time.

General D'Mont was waiting for them, his bent elbow jutting from the back window of a Dern army truck.

"Mr. Pent, we'll be in touch when the storm passes to discuss the modified distributions. The damage is already substantial." He glared at Mara as though she'd caused the storm. Her face remained blank. "You'll make it up to me, won't you? As I'm turning a blind eye to the fugitive you're smuggling off planet. Don't bring her back anytime soon."

Liam nodded. "Yes. Of course. We should be going, before the winds ground the shuttles."

Lightning cracked the sky above them, flashing light snaking through the air.

"Where is Harper?" Liam muttered. "She was to secure transport."

Mara couldn't wait any longer. Her body surged into motion, heading across the street.

"We don't have to walk, my dove. I'm sure the general would be willing to—Mara!"

She slipped between two buildings, under the over-hanging branches of the citrin trees, a momentary respite from the driving rain. Behind her she heard the truck door slam, the engine start. They'd have to go around to catch her, meet her on the Queen's Road.

That was fitting.

The truck pulled up to the corner just after she reached the edge of the tiled street. Liam opened the door and stood to lean over it, shouting against the wind for her to get in. But it wouldn't matter if she did. The Queen's Road was filling with people funneled south by the storm. The truck would never get through.

Mara walked towards the truck, caught in the flow of the crowd. Liam grabbed her arm as she passed.

"What's going on?" the general barked.

"The canal," Mara said. "It's flooded."

He pulled a stone from his pocket and his face twisted when it confirmed what she already knew. What Calvy had told her would happen. The Dern had under-estimated the force of Balti.

"Do you have fires to put out?" she asked the general, his square face red with impotence. "Or are your rigs already underwater?"

"We have to go," Liam said, tugging her into the truck. "Harper will be—"

"No. She won't." Mara's voice had taken on an eerie calm, without any effort. "She's at the factory. Securing evidence. Before the water washes it away."

"Evidence—"

"She knows, Liam. That you've been stamping your weapons with seals of Theos and supplying them to the Dern. I told her about your deal with D'Mont."

"You—you what?"

The general shook his head. "There's no protecting her now, Pent."

Thunder shook the ground and Liam's eyes flicked to some motion behind her. Mara turned her head and found Calvy astride his hoverbike. Rain beaded on his navy jacket and above the irresistible bow of his mouth. His black eyes had never looked so dark, fringed by wet lashes and shadowed by his strong brow. And yet—all Mara saw was the impossible glow that emanated from within him.

The Balti coursed around him but he stayed still, a rock in a stream.

"It's too late," Mara said.

"Hear that, D'Aldiern?"

"No, Liam. It's too late for us. It's too late for you. You can stay to watch, but I wouldn't advise it. You should go, before Harper comes looking for you. Both of you."

Liam let go of her arm and she backed away.

"You can't be serious. Mara. He's nothing. He's not a soldier. He's not a prince."

As if that mattered to her. He was Calvy, that's all she wanted him to be. But she had a better answer now, one that would set Liam reeling.

"He is a prince. I made him one. A side effect of marrying a queen."

"A queen?" Liam's face twisted and he looked to the general for support. "She's out of her mind."

"Better let me take her in. It works in our favor. No one will believe her when she opens her mouth."

They talked as though she weren't there, so she made herself known. "I am the last of the Balti royal line. And I'm not going anywhere because this planet is mine to defend."

"This is insane, Mara." Liam dropped from the truck to follow her, his hand outstretched. But there was already too much distance between them. She was beyond him, where he couldn't reach her. If he tried, Calvy'd be on him in moments. And if one of them came for *her* prince, tried to drag him back to Dern or Theos, moons help them. He was under her protection now.

"Come with me, and we'll get you help," Liam coaxed. "We'll figure it out."

"I already figured it out." Mara continued her progress towards Calvy. "You should know—" she turned to Liam "—that I had two men in my room last night."

The general laughed. "You knew what she was, Pent."

"One was there to give me this." Mara held up her wrist, showing him the neat little laser line, red and raised on her skin.

"What's that?"

"We're about to find out."

"Grab her already!" the general cried, but the soldier he addressed was Runa and she didn't move to follow the order. "I'll do it myself." He lurched from the vehicle.

Liam stood staring at Calvy, caught in Mara's story. "And the other? The other man, Mara?" he shouted.

Mara put one foot on the hoverbike's rail, her hands on Calvy's shoulders. "He gave me a promise!"

Liam blinked his soft green eyes and his voice broke in the wind. "We had a deal!"

She let a perfect smile pull her cheeks apart one at a time, not bothering to shout. Let him read her lips. "I got a better offer."

"Mara—Mara!"

The general had almost reached them when Calvy

kicked the hoverbike into motion. Water sprayed up from the street, splashing dirt into his face as they took off.

Mara stood behind Calvy, the wind and rain swirling around her as they sped to higher ground, to the Pearl.

"You okay?" Calvy shouted over his shoulder.

Mara tightened her grip on the slick wet shoulders of his jacket. "I'm with you."

She hadn't waited until the morning. She hadn't needed the night to decide. Liam had laid it out for her and she'd known immediately what she needed to do. What she wanted to do. Because when she'd closed her eyes, to find somewhere still, somewhere quiet in her mind to think, she'd imagined Calvy around her, not just protecting her peace, but creating it.

Liam had offered her something she hadn't needed. A way to ensure the people of Balti were safe. The people of Balti were hers. She didn't need him to take care of them. She could do it herself. It was her duty.

The wind whipped at her hair; her wet shirt clung to her front and flapped sharply behind her.

Harper had found Arin and Calvy last night. Arin had brought the chip. And Calvy... Calvy had watched her, watched her claim her place, with a smile on his lips.

He had stood by the window, the Balti night at his back. There had been moons behind the clouds. Mara had felt them. The coffee table had been cool against the back of her hand as she held her palm up so Arin could access her wrist. She'd spoken while he inserted the device into her arm. Words that couldn't wait. A request she'd needed Calvy to hear then—right then.

"I want something from you," she'd said, ignoring the pain, the burn on her skin. "I want a promise."

Calvy hadn't missed a beat before answering. "It's yours."

"You don't even know what it is. What if I want you to lock yourself in a pod tower?"

"Unlikely." His smile had faded, replaced by that earnest-eyed gaze of his. That gaze she loved. From the man she couldn't live without. "I know what a promise means to you. I'll do it. Whatever it is. Whatever you want."

"Be with me," she'd told him. She didn't need him to do anything more than that.

"Done," he'd said.

The Pearl loomed in front of them. Arin had deactivated the beams of the fence. Members of the displaced moonclan and soldiers cut off from their base had gathered on the sloped grounds. There was no telling how far the floodwaters would reach now that the Dern had made them all so vulnerable.

"Sixty-meter waves," Calvy told her as they pulled to a stop. "None of those rigs are going to make it. The factory, too, it'll be wrecked."

Mara caught a flash of red in the crowd and locked eyes with Iola. The woman grinned at her, the look full and wicked in the face of chaos.

Mara spun back around and collided with Calvy's chest. She lifted her mouth to his, her heart fluttering in her throat. His lips were warm and slick and yielding as they slid against her own.

"I'm with you," he repeated back to her along with a new promise. "No more waiting, no more searching. For either of us."

Mara's hand went to her wrist.

And she pushed.

The chip gave a soft click under her skin.

She climbed the slope, her eyes on her feet, measuring each step, and stopped on the flat of the last tier of rolling hill. There she turned to face the crowd that had flocked to the Pearl.

Her shirt was soaked and it was hard to see in the blur of wind and rain. But her voice rang clearly through the air.

"This planet was my home," she called out, "before the Dern and their partners stole it, through murder and malice. They paid us nothing but lies and death and destruction. They have pushed us to the brink, taken our lives for their own profit. Today that ends."

She let the words sink in, taking a breath to steady herself. The lightning had subsided, but the air was charged still, charged with her power, her honesty. The people on the hill stood with their chins high to regard her, absorbed in the hope she offered.

"The return of the queen?" A man stepped forward with longing in his eyes.

A woman behind him shook her head, her light hair dark with rain. "Queen of dust—the Dern won't leave until they've drained us dry. The Resurrection is a myth."

Mara dug her heels into the soft earth. She had to let them see, see how much it meant to her. How much she cared. "This is not a resurrection. This is a resurgence. Balti herself has risen to wash them from our planet!"

"And then what?" It was Iola who separated herself from the crowd, whose eyes gleamed with unshrinking audacity. "When the waters recede and they come back to rebuild—who will stop them?"

"We will. I will," Mara said. Iola grinned again and Mara knew that was what she'd been hoping to hear. Emboldened, her voice rose up as she revealed herself.

"I am Mara Leanor Balticourt. And their claim is no match for mine."

And then she saw them. Black marks in the sky, growing closer and larger, swooping and soaring towards the Pearl. Towards her.

Mara craned her neck, lifting her grey eyes to the storm.

Birds. The raptors of Balti—petrels and gulls and ospreys—circled above her. The flapping of their wings filled the air, drowning out the crashing waves that assaulted the cliffs behind her.

Mara dropped down, her face still skyward, her knees sinking into the wet moss. She was drenched from head to toe. But the shivers that spun up her spine weren't from the cold.

The birds formed a ring above her. A crown of feathers, alive with flight.

They had been called here, as she was. Drawn in by the chip on her wrist, activated by the truth in her DNA, here to support her claim. Her claim that she could do better—for all of them. And she would. She would devote herself to it, dedicate herself to Balti. It's all she'd ever wanted to do. For Jimma, for her family, for herself.

This was her place. She'd found it. She'd made it.

She let out a sob, not bothering to hold it back. Until that moment she had still doubted. It had been impossible to believe that the power was within her to reform her world. She didn't have to hold anything back now. She didn't have to wear the mask she'd designed to prove she was Balti enough. Grasping at control, keeping her truth to herself—that was for the Dern. Hard as she'd tried to be Balti through and through, she'd still absorbed those Dern practices, to protect herself.

To survive. She didn't need them now. Couldn't keep them and embrace her heritage.

Mara looked away from the birds to scan the faces of the Balti people—her people. They looked up at the raptors, their mouths open, their eyes wide with credulity and understanding. She had to stand, to be there for them, show them the way: to be open, accepting, willing to take life as it came. They had suffered indescribable loss. Life had dragged them down and never let up. But they were still here. Willing to hope. Looking for the good. Looking for better.

And she would give it to them.

One set of eyes was trained on her and her alone. Calvy watched Mara, ignoring the spectacle above.

You don't need anyone.

He was right—she could do this alone. But she didn't want to. Her hands closed into tight fists as a slow, smooth smile turned up his mouth. His eyes were full of admiration, of adoration. Of love.

It was how he always looked at her. And no matter what else changed, that wouldn't.

She knew it.

She could feel it.

And she'd never let it go.

* * * * *

Acknowledgments

Thank you to Elaine Spencer and Kerri Buckley for finding another of my books a home at Carina Press. Thank you to Stephanie Doig, whose editorial awareness made this manuscript better in every way. And thank you to all the friends who offered insight, encouragement, and enthusiasm in response to the question, "Do you want to read my space nonsense?"

Beyond expressing gratitude, to acknowledge is to accept. I wrote this book in 2019. It was queried, rejected (and rejected), and shelved. Two books later, I tried again and had the most fun revising it for print. This to say: things happen when they happen. Or, if I may, a Whitman: "I accept Time absolutely. It alone is without flaw, it alone rounds and completes all, That mystic baffling wonder alone completes all."

About the Author

A fan of topknots, fried Brussels sprouts, and other people doing the dishes, H.E. Dare lives, laughs, and writes in Chicago, contributing to the world's supply of book boyfriends and girl crushes. She also writes contemporary romance as Hanna Earnest and wants to be friends on Instagram and Twitter @hannaearnest. Find out more at hannaearnest.com.

After secretly eloping, two pop stars agree to a fake feud to keep the real scandal out of the tabloids. But where fake relationships go, real feelings follow...

Keep reading for an excerpt from
All the Best Nights *by Hanna Earnest.*

Chapter One

The drumming was louder now. Three even beats tapped out by two candy-shell nails on the bar, punctuated by a one-count pause held just long enough to infuse the silence with her displeasure before the rhythm repeated.

Meeting Nelle tonight had been a mistake. A year had passed since the magic moment she'd slipped her number into Bran's pocket at the Cleffy after-party, her breath raising the hairs on his neck as she whispered into his ear, "You're it." That last image of her stood out in his memory like the bas-relief of her raised and defined shoulder blades in the open-back dress she'd worn as she walked away from him. He'd been dazzled—there was no other way to describe it—dazed by her radiance. Charmed by her audacity to go after what she wanted, her confidence to approach him even as the requisite supermodel held tight to his arm.

And he'd been an idiot to assume he could recapture that spark. He wasn't the same person he'd been a year ago. He'd cracked and broken since then. And Nelle had changed too. That night she had been green, nominated for best new artist, and now, based on the supercharged buzz surrounding her second album, her star had risen.

Nothing could touch her. Whatever might have fizzed between them that night had gone flat now. Maybe it had never really been there. Maybe he'd just been surprised, lured in by all that gold-tinged skin, by a bold display he hadn't expected from a media darling with a good-girl image like Nelle's.

Tonight he could barely focus on her. The sun had been in his eyes the whole drive into the city, glinting off the skyline as it set at his back, angry and red. He'd spent the day squinting against excess light. Everything had been too bright—the glare off the topcoat of snow covering a field of graves blinding him worse than any stage lights he'd encountered. He'd had no relief from it, his sunglasses broken and twisted in his jacket pocket. A jacket that was woefully thin against Chicago's December chill.

All that sun and no warmth.

It was a good thing he was so numb.

One, two, three, Nelle drummed again.

Bran filled the gap, setting his empty pint glass on the polished wood, the dull thud familiar, a bass note of a chord he'd heard before. They were sat on either side of a rounded corner, an arrangement that afforded room for intimacy had they been angled towards each other, but instead seemed to accentuate their opposition in the moment. They sat as disinterested strangers, each facing the man in rolled shirtsleeves busy behind the bar.

Bran leaned his elbows on the curved countertop and motioned for the bartender, not missing the man's sharp glance at the untouched cocktail in front of the woman next to him. Their server had definitely recognized her, based on the reverence with which he had placed her drink down, a two-handed approach complete with a respectfully low head bow. Nelle's face and voice had been everywhere for the last two years and even in the bar's dim light she was recognizable: amber eyes like scotch on ice under thick dark lashes and thick dark brows set in a heart-shaped face. And that hair—trademark black waves fell over her shoulders as she sat straight in the low-backed bar stool.

"Another Two Hearted," Bran said. The barkeep stalled, waiting for Nelle's reaction. Bran's own fame was apparently of little consequence to the waiter. Sure, his band, Judith From Work, had broken up. But Bran had been on the scene for years before Nelle. And he'd just come off his first solo tour, which had been deemed a critical and commercial success—if not as lucrative as his label had wanted because he'd played smaller venues. And what about hometown advantage? Shouldn't that tip the scales in his favor?

But the barkeep only had eyes for Nelle. She noticed the delay and set the man into motion with a smile. "And can we have some French fries, please, when you have a second?" she added with an aggressive pleasantry that made Bran's molars ache.

"French fries?"

"Did you want a burger?" Nelle's voice, while high in tone, had a steely weight, like it was anchored deep inside of her. Tonight it held an unmistakable edge. The clear metallic scrape of a knife against the sharpening stone.

Bran shifted in his chair. "This is a Michelin-starred restaurant. We don't need to eat at the bar—I can get us a table."

"So can I." Her cheerful yellow fingertips took up

their rhythm on the counter again. "I don't think we'll be here long enough."

He didn't doubt that assertion. There wasn't anything here for either of them, it seemed. And the longer they stayed, the more likely it was someone would notice and think the encounter more than it was.

Across the restaurant a light flashed and Bran and Nelle both swung instinctively towards it to determine the source. But the flare was just a candle flame momentarily enhanced by the curved water jug of a passing waiter.

Bran exhaled slowly. "Because we won't be able to get through a meal before the paps catch us?"

Nelle curved her hand protectively around the stem of her coupe glass, a lemon peel on a metal spear resting across the rim. "Because this isn't going how I thought it would."

Honesty saturated her voice. Genuine emotion that carried through her music, unfiltered even in recordings. And in person it just about devastated him. He'd wanted something else from this too, but he wasn't going to say it. And it wasn't her fault: he shouldn't have agreed to see her. Not today.

Bran rubbed his eyes and looked down, landing on the brimming drink in front of Nelle. She lifted the shallow bowl and Bran followed it up to her mouth as she sipped the cloudy liquid and back down, replaced soundlessly on the bar. His gaze idled on the red smudge of her lips imprinted on the glass.

Okay, so that was one reason he'd gone against his better judgment and come tonight. He hadn't been able to stop thinking about that mouth for months. Every time he heard her voice on the radio or caught a glimpse of her on some magazine cover, he'd obsess about the full-lipped curve of that smile she'd given him when the heat of her skin radiated through the lining of his pocket.

She wasn't smiling now, pulling her hands into her lap and twisting one of a half dozen rings she wore staggered above and below her knuckles like notes on sheet music. The obsidian stone disappeared once, twice, before she released it, squared her shoulders, and tried valiantly to engage him in conversation again. "Don't worry about photos."

"You don't mind?" His head tilted to the side as he considered the statement. Maybe she liked it—the attention. She was good at getting it.

"Of course I mind. But they don't know we're here. They won't bother us."

"They won't?"

"It isn't like that here. It's the Midwest. It's home. It's safe."

Home? Not really. Not anymore.

"It's like that everywhere for us. Don't tell me you're that naïve."

Nelle lifted her glass again. "I'm not. Andre and I have an arrangement."

"Who's Andre?"

Nelle motioned to the barkeep and the garnish slid into her drink with a soft clink.

"You paid him?"

"We took a photo together."

Bran laughed, the sound as hollowed out as he felt. "Oh, that'll stop him. I thought you said you weren't naïve."

A glare narrowed her eyes. "I'm not. There's nothing wrong with trusting people to help you."

She waited a beat for him to respond, giving him the chance to show some willingness, some effort on his part to salvage the conversation. But he was done here. It wasn't enough to risk the blog fodder that would be twisted out of pictures of them having dinner together.

When he didn't say anything, her lips pressed together. She'd reached her limit too. He was surprised she'd let it get this far. Nelle didn't need to sit here. She was like him. She had options, anywhere she went. Better for her to use them. And he'd have the next drink alone. Take a nap in the car. Forget the company he'd hired to ship it back to California, he'd drive it himself. The album he'd promised his label by the New Year hadn't materialized. New music just wasn't coming to him. A spontaneous road trip wouldn't put the album any further off course. Maybe he'd even be inspired. Maybe he'd find what he was looking for rolling across the great American plains. Or maybe the blazing desert sun would leave him as dry and shriveled as his current creative vision.

Nelle uncrossed her legs and inched to the front of her seat. "I really thought you'd be different."

"Yeah?" He spun his own stool to get his knees out of her way, make it easier for her to go.

"But you're just a talented dickhead."

A lot of things had been said about Bran Kelly. He'd worked his way into the spotlight by nineteen, becoming the lead singer of a world-renowned band, so people who'd been inclined to comment had had seven years to come up with some shit. But no one had ever called him a talented dickhead.

And Nelle wasn't stopping there. "If you just wanted to have a drink, flirt a little, go back to my hotel, no pressure—we could have done that. Instead you show up late in that ridiculous car, slam a beer, and call me naïve? At the very least I expected some originality from Bran Kelly—but I've heard this one. A couple versions, actually. And I don't care for a repeat."

She stretched one black ankle boot to the ground while reaching for the big leather bag hanging from a hook under the bar. Behind her, large windows framed the dark city street, his car parked across it next to an empty lot. It unnerved him that she'd seen him arrive, like a perspective in the wrong direction, a Nighthawk looking out, studying him. Headlights from a passing car cut across the room, outlining her edges in a burst of backlighting. Bran's eyes widened, taking in her flared leather miniskirt and tight black turtleneck sweater. A silhouette of black on black. Even her thick hair, loose and cascading down her back, shone with the ebony gloss of night.

Bran had wanted the day to be over and suddenly it was—of course partial credit could be given to how quickly the sun set in December, how early, but for a moment it seemed like Nelle conjured the darkness that appealed to his tired eyes. And she alone was defined in it, by it, fierce and powerful—a goddess whose blessing he craved.

And he felt it—saw again that brazen determination that had mesmerized him a year ago. A shiver rocked his shoulders as the door at his back opened, letting in a gust of winter air. He was awake. He was wired—charged by her tractor-beam stare. The words pulled up from deep inside him, the rush of creation pricking across his skin.

She turned midnight.

A lyric flashed in his mind.

He needed her to stay. He needed her to do that again. Another flash, another spark leaping from her to him, like static electricity jumpstarting his process.

Bran blinked. Then he was on his feet, filling the cramped space between their stools before she could.

"Wait—wait—" Bran shook his hair and settled it back into place in one involuntary movement. He scrambled to remember the reasons she was going. "I've had a long day. I'm sorry. I'll nurse the next beer."

For the first time since landing in the seat next to her he locked his eyes on hers for more than a fleeting glance. They glowed like sun caught in honey and he felt just as stuck.

"I didn't mean to be late. I was speeding. You gotta know I was—who goes the speed limit in a Ferrari, right?"

Her eyes sizzled with annoyance and he remembered her calling the car ridiculous.

Bran was so used to being the force in a room, the sun around which everyone seemed to gravitate. Normally it was his electric-blue eyes that shocked people into stunned silence. He was off balance when he was with Nelle, when it was his body that spun towards hers, his lungs that struggled under her gaze. Whatever he had that drew people in, she had it too. Only hers was fresher. Not yet faded. And it pulled something to the surface in him—something he recognized, something he'd lost.

Queen of light.

Another lyric. Another ray of hope breaking through his blocked mind. The hazy shape of a song formed in his periphery.

He had to make her stay.

Skewered by her gaze, Bran prepared another admission, willing to humble himself to any level, if she'd just sit back down. "Admittedly, yes, the car is a little over the top. It's the first big thing I bought." She had to understand. "You must have done something with your signing bonus?"

"I paid my parents' mortgage."

Maybe not.

He couldn't keep the desperation out of his final plea. "Please stay."

Half standing, she deliberated silently for a long, torturous minute while Bran held his breath. Finally, when his lungs had begun to ache, she settled herself back in her seat. And as relieved as he was, he had no idea why. Maybe she was curious about what had changed his attitude? Maybe she just wanted to finish her drink. It didn't matter. He had a second chance to focus on her. To catch any flashes of her brashness and hope for another burst of inspiration.

She crossed her legs and leaned as far back from him as she could. "I'm not sleeping with you now."

Bran let out a shaky laugh. "I wouldn't expect you to."

As Nelle gulped the last of her cocktail, lips puckering, it dawned on him that was all she'd been interested in. This could have been easy. Both of them intent on quick access to passion—if only he hadn't been so distracted, so stupid. That ship had sailed. But she was still here, the sour twist easing from her mouth. He could settle for a little conversation and a little hope.

He picked up the beer Andre had delivered to take a restorative gulp and caught Nelle's watchful glance. He sipped instead, to prove he could behave. The beer was cold and bitter and he held it in his mouth as she leaned forward. She took the pint from his hand, her eyes locking on his as she swigged it back, leaving him his own print of her lips on the rim as she set it down. Bran swallowed. A hidden sweetness coated his tongue. How had he not been paying his full attention to this girl?

"I'm not sleeping with you either," he told her when he recovered himself.

Unmistakable interest lit her face. "Because you've rekindled things with Francesca."

He raised his eyebrows. "Have I?"

"You haven't heard? They're saying it was backstage at the Victoria's Secret show."

"That's news to me. I haven't been in New York since October."

"*News* is a strong word for it. Same source reported my butt implants." She angled her hips to give him a glance at her backside. "Nice, right?"

And he'd been fixated on her mouth. The things he could do to an ass like that. He swallowed again. "Very natural."

"Well. It is. So." Her gilded lids glittered as she shifted her attention to the barkeep, thanking him with a smile for removing her empty glass. She stretched, the sweater pulling tight over her breasts, her sleek hair dancing over the crescent arch of her spine. Curves and shadows. This was the performer in her, aware of his attentiveness, feeding off her audience.

"I'm not with Francesca anymore. I'm not with anyone." He put his arm on the low back of her chair, thumbing the nailhead trim that lined the edge.

"But you're not sleeping with me?"

"I'm considering celibacy."

She bent towards him. "Bran Kelly. Celibate. This is a line, right? You tell a girl you're withholding your dick from the world to make her want you more? The rock-star thing not working for you anymore?"

It wasn't a line. But a solution he'd entertained earlier—when he wasn't close enough to smell the Chanel at her neck. When it felt like his only option was something drastic he'd never have considered before.

His aforementioned dick twitched at her casual shout-out and Bran tried to quiet that urge. She inspired something more valuable in him, but maybe he could turn this around and satisfy them both. He was aware of the night stretching before them, long and cold.

He had to grip the back of her seat to stop himself from sifting his fingers through the bottom inch of her hair. When Nelle coasted a hand through the waves, Bran swayed forward to inhale. Her hair swung over her shoulders, falling over the back of Bran's hand, and he had the sudden sensation that he had slipped, the stomach lurch of losing your footing.

Black like ice, queen of light, she turned midnight.

The line flickered through Bran's mind and he resisted the impulse to pull out his phone and type it into his notes. That would look like texting—and definitely not help his case. His fingers tensed at his side. He repeated the words in his head, trying to combat the anxiety of losing them, unaware of how the desire tethered itself to the woman sitting next to him.

Nelle pressed forward, still hunting down answers. "What is it then? A New Year's resolution—a quarter-life crisis?"

"More of a clarity thing."

"Pussy clouds the mind?"

A smile tugged at Bran's mouth. "They're wrong about you. You've got an edge."

"Because I said *pussy*?"

"Because you pursued me while I was with someone else."

Now he wished for blaring sunlight, to see for sure that her face had gone pink with a blush of his making.

Andre arrived with a second cocktail, and Nelle swiveled towards him with another practiced smile. "And we're gonna split a burger." She glanced down before meeting Bran's eyes again. "I should apologize for that."

"But?"

"I wouldn't mean it."

A soft silence settled between them, the thick snow outside muffling the sounds of the city. Her mouth curved, finally for him, and an uptick of tempo thumped in his heart.

The candle across the room winked again. Bran touched her elbow, the fabric of her sweater soft, thinner than he'd expected. "You're sure Andre has your back with the paps? I can't help thinking they'd kill for this."

She recrossed her legs, her feet tangling momentarily with his. He widened his thighs, making room for her to fit the V of her stacked knees between them. "*If* this were happening—they'd be all over us in a minute. Reporting our breakup while speculating that we're engaged—contrasting headlines over a photo of us buying groceries and holding hands—"

"That's why I have a no-hand-holding policy. Makes it too easy for them."

"And if I eat one gyro too many: bump watch."

She was right. That's exactly what they always did. Take any scrap of his life they could find to churn out stories he barely recognized as his life. Soon they'd have more than fragments to work with, soon they'd have every detail that made Bran Kelly who he was. The private stuff that made him feel like a real person.

And he didn't know how to stop it.

"Everything they can find, sold to the highest bidder." He moved his hand from her sleeve before his grip tightened. He shouldn't be talking about this. Not when he was trying to focus on Nelle, let her be the distraction from his other problems.

But she was nodding, rebalancing the metal toothpick across her glass. "Better than making things up."

His response arose from the ease of talking to someone who really understood. "Does it bother you more when they're wrong or when they're right?"

"It bothers me that I can't have any secrets." She gave up on balance and let the lemon peel splash back into her drink. "It bothers me that I don't think I can keep any."

"Then you need a tighter circle. Or a smaller one."

"Is that what you do? Keep a circle so small and tight you suffocate inside it, your secrets preserved as your body rots?"

"You're pretty dark for a pop princess."

"You're pretty chaste for a rock god."

A second line flared in his mind, warm with the possibility of what it could become, and he tried to burn it to his memory.

The French fries arrived in a paper cone with a little dish of pale aioli. The smell filled Bran's nose and his mouth watered. That numbness had kept him from registering how hungry he'd gotten.

Nelle had a crispy golden strand in her hand before Andre had managed to set the plate down. "And you know how they call you Bran and Fran? If we got married they'd call me Nelly Kelly."

Bran froze, hot fries searing his fingertips. "Would they?"

This time it wasn't a lyric rising in his mind. But an idea that only a man as blindly desperate as he currently was would consider.

She nodded with confidence. "Of course they would."

Even if he was in straits dire enough to come up with a scheme like that, Nelle certainly wouldn't accept. She was a catalyst, and he was reacting too quickly. Besides, she didn't need a last name. Why would she take his?

So Bran filled his mouth with fries and swallowed the idea with them.

Don't miss All the Best Nights *by Hanna Earnest, available now wherever books are sold.*

www.CarinaPress.com